Balances

CONTENTS

Day Zero

Deserter and Sorcerer

Audience with the King

Headaches

Sir Marek

Dinner and a Scheme

On the Job

Family

Charitable Enterprises

Practice

Dinner and a Show

Cousin

Zero Hour

Truth

Wait, What?

On the Move

Path-Mate

They

Whoops

Aftermath

Good

Tymirin

Isle of Dragons

Dragon Things

Prince of Seyzharel

Home Again

for Pickle

who loved these characters

somehow even more than I do

Balances

Bethany Laurel

DAY ZERO

Darkness pressed inward, close and suffocating as ever.

Trailing his left hand along the wall, Akieryon paced and paced. Seven steps. Turn. Ten steps. Turn. A predictable rhythm, the heartbeat of his incarceration, the flimsy thread by which his sanity dangled. Twelve circuits completed, he reversed direction, his right hand tracing the track he had long since worn smooth.

Food would appear soon, delivered by magic, denying him even a few seconds' contact with another living being. He had stopped counting the meals after what he guessed was a decade. What did it matter? He'd been forgotten in this windowless cell. He had always been alone. He would always be here, a deeper shadow in the endless night. Seven by ten. The dimensions of his entire world.

A soft chime preceded the arrival of his meal, a reminder that he still heard sounds outside of the ones he himself made. Akieryon seated himself at the foot of his cot, and he waited.

A sliver of light speared through the perpetual darkness of his cell. With a shriek of pain, Akieryon scrambled backward over his cot, upsetting the tidy folds of his bedding. One hand shielded his eyes from the light, and yet it *hurt*. Tears streaming down his cheeks, he cowered and squinted, and utterly failed to understand what was happening.

"Come on." A hand closed around his wrist and gave a short yank, exposing his entire face to the cruel light. "We have to go. Now."

Akieryon stumbled to his feet and tripped along after this stranger, out the mysteriously open door, and into the blurry gloom of the corridor. He blinked rapidly, blinked hard, but nothing came into focus. The stranger was babbling.

"I'm Zephael. Zeph. I'm a Birthbringer—I oversee the birth of kittens—so I really have no business being in a place like this. But neither do you. You haven't been forgotten, but now you have to *go*." He dragged Akieryon out into the sunlight, which was worse. Akieryon cowered. A guttural growl rose from somewhere deep in his chest, but he had no time to wonder at it. "Sorry," Zeph was saying. "But I can only open portals to one place."

He gave Akieryon a gentle shove. The ground opened up beneath him, and he plunged from one world into another.

Though he only fell for a second or two, Akieryon landed as though he had been launched from a trebuchet. Knee, shoulder, hip, and finally his head struck a deep furrow in damp earth. Soil burst out in all directions, in his hair, his nose, his mouth. Clods of dirt rained down as he finally tumbled and skidded to a stop, at a depth somewhat below the topsoil. Somewhere nearby, a horse screamed.

Choking and sputtering, Akieryon tried to push himself up out of his private crater. His arms buckled, and he collapsed face-first in the dirt. At least it blocked out the horrible, stabbing sunlight.

"Hey… are you okay?"

Every muscle along Akieryon's spine tensed, and he managed to lift his head enough to gulp in a little air. "I don't know where I am." His voice sounded thin and dry, alien with disuse. Every instinct told him to turn his head, to try to look at the stranger standing over him. But what good would it do, when the light would blur his sight and stab his brain?

"You need help." Not a question. The stranger shifted, crouched, and Akieryon sensed rather than saw a hand extended to him. "Can you stand?"

With more effort than it should have required, Akieryon pushed himself up onto his hands and knees. He took several slow breaths, steadying himself, mustering his strength. The air felt thick and charged with conflicting energies. Separate worlds compressed into one. Aftermath of cataclysm long gone. "Oh," he blurted. "This is the Mortal Sphere."

"Seems to be, yeah. You're in Davenz, about three leagues from the capitol."

Hearing humor in the stranger's voice, Akieryon dared a glance at the man who crouched nearby. He wore riding leathers—good quality, well kept, but fairly plain. He had twisted his black hair into several plaits, several days or leagues ago. He had tattoos on his cheeks, and his silvery green eyes were a little less than human but a little more than kind. When Akieryon flinched back from the light and covered his eyes with one hand, the stranger began fumbling around in a pocket.

"Here." Gentle fingers pulled Akieryon's hand away and rolled a layer of gauze across his eyes. "How's that?"

Akieryon blinked several times, testing the push of his eyelashes against the gauze, sampling the faint light that filtered through. His eyes may water a bit, but they no longer stung and stabbed and burned. "Better," he whispered, his voice abruptly gone hoarse. "Much better."

"I'm Tempest," the stranger said, his deft fingers securing the blindfold. "Just Tempest. I'm in the middle of some dull political work, but if you like you can accompany me."

Despite the uncertainty thrust upon him, despite the sudden realization of how much the world hurt, Akieryon found himself smiling. "Dull political work sounds like all the excitement I can handle today," he replied, and Tempest laughed.

~⋄✦⋄~

Akieryon's education had neglected to include horsemanship, for obvious reasons. Portals and wings made for more efficient travel, generally. His ignorance on full display, Akieryon leaned awkwardly against Tempest and kept both arms wrapped around his waist. After the cool darkness of his cell, the intensifying sun—afternoon?—sapped what remained of his strength. Pressing his cheek to Tempest's back, Akieryon drowsed.

He hardly noticed when he sagged to the side, but Tempest clamped one hand over both of his wrists. "No, you don't," he said, jerking Akieryon out of his daze.

"Sorry."

Akieryon felt rather than heard Tempest's soft scoff. "For what? Nearly falling off, or generally for sitting a horse like a sack of dried peas?"

Shame bloomed heat into Akieryon's cheeks. He sat in silence for a few strides before he said, "I never had cause to learn."

"Until just now. Here, switch with me." Whereupon Tempest proceeded, by some arcane means, to maneuver himself into the saddle behind Akieryon without so much as slowing the horse. "Straighten your spine and relax your hips."

"How am I supposed to hold on if I relax my hips?" Akieryon protested, and Tempest's chuckle stirred the hair near his ear.

"I won't let you fall. But you have to trust me."

Did he trust Tempest?

Did it matter?

For an hour or so, Tempest gave patient directions and gentle corrections. When he had a chance to think of something other than his seat on the horse, Akieryon wondered at it. None of his teachers had ever shown him quite so much grace. When the lesson drew to a close and Tempest began to signal to someone ahead of them, a twinge of sadness twisted in Akieryon's insides.

Their pace slowed as the horse's hooves struck a hollow rhythm on sturdy wood planks. Ahead of them, voices chattered in a low hum, ropes and axles creaked, and a donkey brayed. A city? Too small to be a city. Too quiet and too clean. They paused for a minute or two, and Tempest answered a few cryptic questions put to him by a gruff voice from about the height of their elbows. Then they were on their way again, crossing more planks of wood, with a broad river rushing beneath.

Beyond the bridge, Tempest answered more questions, and the smells of the city finally caught at Akieryon's nostrils. Smoke and washing. Goats and hens. Dyes and leathers. Water, both fresh and otherwise. Somewhere nearby, the steady music of a smith's hammer rang out. People called to one another, cheerful or angry or urgent. When they passed a public house, Akieryon could smell the ale.

"Is this the capitol?" he asked when he thought his senses could take no more. How many people lived here?

"It is. Not much farther now."

Tempest's word proved true. Soon heavy chains rattled, and the noise of the city faded a little into the distance. Someone gave a sharp whistle.

"Ho there, Tempest!" called a higher voice. "What have you dragged in this time? New recruit?"

"This is Akieryon," Tempest called back. "He's my guest."

Guest.

When had he ever been anyone's guest?

"All you miscreants will abide by Hospitality," Tempest added, and maybe half a dozen people laughed and fired back goodnatured jibes. Ignoring them all, Tempest dismounted and reached up to help Akieryon off the horse.

"Why the blindfold?" asked the woman who had first spoken. "That's hardly hospitable."

"It is when the light hurts," Akieryon ventured, scarcely above a whisper. Somehow, his voice had all but frozen in his throat.

"Tell Caspar I'll be along directly," Tempest said. "After I show Akieryon up to my suite."

"Your *suite?*" Akieryon repeated. He tripped along as Tempest steered him down a path, then up an outrageous amount of stairs. Akieryon ached from the riding lesson. "You're someone important."

Tempest made a noncommittal noise. Akieryon supposed he would have to wait a little longer to learn what this man really was. He gripped Tempest's arm, and he walked onward.

DESERTER AND SORCERER

Tempest's suite consisted of an antechamber, a combination wardrobe and armory, a bedroom, a bath with what could have passed for a pool, and a tiny private library. When Tempest had secured heavy curtains over every window, Akieryon tugged the blindfold from his eyes and peered around, grateful for the gloom. His eyes still tired quickly, and he found himself pressing fingertips to closed eyelids more often than not. Tempest had disappeared into the wardrobe.

"Feel free to poke around," he called out to Akieryon. "Help yourself to a bath—pull the copper chain for hot water—and a change of clothes. Nap if you want. Whatever." He emerged, fastening a sword belt over an embroidered long vest. "I don't know how long I'll be in conference with the king. Here, are you well?"

Akieryon lowered his hands from his eyes yet again. "Yes," he replied, embarrassment creeping warmth up his cheeks. "I haven't used my eyes so much in a very long time. I'll adjust, I promise."

Tempest gave him a sidelong look, but nodded. "I'll have some food sent up as soon as I can." With that, he slipped out the door and closed it softly behind him.

Panic leapt up within Akieryon, battering wildly at his ribs and pushing the breath out of him. He doubled over, his hands on his knees, gasping for air as the plush rug beneath his feet faded before his rebellious eyes. He would faint. He would faint and he would fall, but at least he would hardly bruise himself on the sumptuous carpet.

No.

No, he refused.

He drew a deep, shuddering breath and held it for four thundering beats of his heart. He released it, counting six. Four beats in. Eight beats out. He forced himself to continue breathing and counting breaths until everything steadied. Then he tiptoed across the antechamber to try the door. He had to.

It sighed open when he pulled on the handle. Sobbing with relief, Akieryon pushed it closed again. He stood there for a long while, trembling, his forehead pressed to the inside of the door. He was free to go, if he so chose.

He chose instead to have a bath.

The tiled bathtub, Akieryon reflected upon inspection, likely could have held half of his graduating class from the Academy.

Who needed a bathtub that comfortably seated six? He located the copper chain, and he gave it a tentative tug.

A gurgle and a splashing noise preceded the water, which sputtered forth from a spout fashioned in the shape of a dragon's head. While the tub filled, Akieryon shucked his clothing. The black sash fell away in tatters. The white trousers had turned ivory with age, and he had worn the inseams almost completely through. The shirt could have doubled as gauze. He folded each piece with care, trying to avoid doing further damage. Then he stepped into the bathtub, which had somehow already filled almost to the level of his knees.

The warmth startled him, as did the silken touch of the water itself. For how many years had he passed each day washing up from a simple clay bowl of water? His skin had forgotten how it felt to submerge. Perhaps he would dissolve and drift away. He closed his eyes. He drifted.

Akieryon startled back to himself when the water lapped at his chin. Scrambling across the tub, he yanked the copper chain, and the flow of water splashed to a stop. He sank to his eyes in the bath, letting the warmth seep through his entire body. When he could hold his breath no longer, he resigned himself to the arduous task of washing his hair. He had given up on his hair decades ago.

Maybe, if he searched long enough, he would find scissors.

Akieryon finished washing, and he remained in the bathtub until the water had cooled nearly to the temperature of the air. It took him two tries to locate the lever that drained the water. For a vague moment he wondered where it went. Down. Down where? Then, rousing himself, he pulled a slate-colored dressing gown from a hook on the wall and wrapped it around himself. He walked a circuit around the bathroom, and he found a pair of gilt-handled scissors lying out on the long dressing table. He raised his eyes to the mirror, and he shied from his own reflection. When had he grown so frail? Gripping the scissors in one hand and his dripping hair in the other, he sheared it to a more appropriate length. Just barely too short to tie back.

Regulation.

Akieryon threw the scissors back down on the dressing table and turned his back to the mirror. Clothing. He should borrow something from the wardrobe. He opened the door, and stared at a wall full of assorted shades of black. He touched the nearest item, a coat, and his thoughts flew far away, to the blue uniform coat lovingly folded and tucked beneath the foot of a cot in a dark little cell.

Hours later, Tempest found him curled on his side on the bed, still wrapped in the dressing gown. The mattress sank under Tempest's weight as he settled in, lying down to look into

Akieryon's eyes.

"You cut your hair," he said.

Akieryon scoffed and looked away. "Not well."

"We can even it up in the morning."

For a while, they simply stared at one another. Akieryon wondered that someone so obviously near to the throne could take in a stranger he found stranded on the road. He studied the slopes and angles of Tempest's face, trying to guess answers to a dozen different questions rattling around in his skull. Unable to utter even one, he reached a trembling hand toward Tempest's cheek.

Tempest caught him by the wrist. "No," he said, his voice soft but firm.

"No?" Akieryon repeated, baffled.

"You owe me nothing."

Akieryon stared at the fingers wrapped around his wrist, at the thumb resting against the heel of his hand. "I… I didn't mean…" He cleared his throat. "Why did you decide to help me?"

Rolling onto his back, Tempest gazed up at the ceiling. "I suppose," he said, "because helping people is the only evidence I have of my own humanity." He flashed Akieryon a wry smile. "Purely selfish motivation, isn't it?"

"Is it selfish of me to say your motivation doesn't matter?"

"Of course," Tempest said, but his eyes danced and his smile warmed.

Akieryon hugged an overstuffed pillow to his chest. Had he truly begun this day still locked away in darkness? It seemed so long ago.

So very long ago…

"Say, Tempest?"

"Hmm?" came a drowsy reply.

"What year is it?"

"Year?" A pause. "By whose calendar?"

Akieryon chewed his lip while he considered what human calendar systems Tempest might know. He had said they were in Davenz. "Is the Tymiri calendar still in use?"

"Yes," said Tempest, sounding a little more engaged in the conversation. "The year is thirteen seventy-three."

A shock speared through Akieryon.

He had been locked in darkness for nearly five hundred years.

Sunlight warmed the curtains when Akieryon awakened, but Tempest had left them drawn tightly closed. Birds cried outside, and a breeze stirred one curtain. Akieryon pushed blankets and pillows aside. His body ached with long hours of sleep, yet still he felt tired. Why did he feel tired? He had done *nothing* for centuries!

His feet squished into the plush rug as he stood up, and abruptly he remembered the riding lesson of the day before. More acutely, the muscles in his legs and back remembered, and reminded him rather more forcefully than he enjoyed. Half-shuffling, Akieryon crossed to the open window and nudged the curtain aside with one fingertip. A thin blade of sunlight lanced across the carpet. Akieryon winced, but it hurt less than yesterday.

He left the curtain slightly open.

In the wardrobe he selected a pair of trousers and a shirt—both black, neither a good fit. Cuffing the sleeves three times, he wandered the rooms, trying to imagine what sort of man belonged here. The library contained tome after tome of different disciplines of sorcery, and little else. The chairs looked unreasonably comfortable. A water clock in the antechamber chimed the hour, and Akieryon followed the sound. Beside the clock he discovered a breakfast tray. His stomach gave a loud rumble.

The clock had not yet chimed again when Tempest returned. He shoved the door open, then closed it with a disgruntled kick. Akieryon dropped the toast he had just buttered, and Tempest froze, staring down at him with an unreadable expression.

"Was... was this for me?" Akieryon gestured at the remains of the breakfast tray. He had already annihilated the fruit compote and the smoked fish, and moved on to cold roast chicken, toast, and soft cheese. Tempest's odd inhuman stare softened.

"Of course." He crouched and stuck a finger in the cheese. "Why are you sitting on the floor?"

"Um." Akieryon blinked around at the ruins of his breakfast. "I… didn't really put much thought into where to sit."

"Clearly." Tempest sat beside him and grabbed a triangle of toast.

Akieryon nudged the cheese closer to Tempest. He wanted to ask what had annoyed the man, but could not work his brain around the right phrasing. He wanted to ask what boring political work occupied Tempest's time, but hesitated to pry. They ate together in silence until the last crumb had vanished. Then Tempest stacked the dishes neatly on the tray and placed it on a small table beside the door. Akieryon struggled to his feet, his muscles screaming all the while.

"Ready for a haircut?"

Akieryon startled at the question, then remembered a drowsy moment with Tempest inspecting his raggedly chopped hair. Right. Haircut. He nodded, and followed Tempest into the enormous bathroom.

"Do you want to watch in the mirror? Yell at me if I'm cutting too much?" Without waiting for a response—or perhaps Akieryon hesitated for too long—Tempest steered him to the mirror and snatched up the scissors. He snipped away at the top and sides, occasionally pausing to ask Akieryon's opinion. As he trimmed the front, Akieryon caught him frowning in the mirror.

"What's wrong?"

Tempest gave a little shake of his head. "You kind of look like someone I know. I'm sure it's coincidence."

He moved around to the back of Akieryon's head. The scissors snipped twice more, and then stilled. Panic sank like a stone in the pit of his stomach, and he resisted a fierce need to slap a hand over the back of his neck.

"What's this?" Tempest breathed. Not alarmed, not angry. Not yet throwing him out into the Mortal world to survive on his own.

"It's called a Lineage Mark." And it was the reason he had had a dozen foster homes as a child. No one wanted to keep him around once they saw it.

"Does it mean something?"

Akieryon shrugged. "No one will even tell me what it looks like."

"Opposing spirals crossed by a wavy line."

Opposing spirals indicated the bloodline of a Fallen. At least that explained… everything. But what did the wavy line mean?

"Does it mean something?" Tempest asked again, his voice softening, gentling.

"Probably that my parents made poor life choices," Akieryon said, and Tempest laughed.

"I'm rather certain we can all say the same."

Akieryon met Tempest's eyes in the mirror, and they shared a smile.

~⚜~

For two days, Akieryon saw nothing of Davenz beyond the interior of Tempest's suite. When his eyes had recovered enough, he opened the curtains. He passed his time reading Tempest's books, or testing the weapons tucked tidily away in the wardrobe. He began the arduous task of restoring his body and his mind to peak condition. Fighting fit. Midmorning on the third day, Tempest discovered him standing on his head.

"What are you doing?"

Embarrassment warming his cheeks, Akieryon lowered his feet to the floor and stood up. "A little light exercise."

"If by 'light' you are referring to your body weight."

"Hollow bones," Akieryon mumbled, his face reddening further. Sure, he had grown thinner in his cell, but one could hardly describe him as skeletal.

"What," said Tempest.

Akieryon closed his eyes. Better to reveal the truth now. Better to shock sooner, better not to have to lie. He drew a deep breath, and he unfurled his wings, tipping the balance of them from energy to matter. By a subtle magic they passed right through the borrowed shirt he wore, doing no damage to the fabric. His white feathers shimmered with a soft light of their own. "I have hollow bones," he repeated in a whisper, barely forcing the words past the fear constricting his throat.

What if Tempest hated him now?

"Huh," said Tempest, and Akieryon's eyes snapped open. The man wore a bland contemplative expression. "I've never met an angel before." He paused, and a slow smile tugged at one corner of his mouth. "Certainly not one who ate quite so much road dust right in front of me."

Akieryon crinkled his nose. "I doubt that's terribly common." Unless Zeph went around pushing people through portals every day.

"And angels require exercise." Tempest's tone shifted from teasing to scholarly as he paced around Akieryon, peering at his wings with interest. "And can be sensitive to sunlight?"

"Yes on the exercise, no on the sunlight. Not usually." Might as well come clean. "I was imprisoned. In darkness."

"Oh, you're a criminal?" Tempest asked without judgment. Purely curious. Still, Akieryon drew his wings closer to himself.

"No. Maybe? I mean, I suppose I am, now that I've run away."

He clenched his fists to stop them trembling. "I injured a superior officer, so I was locked away." He rather understated the situation. Five hundred years later, the extent of the damage he had done still haunted his nightmares.

"May I?"

Akieryon glanced up, and he startled at the sight of Tempest's hand hovering near his wing. He shied, then fought against the instinct to do so. "Yes." How had he made his voice so steady?

He braced for the moment of contact, for a push against his skin, a tug on his feathers. Instead, Tempest's fingertips barely grazed his feathers, his touch as light as a breeze. "Fascinating," he murmured. "It feels like they're made of light."

A fresh blush heated Akieryon's cheeks, and he took a small step to the side. "Are you a sorcerer?" Considering the books in the little library, that was probably a stupid question.

"Merely a hobbyist," Tempest replied a little too quickly. "Are you ready to see more of the castle?"

"Sure?"

"Good." Executing a swift turn, Tempest led the way toward the wardrobe. "Let's get you into something a little nicer. The king would like to meet you."

Akieryon snapped his wings back out of sight, back into the space between matter. A self-protecting gesture. "What? Why?"

Pausing with a hand on the door, Tempest lifted one shoulder in a shrug. "Perhaps because the guards are gossiping about whether you and I are lovers." When Akieryon goggled at him, he added, "I blame Dani for this—she's the one who asked if you were a new recruit when we arrived."

"I'm… I'm not."

"A new recruit, or my lover?" With a flash of a grin, Tempest vanished into the wardrobe. Akieryon stood alone on the plush rug, struggling to work out whether he had meant that as flirtation or humor.

AUDIENCE WITH
THE KING

Tempest's clothing all hung a bit too slack in the shoulders. Akieryon stared at his reflection, picked at the hem of the quilted doublet, and longed for his uniform coat. Tempest caught his dubious glance and misinterpreted it.

"You look fine."

Akieryon hadn't worn anything other than his dress uniform in formal settings since before graduation from the Academy. Blue with black facings and gold braid. A high collar. White gloves. Three swords. In Tempest's shades of black, he felt hopelessly underdressed. "I guess," he mumbled.

"Don't you trust my judgment?"

Tempest's smile reappeared, swift and teasing. Again. Akieryon wanted to shove him, but physics would favor Tempest. "Is this really appropriate for meeting a king?" he asked instead.

Turning away from the mirror, Tempest rubbed at the back of his neck. "You'll stand out," he admitted. "And everyone will know the clothes are mine."

"This will do nothing to quiet the rumors about us," Akieryon predicted. Tempest left his question unanswered, but it didn't matter. Without his uniform he would always feel undressed. Squaring his shoulders and lifting his chin, Akieryon followed Tempest from the wardrobe through the antechamber, and out into the corridor.

The last time he had been outside Tempest's rooms, he had had nothing more than the gentle pressure of Tempest's hand on his arm to guide him. Now he peered around with interest, taking in every detail. Walls paneled in cedar stretched away in either direction, punctuated at intervals by heavy tapestries. The blonde wood of the floor gleamed with frequent polishing, and looked to have been replaced at some time in the last decade. Tempest caught him staring, and nudged him with an elbow.

"Did you expect a utilitarian fortress of rough-hewn stone?"

"It would suit your temperament better," Akieryon blurted before he could stop himself. Tempest stared at him for half a stride, then laughed.

"You catch on quick, my friend," he said, and something in Akieryon warmed at the word. Friend. When had he last had friends? In school? Before Raaqiel had labeled him Chess Nerd, a name that had unfortunately followed him for decades?

Tempest led him down two flights of stairs to a corridor that sported much the same decor, but with greater detail. Guards stood at intervals, their hands clasped behind their backs. Tempest nodded to them, and they nodded back. At a double door with mother of pearl inlay, Tempest paused.

"Ready?"

Swallowing a sudden wave of nerves, Akieryon nodded. The guards opened the doors, and a burst of noise struck them. Akieryon almost shied from it. People of all ages, sizes, and shades of human milled about ahead of them, draped in colorful silks and velvets. Tempest stepped forward, Akieryon followed, and a hush radiated out around them. People parted to let them pass. The doors swung closed with a hollow thud that sounded a little too final.

Beyond the colorful crowd, Akieryon noticed a platform raised two steps above the rest of the rectangular chamber. Upon it, a man perhaps a few years younger than Tempest sat at the very edge of an ornate chair. He propped his chin on one brown hand, observing everything. Akieryon should have observed him in turn, but the woman standing a step behind him caught his eye instead. Rather, her vibrant red hair held Akieryon's attention. Heaven had few redheads, a thought which had him forcing himself not to tug at his own auburn hair.

"Tempest." The man on the edge of his seat, the king, beckoned to the both of them. "At last, you've brought your guest."

Akieryon felt a blush creeping up his cheeks, but Tempest nudged him forward. "King Caspar, may I present Akieryon."

One of the king's eyebrows flinched upward. "Just Akieryon?"

A grin flashed across Tempest's face. "Have I ever lied to Your Majesty?"

"Unfortunately not." King Caspar beckoned again. "Approach, Akieryon. Let me see what sort of man can have Tempest so preoccupied."

"Sire," Tempest objected, and Akieryon stepped closer to the smirking king. His gaze wavered, darting again to the redhead. She watched him with a wary eye.

"Where do you hail from, Akieryon?" His voice was pitched low, almost conspiratorial. His words carried no farther than he wished, even in this crowded chamber. The question snapped Akieryon's attention back to the king.

"Ah, I'm not certain how to answer that, sir."

"I would prefer honesty," Caspar said with a disarming smile.

Akieryon shifted his weight, resisting an impulse to nudge his toe against the the lower step. "The Sixth Sphere," he said, almost in a whisper. "I doubt anyone here has heard of it, sir."

The redhead leaned forward and murmured something to the

king, who nodded. He opened his mouth to speak again, and Akieryon braced for another prying question. "Come closer," Caspar said instead. Akieryon took a tentative step forward. Upward. Caspar rose from his seat and descended one step to meet him. "You look like an earnest young man, Akieryon."

"Not so young as you might imagine, sir."

A hint of a smile played about Caspar's lips. "How long have you known Tempest?"

Where were these questions leading? Akieryon glanced over his shoulder, but Tempest's impassive expression offered no help. "A few days, sir." He barely gave the words any voice. All but the most dedicated gossips gave up on eavesdropping and returned to their murmured conversations. "We met on the road." More or less.

"And you're staying with him. Fascinating." A flash of humor danced in the king's eyes as he looked toward Tempest. "Indefinitely?"

Heat flooded Akieryon's face. "I, uh, I haven't actually asked —"

"For as long as he wishes to stay," Tempest interrupted, his voice unusually firm. "Sire." Something in the tilt of his head carried a subtle warning, which Caspar blithely ignored.

"Indeed? You must be something special."

Akieryon remembered what Tempest had said to him about

helping people. "I think he would have extended the same kindness to anyone in my situation."

"*Do* you?" Caspar placed a hand on Akieryon's shoulder and turned him slightly to face Tempest. "You see, Akieryon, I've known this man here for over fifteen years, and I feel that you really should know… How shall I say this? Tempest, he has good in him, truly he does, but, well… Sometimes he's… Ah, he can be… He can be a bit…"

A flicker of a reflection gleamed in the midst of the assembled crowd, light on steel. A blade raised for throwing. By the time Akieryon had stepped in front of the king, Tempest had already thrown two courtiers aside. People screamed and scattered as he surged forward. Tempest had a dagger in his hand, which Akieryon had not noticed on his person. He rammed the blade into the stomach of the would-be attacker, raising him off his feet with the force of the impact. More people screamed. Deaf to the noise, Tempest dragged the dagger upward, punched his free hand into the wound he had made, and yanked back a fistful of entrails as the man fell back from him.

Caspar heaved a world-weary sigh. "Excessive," he finished with a little shake of his head.

Tempest crouched over the dying man, growling questions and listening for answers no one else could hear. The other people had retreated to the edges of the room, many of them pallid with shock, a few of them spattered with blood. The guards stood blocking the doors, permitting none of them to flee. When at last Tempest straightened, he gazed impassively at the body at his feet.

"Would anyone else care to try to harm the king?" he asked, his voice quiet, even mild.

The redhead sauntered to his side and punched him in the arm. "*I'm* the bodyguard now, *ambassador*," she said, and Tempest gave a rueful laugh.

"Old habits die hard." He looked downward one last time. "Assassins, not so much."

Akieryon turned to Caspar. "Does this happen a lot?"

"More than I'd like." The king shrugged. "Some people object to my ideas of governance."

Some people with pockets deep enough to hire assassins. Akieryon thought of his last encounter with an assassin, and he grimaced a little. Caspar misread his expression and turned him a little away from the body. He shook his head, but his gaze ran over the crowd, alert for more danger. Waiting for the inevitable.

Some of the bystanders clung close to the walls, wide-eyed and traumatized, but a few had begun to edge toward Tempest, peering at the body of the assassin in morbid curiosity. Akieryon hung back, close beside the king, dread knotting in the pit of his stomach as a portal opened, unnoticed by the humans in the room. A Ferryman stepped through, planted her fists on her hips, and surveyed her task.

Akieryon wished he had learned a spell to make himself invisible, but of course the Ferrymen had ways of seeing the unseen. This one muttered something under her breath, sighed, and extended one hand. At her touch, the soul of the slain assassin became visible to Akieryon's eyes. He stared down at the empty shell he had inhabited, now a wretched mess on the floor.

"Not human," the soul whispered over and over. "He can't be human."

"Of course he's human." The Ferryman tilted her head. "He's just… different. Come. Let's get you home."

Home meant the Void, where every living soul began its journey after parting from its flesh. The soul of the assassin looked up, and saw Akieryon watching them.

"That one. What does that one want with me?"

The Ferryman rolled her eyes. "Absolutely nothing. And consider yourself fortunate for it, for you'd never stand a chance against one of Lord Michael's." She caught the fearful soul by the scruff, and they both vanished through her portal.

"Is it true that you're a soldier?"

Akieryon startled at the sound of the king's voice. He blinked and rubbed at the back of his neck, at the Lineage Mark there. "Who said so?"

"Dani did." Caspar tilted his head to indicate the redhead beside Tempest. "She's right, isn't she?"

"I… I *was* a soldier." Akieryon forced himself not to fidget under the king's appraising stare. "I don't know what I am now." A fugitive, probably. If the Ferryman said anything to her superiors about seeing him here, he would have to flee.

King Caspar merely nodded, as though such a statement required no further explanation. The guards, Akieryon noticed, had begun allowing people to leave one at a time, presumably after thorough questioning. When Caspar strode over to Tempest, Akieryon was all too happy to follow.

"The usual?" Caspar asked, bumping his shoulder against Tempest, who nodded.

"The latest."

"A pity. This sort of thing is a senseless waste of resources. A parliament will convene, with or without the approval of the nobility." Caspar shook his head. "With or without me even, at this point."

"It's performative." Tempest crouched and searched the body for weapons to add to his cache. "Someone is willing to waste lives to demonstrate displeasure." When he stood up, Caspar met his stare levelly.

"You see why I sent for you," he said. "Why I want you by my side until this business is settled."

"You've had better plans."

Caspar scoffed. "You, of all people, have no right to say that."

"There is nothing wrong with my plans," Tempest objected.

"Carnage aside?"

"Obviously."

"Obviously," Caspar repeated. He shot a meaningful glance at Akieryon, who failed to interpret it. "What do you think?"

"I think this one didn't come cheap." Tempest handed a silver-hilted dagger to his king. "I think we need a list of people who can afford this kind of expense." He chewed his thumbnail until Dani swatted his bloodied hands away from his face.

"Gross," she admonished, and Tempest ignored her.

"I think we need to know what people are really saying about this parliament of yours."

Caspar nodded. "Good. The two of you will find that out for me." He turned an apologetic little smile toward Akieryon. "Always more work. Two nights hence, let's dine privately, the four of us." His smile broadening, he plucked at the quilted doublet Akieryon wore. "And let's get you some clothes that don't belong to Tempest, yes?"

"I'd like something in blue," Akieryon blurted before he could think better of it. Did he really think he could replace his uniform coat so easily?

"Blue you shall have." Caspar clapped him on the shoulder in a friendly gesture that Akieryon only just managed not to shy from. "Right, Tempest?"

"Blue is good," Tempest agreed in an absent manner, his thoughts straying far away as he contemplated the body at his feet.

Tempest chewed his thumbnail all the way back to his suite. He took long strides, leaving Akieryon winded from the effort of keeping pace with him, and he said nothing. Akieryon watched his expression, trying and failing to read his thoughts by the slight furrow between his brows.

Tempest slammed through the door into the antechamber, and Akieryon eased it closed behind them. Given Tempest's state of agitation, Akieryon expected him to pace the room. Instead, Tempest slammed through into the bathroom. He barely kicked his shoes off before stepping into the enormous bathtub and yanking the copper chain. The pipes burbled, and water streamed from the dragon-head tap. Tempest stood directly beneath it, unbraiding his hair as the water soaked him to the skin. Rusty swirls of diluted blood dribbled from his clothing and ran down the drain, which remained open.

"You need a showerhead," Akieryon remarked, realizing too late how rude it was that he stood gawking in the doorway. Tempest blinked at him from beneath the steaming water, apparently unbothered.

"A showerhead?" he repeated, unfamiliar with the word, or the concept, or both. Akieryon fumbled through an explanation, describing the way a spout with many holes scattered the flow of water, making for more efficient washing. His cheeks had warmed by the time he fell silent.

Tempest nodded. "I'll have one made," he remarked, his tone impossibly light for a man who had just started peeling off layers of sodden, bloodstained clothing.

His blush intensifying, Akieryon turned away. The rush of water and the splashing of Tempest scrubbing the blood away followed him through into the bedchamber. His thoughts full to bursting, he stripped down to shirt and trousers, sat on the bed, and pulled his knees up to his chest. He would have a new blue coat. Someone wanted the king dead. Tempest killed like a demon and no one cared.

No one cared.

Why did no one care?

A scene flashed through his mind. A sizzle of magic. The stink of flayed flesh. Bare bone and blistered skin. Oily smoke seething along the edge of his blade as though it belonged there, as though he had called it forth on purpose. As though he had any idea how to banish it. Crushing his eyes tightly shut only brought more memories, and Akieryon buried his face in a pillow to stifle his shuddering breaths.

The air had become too heavy to fill his lungs.

Impenetrable darkness surrounded him.

His world was a tiny, dark cell.

Forever.

"Akieryon."

Tempest's voice held a note of urgency, a note that suggested he had called Akieryon's name several times already. Akieryon forced his head up from the pillow, and he noticed in an oddly detached way how his body tilted toward the place where Tempest's knee pressed down into the mattress. How had he not felt that?

"You're shaking." Tempest's hand hovered above his arm, ready to offer comfort, unwilling to touch too soon. "Has something happened?"

Akieryon looked at the hand, still paused a breath away from his skin, the wordless offer of a man who understood too well.

"I… I did it. I deserved… Well, that's a bit of a stretch, isn't it?

But I did nearly kill a superior officer. My mentor. My teacher." Pausing to gulp for breath, Akieryon leaned into Tempest's touch. "I never meant to do it, I didn't even know I *could* do it, and then everything happened so fast..." Akieryon looked down at the pillow in his lap. "Maybe I really am a monster."

With a firm tug, Tempest pulled Akieryon into his arms and held him to his chest. "You're no monster. Trust me, I'm something of an expert on the matter."

"You don't know." Akieryon turned his face against the damp towel that hung forgotten across Tempest's shoulders. "I tore the flesh from Master Seikhiel's bones. It was a routine training exercise. I... I didn't know I could use non-celestial magics. I certainly couldn't control it. I was a danger to everyone." When had tears started to strangle his words? "I think that's why he locked me away. I was a danger to everyone."

Tempest sat in silence, his arms secure around Akieryon and his heartbeat heavy enough to feel between them. What had he done? Why had he said all that? If he presented a danger even to his own kind, surely these humans would want him gone.

"Why did they not teach you to control it?"

Tempest's words burst through his expectations, shattering his fears and dashing a shock like cold water across his self-recriminations. Phrased thusly, it sounded so sensible. So simple.

Akieryon drew back, drew a shuddering breath. "I… don't know? I'm an angel who can use demonic powers." His thoughts flew to the back of his neck, to the double spiral mark. Those who had seen it might know. "I'm an abomination." Master Niseriel's word for him, now upon his own lips. "My commanding officer must have known. He used to push me to train harder than everyone else. To learn to defeat even the most lethal of demons."

To fight losing battles.

It struck him suddenly that Niseriel had never meant for him to survive his first few missions, and when he had, his commander had only pushed him toward more dangerous work.

Toward the hunt for a notorious criminal.

Akieryon scrubbed at his eyes with the edge of Tempest's towel. "I'm not sure what to think any more," he admitted, perhaps more to himself than to this strange human who showed him limitless compassion. "Maybe I never could tell who was my enemy."

Tempest made a small, thoughtful noise. "If you wait long enough," he said, "they often reveal themselves without too much effort on your part."

Of course a man like Tempest had enemies. Ambassador. Bodyguard. Sorcerer of some sort, if the books in his library were any indication. And yet, his steadfast presence, his willful kindness toward a stranger he had met on the road, these thoughts gave Akieryon just enough room for doubt. Who could truly dislike Tempest?

Well. Apart from the occasional bloody spectacle, apparently.

"Why does someone want to kill the king over a parliament?" Akieryon blurted, awkwardly voicing the thought as soon as it popped into his head. Tempest let out a long-suffering sigh.

"Because it will include representatives from the merchant and working classes."

Confusion skittered across Akieryon's face, pulling his brows downward. "Isn't that good?" Did he truly understand so little of human governments?

Tempest scoffed. "Not to the wealthy and the titled. They hate this parliament with a venomous fury, and it hasn't even convened yet."

Feeling something of his old self, Akieryon lifted his chin. "Then we shall have to ensure that it does."

Tempest pulled him forward into a warm hug. Akieryon closed his eyes, breathing the scent of damp skin and soap.

You're no monster.

For the moment, at least, he could believe it.

HEADACHES

Akieryon awakened alone again. Sunlight streamed in the open windows, and the curtains fluttered in the morning breeze. In a haze of drowsiness, he fumbled for Tempest's pillow, and he found it still warm. Akieryon wrapped his arms around the pillow and pulled it to his chest.

A dull ache throbbed behind his temples, a charming souvenir of yesterday's upset. He needed water. Moving would bring more pain. Holding the pillow tightly, Akieryon rolled onto his back and stared at the now-familiar ceiling.

Less than a week had passed. Mere days ago he had still paced the darkened rectangle of his cell. How had he grown so accustomed to these rooms already? When had he become so comfortable here that he thought of Tempest's grand bed as his own?

A knock at the outer door jolted his heart into his throat and sent all the blood in his body to hammer at the inside of his skull. Pressing a hand to his brow as though that might somehow keep his brains in his head, Akieryon levered himself upright. He dug his bare toes into the plush pile of the rug, gripped a bedpost, and dragged himself to his feet. One step at a time, one careful breath per step, he shuffled forward.

Arriving at the outer door, Akieryon grasped the handle and pulled. In the corridor beyond, a short woman met his bleary stare with a benign smile. She held long, narrow swatches of blue fabric over one arm, and the tight bun of her dark hair bristled with pencils.

"You'd be Akieryon, then." When he stepped back, she breezed into the antechamber. "I'm Cori, journeyman tailor, here for your measurements." Akieryon watched as she tossed the swatches onto a slender chair and took a tape from her belt. "Let's get to it."

She measured every possible line and angle of him, and perhaps invented a few, scribbling each number in a tiny notebook with a pencil snatched from her hair. She chattered a bit about fashions, fabrics, and how great a shame it was that Tempest had taken every scrap of color in his wardrobe away to his posting with the Lenyr. Akieryon itched with questions, but he held them back. Perhaps it was too soon to pry.

"A'right, then." Cori waved him toward the chair. "Pick a fabric, and we'll talk details." She focused for a moment on rolling her tape and stowing it back on her belt. Akieryon thumbed through the fabric swatches. He lingered for a moment on the shade he knew so well, the shade he could picture every time he closed his eyes. He was a deserter. He had no right to it. Drawing a deep breath, he selected a darker blue.

Cori swooped in, plucking the fabric from his hand and wrapping it around her little notebook. "Oh, that will look simply dashing with your coloring. What about facings? Silver?"

Neither white nor black. Akieryon nodded in silent gratitude. He would no longer look like a Demonslayer.

"Would you prefer pewter or enameled buttons?"

"Enameled?" Akieryon repeated, intrigued by the idea. Cori beamed at him and bounced on the balls of her feet.

"When this is done, Tempest will have a tough job of it keeping you to himself." She gave his arm a friendly pat. "I can see why he hasn't let you out much," she added, winking.

"Oh, no, I'm free to come and go as I please," Akieryon blurted, his stomach twisting at the suggestion—even in jest—that Tempest might keep him locked away. "I just… I don't want to go out yet."

"Well, no. Not dressed like *that* ." Cori cast a playfully judgmental eye over his borrowed shirt and trousers. "Don't worry. We'll fix you right up." With a breezy farewell, she swept back out the door and slammed it a bit too hard for Akieryon's headache.

Breakfast might help, he reasoned, and a bath. Beyond that, he had little access to restoratives from within Tempest's suite. Locating the usual breakfast tray on the side table, he started with fresh fruit and some sort of buttery bread. As he nibbled, Cori's words haunted him. *I can see why he doesn't let you out much.* Was that what people thought? That Tempest told him what to do?

Frowning only made his head hurt worse. He directed his energy toward his breakfast instead. Later, he couldn't remember what he ate.

A bath only made Akieryon's headache worse. Tempest returned some hours later to find him kneeling beside the bed, his face pressed against the coverlet. Somehow, Tempest seemed to take this latest odd behavior in stride. He settled himself on the floor, near enough to touch, and he waited for Akieryon to speak. With some struggle, he gathered his thoughts.

"Everyone thinks you're kind to me for my looks." Akieryon rolled his head to the side just enough to peer at Tempest from the corner of his eye. "Am I so beautiful to humans?"

Tempest pressed a fingertip to his chin, which Akieryon had begun to notice he did often when a question took him by surprise. "Perhaps," he conceded, as though he had no means to gauge a person's beauty. "Or perhaps they sense something ethereal about you."

"Did you?"

"I sensed your magic," Tempest said with his usual bluntness. "When I first touched you, it seemed like there was a—a sort of push and pull beneath your skin. What?" He frowned as Akieryon shifted around to face him properly. "Have I said something to give offense? You look so serious."

"Angel magic functions on the manipulation of opposing forces. That's what you sensed." Akieryon watched as Tempest considered this information. Once again, he seemed blandly curious.

"How does that work?"

"With a lot of concentration, mostly," he said, managing a shadow of a grin. Tempest gave a soft chuckle. Akieryon enjoyed the moment of shared amusement, but too soon another thought tumbled out of his poor sore head. "The king," he said. "He's the only person who hasn't treated me like I'm—I'm uncommonly pretty or something." When Tempest went still, Akieryon knew the truth. "You told him about me."

"Of course I did," Tempest said, as though it should be obvious. "I can't lie to Caspar."

"Because he's the king?" Akieryon had always struggled to follow human politics. Short lifespans always seemed to complicate matters.

"Because he's my friend." When Akieryon did not immediately register comprehension, Tempest added, "He's a Person and he's mine. He can tell when I'm keeping something from him."

"What do you mean, Person?" Akieryon tried to give it the same emphasis Tempest had. Tempest waved one hand in a vague gesture.

"Most people aren't, you know."

Akieryon tried to contest the point, but the mental effort of the conversation proved too great. Closing his eyes, he sank against the bed again. He felt his hair stir a moment before warm fingertips brushed against his forehead.

"Are you well?"

"Headache," Akieryon mumbled, though by now the word rather understated his suffering. Every movement lanced fresh agony through his skull.

"Here." Tempest pressed a glass of water into Akieryon's hand. There had been no water in the bedroom. Akieryon looked at the glass, lovely etched crystal with a thin band of gold at the lip. He looked at Tempest, and he raised an eyebrow. Tempest grinned at him. "Drink," he encouraged.

"You got this with magic."

Tempest shrugged one shoulder. "Yeah."

Akieryon took a careful sip of the water. "You say you're not a sorcerer," he accused, but he continued to drink from the extraordinarily fancy glass.

"No, a sorcerer does magic professionally."

"You're just being pedantic, *ambassador.*" Akieryon finished the water. Tempest touched one finger to the side of the glass, and it refilled. "You have small enchantments all over these rooms."

Tempest's smile turned faintly sheepish. "It's very difficult to get blood out of velvet."

"It's not just your wardrobe." Akieryon sipped the second glass of water. "What does the enchantment on your bed do?"

"It's always the right temperature." Tempest paused, then added, "And the pillows don't fall on the floor."

"You use magic for convenience!" Accustomed to magic requiring concentration and precision, Akieryon struggled to understand Tempest's casual enchantments.

"I can't think of a better use for it." Taking the empty glass from Akieryon's hand, Tempest set it aside. "Can you stand?"

Akieryon tried. One of his feet had stealthily gone numb. His second attempt involved gripping the bed frame and pushing himself upward. Gravity was definitely increasing. He sank back down again and gave a cautious shake of his head. "You've enchanted *me* now."

Tempest looked embarrassed. "I was trying to ease your pain. It seems I've made you drowsy instead." He scooped Akieryon up in his arms and lifted him onto the bed. "Perhaps sleep is what you need."

"You didn't use magic for that," Akieryon teased as Tempest arranged pillows and blankets around him. He struggled to keep his eyes open, and a sudden panic stabbed through him. He was helpless.

He was trapped.

"Akieryon." Tempest took hold of his wrist and felt for his pulse. "What's wrong?"

Akieryon made a small, desperate noise. Tempest leaned closer, and Akieryon tried to hold tight to his sleeve. "Stay," he managed, his voice thin, his breathing shallow. "Please stay."

"Of course." Tempest stretched out beside him, his familiar warmth pushing back the panic. Akieryon rolled his head against Tempest's shoulder. The room wasn't dark, the door was unlocked, and he was not alone. Gradually, the pounding of his heart slowed. He could let himself be vulnerable. He could sleep.

~⸳❧◆☙⸳~

Akieryon startled awake. Immediately, Tempest's arm around him tightened. Akieryon blinked and squinted, struggling for a moment to comprehend the afternoon sunlight streaming in through the windows. While he blinked away the fog of sleep, Tempest's protective grip softened. Akieryon pulled a pillow between them and hugged it to his chest.

"You stayed."

"You asked me to." Tempest set aside the book he'd held in his free hand. "How are you feeling?"

Akieryon tilted his head at experimental angles. The sharp pain of earlier had gone, leaving vague malaise in its place. "Better. Much improved." He could feel a warmth creeping up his face, and he buried his chin in the pillow. "You're very patient with me."

"I do know something of what it is to be imprisoned."

"You?" Akieryon gasped before he could stop himself. It seemed impossible that any mere prison could hold Tempest. Tempest was strong and confident. Tempest casually wielded complex magics.

Tempest tore a man's guts out with the liquid grace of a born predator, and then chewed his bloody fingernails afterward.

Akieryon wondered if he would ever sort out this puzzle of a human. Some nagging doubt in the back of his mind told him he should fear Tempest, and yet what could a former Demonslayer have to fear from a human?

Tempest shrugged. "It was a long time ago."

Long ago... but how long? How old could Tempest be?

Akieryon opened his mouth to ask. "Will I ever feel normal?" he said instead.

Tempest shifted, and for a moment Akieryon thought he might reach for him, might pull him close. Instead, Tempest sat up. "I don't know what normal is," he said flatly. He swung his legs over the edge of the bed. "I don't know that it matters."

Pushing himself up on his elbows, Akieryon watched the line of Tempest's shoulders, looking for tension, for signs of unhappiness. Nothing. "You must be either very strange or very wise."

"Probably both," Tempest agreed with a chuckle. He stood up, taking his book with him. "I'm to meet with the Draycens about this latest assassination attempt." The water clock chimed, and he tilted his head at the sound. "It seems I'm late."

He left Akieryon sitting alone in the great bed, wondering who or what the Draycens might be. Akieryon stayed still for a little while, trying to sort out his muddled thoughts. Humans were meant to be simple creatures, all driven by the urgency of living for a single century at best. Not Tempest. Tempest acted with deliberation, as though time meant nothing to him. Tempest had to choose to maintain his humanity.

Without thinking, Akieryon hugged the pillow again. It gave off a faint scent of smoke and sandalwood and vast empty spaces, the same smell that always clung to Tempest's hair, even when freshly washed. It tingled Akieryon's nostrils and tugged at his memory. He knew that smell from long ago. How could he know that smell?

A knock at the outer door had him flinging the pillow aside and lurching to his feet. The pillow rolled to the edge of the bed, rocked against an invisible barrier, and stilled. Akieryon hurried through the antechamber and yanked the door open.

A liveried servingboy stood there, posture rigid, a silver tray held before him. Warily, Akieryon lifted the little ivory card that lay upon it. *Sir Marek, Lord Draycen requests your presence at the sixth bell.* Akieryon looked at the boy, who would certainly be too young to be a cadet, but he could not guess an age.

"Me?"

The boy nodded.

"Where?"

The boy shook his head.

"Thank you," Akieryon said. "You've been very helpful."

The servingboy tucked his tray under one arm, executed a brief bow, and strode away down the corridor. Akieryon closed the door. The sixth bell. When was that? He went to examine the water clock.

The device, he realized, was quite complex. In addition to

chiming the hours, it displayed the season, approximate sunrise and sunset times, the temperature and air pressure, and other measurements foreign to him. He had never seen Tempest maintain the thing, nor ever do more than glance at it. If he investigated more closely, Akieryon wondered if he would find more hidden magic, more enchantments purely for Tempest's convenience. Probably.

According to the clock, he had a little more than an hour before he needed to meet with this Sir Marek. He wandered into Tempest's wardrobe, hoping to find some clothing to borrow that would feel at least somewhat appropriate. What did one wear to meet a stranger of unknown station?

A uniform.

Batting the thought away, Akieryon rummaged through black silks and black velvets and even black leathers. He would use what he had at hand. What else could he do?

SIR MAREK

A little before the sixth bell, Akieryon stood at the door to the antechamber. He tugged at the hem of his borrowed vest. Somehow, without Tempest beside him, it bothered him more that nothing fit properly. He had decided on a less formal look in favor of freedom of movement, which he figured this Lord Draycen might take as a grave insult. He would have to live with that. The more pressing concern, really, was where to meet the man.

Should he try to figure it out for himself? Akieryon's hand hovered above the door handle. He was no longer a prisoner, and still his world consisted of only a few rooms. Worse, he had never actually gone anywhere in this castle without Tempest. Suddenly he regretted not thinking to explore, but how would that even help him now?

After an agonizing moment of deliberation, he pulled the door open. On the opposite side of the corridor, the silent servingboy leaned against the wall, looking bored. Upon seeing Akieryon, he straightened.

"So," said Akieryon, relieved to see him, "where are we going?"

The boy tilted his head, indicating a direction. Without a word, he turned and walked away, leaving Akieryon hurrying to catch up. At first, it looked like they retraced the steps to the king's audience chamber. Then the boy veered off to the right, through a series of arches and down a tight spiraling stairway that ended in a sort of enclosed garden. Baffled, Akieryon looked around him. The ceiling and two walls opposite the stairs were made of glass fused to an intricate metal mesh. Potted fruit trees lined the walls, interspersed with planters full of vibrant flowers and lush greenery. A large fountain dominated the center of the space, not quite impressive enough to make Akieryon miss noticing the scorch marks on the wall beside the stairs.

A man waited beside the fountain, a book in his hand. He faced slightly away from the stairs, careless in his demeanor, absolutely contrived. His carefully groomed hair blazed the same vibrant red as Dani's.

Akieryon stepped forward. "Lord Draycen, I presume?" He hadn't meant it as a question. The man set his book at the edge of the fountain and turned, his deliberation pure artifice, his smile false.

"Ah," he said. "Akieryon. Tempest's guest."

"That's correct." Uncertain how to react to this man who studied him as though looking over goods in a market and finding them wanting, Akieryon fell back on his military training. He stood at rigid attention, his hands at his sides, his gaze fixed ahead, not quite looking at Lord Draycen.

"My sister thinks you're military."

So Dani was Lord Draycen's sister. Tempest had met with both of them earlier. "Oh," said Akieryon.

"Oh?" prompted Lord Draycen. He had begun to pace around Akieryon, inspecting him from every angle.

"The resemblance is—"

"Almost entirely in the hair," interrupted Lord Draycen with a scoff. His pacing, his scrutiny, and now his dismissive demeanor all put Akieryon on the defensive. It felt a little too much like standing before Master Niseriel, awaiting judgment. "If you're a friend of Tempest's," he said in a distinctly unfriendly tone, "then you must call me Sir Marek."

Akieryon tried to swallow his rising unease, and he found he had no voice. Was he friend to Tempest? He certainly hoped he was. He gave a tiny nod. Sir Marek watched the muscle clenching in his jaw.

"Who are you really?"

"Akieryon." His voice came out in a whisper. "Formerly of the

Fifth Sword. Son of nobody, out of the Sixth Sphere."

"Why are you here?" Sir Marek persisted, his questions coming as demands. He stepped closer, a frail human shadow of Master Niseriel's unpredictable menace. Akieryon's gaze dropped to the flagstones beneath his feet.

"I had nowhere else to go."

"And you just happened upon Tempest on the road? Less than a day out of the city?" Sir Marek's hand shot out and caught Akieryon by the arm. "Now, when King Caspar's life is in peril? You expect me to believe that this is all coincidence?" His grip tightened, his fingers finding pressure points and digging in. Akieryon looked at the hand that held him, observing in detached fascination. What did this man hope to accomplish? Sir Marek loomed close, too close, and gave his arm a rough shake. "Answer me," he growled.

As soon as Akieryon released the tension holding his body rigid and his jaw shut tight, muscle memory took over. He broke Sir Marek's grip and caught hold of his wrist in a single motion. Akieryon yanked him forward while thrusting one foot out, breaking his stance, overbalancing him. Then he dropped low, and a precise jab with one elbow sent Sir Marek toppling into the fountain with a yelp of surprise.

Akieryon stood over him, looking down, his expression as cold as Sir Marek's voice had been a minute ago. "I am a Demonslayer of the Fifth Sword. If I meant your king harm, he would be dead already."

He did not wait to watch the shock on Sir Marek's face turn to any other emotion. Instead, he turned toward the spiral stairway. Still feeling the pressure of a delicate human wrist in the palm of his hand, Akieryon numbly retraced his steps back to Tempest's suite.

He was no longer a Demonslayer. He was a deserter.

He deserved whatever Sir Marek had intended.

The outer door slammed, and Akieryon flinched at the sound. "I heard you met Marek," Tempest announced from the antechamber. He sounded amused. He knew something of what had happened. Heat rising in his face, Akieryon sank down deeper in the bath.

"I did." The words came out sullen. Why had he not closed the door to the bathroom? He strung together vague memories of returning here in a daze, of casting aside his borrowed clothing and pulling the chain for hot water. Footsteps approached. Tempest would find him here, would discover the rumpled heap of discarded clothing. Akieryon shifted to hide his arm from view, to conceal how he had tried in vain to scrub away the memory of Sir

Marek's touch as well as deeper, older memories, memories from before the dark.

Tempest appeared in the doorway, his smile dying as he saw Akieryon. "Oh." In a moment he was at the edge of the tub, kicking his boots away and plunging his feet into the water. He sat, and he pulled Akieryon over against his knee. "Tell me."

Akieryon closed his eyes, and suddenly only the solid warmth of Tempest was real. The memories were shadows once more, too distant to hurt him. "He was just…" He sighed. The right words to describe Sir Marek eluded him.

"A dick."

Tempest's flat tone startled a laugh from Akieryon. "Yes," he admitted. "Yes, he was."

"He never does make a good first impression," Tempest said. His grip tightened a little. "Did he frighten you?"

Frighten? "No," Akieryon replied slowly, considering his own reaction to Sir Marek. "No, I don't think a human *can* frighten me. But… But he did remind me of someone else…" He shuddered. Master Niseriel had handled him roughly in the past, had punished him and torn feathers from his wings, but he knew others had suffered far more. And now he knew why. His fingertips strayed to the back of his neck. Master Niseriel would threaten and intimidate and inflict small torments, but he would not contaminate himself.

He disdained Fallen and demons too much for that.

"Here, what's this?"

With Tempest's fingertips gentle on his wrist, Akieryon froze. He had forgotten that his skin still glowed pink with scrubbing. "I…" He gulped for breath. "I tried… I tried to wash it," he managed in a whisper. He stared down at Tempest's hand on his arm, watched his thumb start to move in a soothing caress. "I don't know…" That wasn't true. "I didn't want to remember."

Tempest didn't say anything to that. He just sat with him and held him until the memories faded back to where they belonged. Later a supper tray arrived, and they ate together, Akieryon wrapped in a dressing gown and Tempest with his legs still wet. When Akieryon smiled, Tempest looked as though a weight had lifted from him.

DINNER AND
A SCHEME

In the morning, new clothing began to arrive for Akieryon.
First came a stack of shirts and trousers, neatly folded, all in shades
of slate. Next, a blushing page delivered stockings in silk and
wool, a pair of shoes that laced to the ankle, and two black vests.
This is a uniform, Akieryon realized. *They're dressing me to match
Tempest.*

It suited him just fine, and so he dressed himself in his new
clothing. As he stood in stocking feet, scrutinizing the impeccable
fit in the full-length mirror, Tempest came in. He stopped short,
hesitated for just a moment, then grinned.

"It's nice to see you in something that fits."

Akieryon felt a warmth creeping up his cheeks. He turned back
to the mirror. "I don't like the shoes." Did he sound ungrateful?

"Neither do I," Tempest said, picking one up to examine it.
"But your new boots will take another week, probably, so we shall
have to suffer." He handed the shoe to Akieryon, who sat down on

a cushioned stool to put it on.

"I'm…" He pulled the laces too tight, and paused to adjust them. "I don't know how to repay you for all of this."

Tempest made a dismissive noise. "I never spend all of my wardrobe budget, and Caspar has been curiously willing to lend his own tailors to the task of clothing you."

Akieryon studied the neat stitching on the cuffs of his shirt. "Is that unusual?"

Tempest gave him a bit of an odd look. "The royal tailors don't tend to do work for anyone but the king. Of course, Caspar is not the typical monarch, so make of that what you will."

"Yes, I'm eager to hear more about his parliament."

"You will." Tempest grimaced. "At great length."

Akieryon busied himself with putting his new clothing away in the space Tempest had cleared for him. "Did you know they'd bring me so many things?" he wondered, and Tempest shrugged.

"The shirts and jerkins take only slight alterations, so I assumed so."

Akieryon had to admit that he knew little about tailoring—and fashion in general—even in his home Sphere. He had received his uniforms, and had followed instructions regarding wearing and caring for them. Before that, he had worn whatever his foster families had cared to provide. Trying not to think too hard about it,

Akieryon went to sit quietly until the time came for them to meet with the king.

Cori arrived first.

She swept into the antechamber, proudly holding up a magnificent blue coat. It had a flat collar and belled sleeves. The shining enameled buttons had nothing to do with fastenings and everything to do with opulence. The tailor held it open, and Akieryon shyly shrugged into it. The weight of it settled over his shoulders, forcing him to stand a little taller.

"How did you do this in one day?" Akieryon breathed, mesmerized by how the fullness of the coat followed his every movement.

Cori waved a dismissive hand. "Staying up all night, mostly. But you are almost the same size as Sir Marek, and that made it easier. Also you don't demand quilting and embroidery, so that helps."

"Cheek," said Tempest from the doorway. He smiled, and Cori grinned and bobbed a brief bow at him. "The coat looks good," he added, his gaze lingering on Akieryon in an appraising manner that made him flush to his hairline. Cori excused herself and closed the door softly on her way out.

Akieryon held his arms out to his sides. "I don't understand."

Tempest shrugged. "Neither do I," he said. "Tailoring is a

particular magic that I've not studied."

"But why go to so much trouble for me?"

"You'll have to ask Caspar." Tempest pulled the door open. "Ready?"

Was it time already? Hugging the full sleeves of his new coat across himself, Akieryon stepped out into the corridor. He had too many questions. How would he ever find any answers?

Two guards stood at the door to the chamber. Akieryon might have sized them up, but Tempest strode boldly between them and pushed the door open for himself. With nothing to do but follow, Akieryon stepped inside.

Two more guards stood just inside the doorway, but they saluted and stepped out when they saw Tempest. Caspar came to greet them, but Akieryon's attention was snared by a lingering feeling of fire long past. Glancing around the comfortably appointed chamber, he saw that the luxurious tapestries concealed scorch marks up the walls. Someone had deliberately chosen not to scrub and whitewash over them. Why? The floor likewise bore scars, peeking out from beneath colorful rugs. Caspar had to have told his people to leave the traces of trauma past. Akieryon tried anew to get the measure of this man, this friend Tempest now greeted as a brother. What sort of a man was he?

Stepping back from Tempest's embrace, Caspar beamed at Akieryon, teeth flashing a bright white contrast to the soft brown of his skin. Angels were always lighter or darker than he was, and Akieryon had to struggle not to stare in admiration. "I see my tailors have been busy." The king clapped Akieryon on the shoulder. "As have my cooks. Come."

Baffled by Caspar's friendliness—all warmth and no artifice—Akieryon allowed himself to be led to a low table set with four places. Dani already sat there, apparently not prepared to stand on ceremony, in figure or in fact. She looked up at them, and she flashed Akieryon half a grin.

"I saw what you did to my brother." For an instant, Akieryon's chest tightened as he imagined Dani watching their exchange from behind a potted lemon tree. "He came in absolutely flummoxed and dripping on the good carpets," she continued. "I'm sure he earned a dunking."

"Doesn't he always?" Tempest settled himself on the cushioned bench beside Dani, leaving Akieryon the place at Caspar's right. Akieryon felt a hint of warmth creeping up his cheeks. This was all too informal, wasn't it? Caspar was a *king*.

Caspar sat, pulling Akieryon down with him. "Relax," he said with another smile. "No harm was done, and even Marek's bruised pride will heal in short order." He reached to the center of the table and helped himself to a bowl of fresh fruit and a platter of cheese. Tempest and Dani followed his lead with no thought to precedence, nor even any particular manners. Tempest lifted his selections on the point of his knife. Dani used her fingers. Akieryon clenched his fists in his lap until Caspar noticed and nudged him with his shoulder. "It's fine," he said, all encouragement. "We're all exiles here."

"I don't understand," Akieryon said, but he nervously moved a halved plum and two kinds of cheese to his own plate.

"Tempest didn't tell you?" Caspar looked to Tempest, who shrugged and gestured vaguely with his knife. "When I was nine," he said between bites of his food, "my parents died. My uncle assumed regency and immediately tried to have me killed." He lifted his eyebrows and tilted his head, indicating the scorched walls. "I escaped—a debt I may never repay—and I fled. I met Tempest not far along the Old Tymirin Road."

"A good thing, too," Tempest said.

"Yes, I never would have made it out of Davenz without you," Caspar agreed, all good cheer. To Akieryon he said, "I made him my bodyguard on the spot, and he protected me from bandits and assassins all the way to Tymirin, where the Empress granted me asylum. It turns out Dani was already there, studying under her captain of the guard, Sir Rynan. Marek found us a few years later.

When I was old enough to claim my throne, we all returned together."

Akieryon had a feeling that Caspar was leaving out a mountain of relevant details. "What happened to your uncle?"

"He's in a bottle on my mantelpiece." Caspar took a large bite of stewed apple that must have been preserved from last autumn, and he chewed with self-satisfaction. Alive or dead? Akieryon hesitated to ask.

"All these two did in Tymirin was read," Dani said, a note of teasing in her voice. "Anything and everything they could get their hands on."

"That's where he got the idea for a parliament," Tempest added. His cool green gaze regarded Caspar with mingled reproach and amusement.

"If I'm going to be a target either way, I might as well have some help with writing laws."

"It won't do you any good unless we can flush out the people behind the attacks," Dani pointed out. She sounded worried, and she gave a firm impression of having wanted to use a stronger word than *people*.

"I have an idea," Akieryon blurted as soon as the thought popped into his head. Everyone turned to look at him, so he soldiered on. That was what he did, wasn't it? Soldier. "How many people know how I came to be here?"

"The four of us," Caspar said, a shadow appearing between his brows. "And Marek. I doubt he'd tell anyone."

Some excuse would have to be made for why he had arrived in a blindfold, and why he had come with no personal effects, but they could work out the details together. "Then put out a rumor that I'm an expert come from a foreign land to help you with your parliament." Akieryon gave him an apologetic little smile. "Of course, you'll have to teach me all about it first. My home is governed by oligarchy, and always has been."

"I can't put you in danger," Caspar protested, but Akieryon would not relent.

"If I can draw out the conspirators, it will have been worth the risk. Besides," he added with a shiver of pure anticipation, "I assure you, I am far harder to kill than you are." His training forbade him to harm humans, but he could disable them in many satisfying ways, as Marek had already learned.

Anyway, he was one of the exiles now. Perhaps he could unlearn some of his training.

Caspar gradually warmed to the plan, and over roast meats and root vegetables he animatedly explained how his parliament would include representatives from the nobility, the trades, and the farming communities in equivalent proportions. The nobility took issue with this plan, but they had yet to succeed at stopping it. Akieryon nodded along, making mental notes to ask for more detail about the granges and the guilds later.

"So," said Akieryon, tapping one finger against the stem of his crystal goblet, "traditionally the king makes all the decisions regarding laws and foreign policy and all that, but the nobility have been able to influence him rather a lot in the past to act in their interest. This new parliament will take a great deal of power out of your hands, diminishing their overall influence. Have I got that right?"

"More or less," Caspar said, apparently pleased with the summation.

"And the granges and the guilds are allotted representatives based on population density, while the nobility—" Here, Akieryon's understanding faltered. "I… What are Houses, and why does each get one representative?"

"Don't worry about it," Caspar assured him. "You're not supposed to be an expert in matters that are specific to Davenz."

"Can you explain more about their complaints that outsiders will have power in the government?"

"Tempest didn't tell you?" Caspar shot an amused glance across the table. Dani snorted. Tempest scooped a heap of strawberries on top of something that looked like savillum and ignored everyone else. "He gave me his kingdom to rule."

Akieryon's confusion deepened. "You're a king?" he ventured, his voice coming out small and uncertain. Looking up to meet his questioning gaze, Tempest gave a firm shake of his head.

"No. I'm not suited to it." He glared at Caspar. "I went back to Arum just long enough to sign the act of annexation."

"There is no one else who could rule," Caspar said softly, just for Akieryon's ears. "He wouldn't have told you that either."

His eyes on Tempest, who settled in with apparent indifference to eat his dessert, Akieryon said, "So the nobility of Davenz thinks of the representatives that will be coming from this newly annexed territory as foreigners?"

"I think you grasp the situation." Caspar shook his head. "The old system clearly wasn't working. Between my uncle here and the coup there…" He sighed. "Anyway, it's time we tried something new."

Akieryon contemplated his own dessert. Something still bothered him, but he couldn't quite sort out what. He took a bite. The savillum tasted of honey and cardamom, just like Enoch made. A twinge of homesickness speared him, and he squashed it.

"Akieryon," Caspar said gently. "Does the cake offend you?"

Realizing he had given the savillum several fierce stabs, Akieryon felt shame coloring his cheeks. "No. I just…" *I wonder if my old friends miss me at all.* He himself could barely remember their faces. Except for Raaqiel, who had nicknamed him Chess Nerd. Akieryon drew a deep breath. "If people are trying to kill you, they must have a contender for the throne?" Yes, there was the nagging thought. Politics of heredity and all that nonsense.

"Undoubtedly. Half the peerage are my extended family." Casper took a long drink of his wine. "The rest have been elevated at some point for distinguished service to the crown."

"But they let your uncle rule in your name?" Akieryon said, frowning.

"Yes, because he was scary."

"Not scary enough," Tempest said with a note of dark satisfaction. A shiver raced down Akieryon's spine. Trying to hide his reaction, he stuffed his mouth full of soft, cheesy dessert. He apparently failed, for after the dishes were neatly stacked and the benches pushed back from the table, Dani drew him aside.

"I know," she said, which seemed to Akieryon a strange way to open a conversation. "Tempest is dangerous and baffling and all manner of alluring. I get it. Just, try not to get too attached."

A bit late for that. "He won't hurt me," Akieryon said, struggling through another wave of confusion.

"Look," Dani said, placing a sympathetic hand on his arm. "You're a nice kid—"

Akieryon cut her off with a laugh. "Kid?" he repeated. "Oh, no, is that why you're all so keen to warn me off of him? How old do you think I am?"

Dani hesitated, sensing a trap. "Twenty?"

Akieryon scrubbed tears of mirth from his eyes. "Not even close." At twenty he had just been turned out from his first foster home. When Dani looked a question at him, he said, "Nearer to eight hundred."

"You're no elf."

Taken aback by her skepticism, Akieryon shook his head. "I'm not," he agreed. "I'm from a lot farther away."

Dani tilted her head, her eyes narrowing in a way too like her brother. "If you hurt Caspar—"

"Tempest trusts me not to hurt Caspar," Akieryon interrupted. "I take it he's not easily misled."

Dani harrumphed, which Akieryon chose to interpret as assent. This Caspar must be something remarkable, to engender such devotion. Perhaps he would see why in time.

"Just don't expect him to love you," Dani added, her voice knifing through his thoughts. "He doesn't do that."

"Tempest?" Frowning, Akieryon looked across to where Tempest and Caspar stood beside the fireplace, their heads bent together, their conversation animated. They looked closer than brothers, two hearts beating a counterpoint to the world around them. He gestured. "Is this not love?"

Dani gave him a patronizing smile. "Eight hundred years?" she said. "Really?"

~ ⋆ ◆ ⋆ ~

"I don't like it," Tempest said as soon as the door closed behind them. "But," he added before Akieryon could protest, "you're right. The plan is solid."

Akieryon glowed under the praise. "I promise, I'm sturdier than you are."

"You're still under my protection." Tempest stepped out of his boots and peeled away his outer layers of clothing. "If any harm befalls you, I'll feel compelled to make a mess."

Akieryon grinned after him. "I don't really see how that's my problem." He went into the wardrobe to put away his delightful new coat, and he found Tempest clearing a large space. "Are… are you getting new clothes?"

"No." Tempest sounded amused, but he kept his attention on his work. "But you are."

Akieryon looked down at himself, then back to Tempest. " *More* new clothes?"

"Oh, yes. If you're Caspar's special guest, as this new intrigue would have people believe, and you've somehow lost all of your court attire, then he's bound to have his tailors hard at work for a month to clothe you."

Akieryon chewed on this thought. "Any chance we can talk him down to two weeks?" he ventured, and Tempest laughed.

"You're welcome to try."

They passed a quiet evening together by the fireside. Tempest had produced a volume on parliamentary government from somewhere, which he presented to Akieryon before selecting a book of sorcery for himself. They sat together in matching chairs, each absorbed in his own reading. Worries could come later.

They always did.

ON THE JOB

The morning sun brought with it a strong wind out of the east. It smelled faintly of brine, and seabirds screamed in the distance. Was there an ocean nearby? Akieryon headed for Tempest's little library in search of a map. A knock at the outer door waylaid him.

Akieryon pulled the door open. There stood Cori, a new shirt in her hands—a thin linen excuse to talk to him. She thrust the shirt into his hands. "I don't blame you for holing up in here for a week," she said bluntly.

"Um," said Akieryon.

"Don't you worry." Cori gave him a friendly pat on the arm. "You've chosen the safest place in all of Davenz."

"Yes," Akieryon agreed. He thumbed the fine embroidery on the charcoal linen in his hands. "Tempest is formidable."

Obviously losing a battle to contain a flood of words bubbling up within her, Cori leaned a little into the antechamber. "I'm so glad he saved you from those bandits. Such a shame about your retinue." Clamping both hands over her mouth, she bounced twice in place and made a squeaking noise between her fingers. "Sorry. You probably don't want to talk about it."

Akieryon found himself smiling a little at Cori's prattle, despite his confusion. He sensed that he ought to play along. "Someone's been talking about me."

"Nnnnnnyeah." Cori gave him an abashed grin. "I overheard one of Lord Draycen's pages telling one of the apprentice lacemakers about how you were attacked on your way on the Old Tymirin Road, and then Tempest swooped in and saved you and brought you here safe and sound but all your people and all your things were lost. I'm sorry!" She clutched her hands to her mouth again. "It must have been a terrible shock for you, and I don't want to cause you any more suffering by talking about it!"

"I'm... processing it," Akieryon said softly. "I am tremendously grateful for everything Tempest has done for me." He would have to ask Tempest about this new rumor. "And you also. Please convey my thanks to your fellow tailors."

Cori flushed with pleasure, bobbed in place, then hurried away to tell everyone what he had said. Mystified, Akieryon went to put his latest garment away. He had finally made his way to Tempest's little library when the outer door opened. His hand hovering over a promising-looking volume, Akieryon sighed. In five minutes would he even remember that he wanted a map?

Tempest found him just as he turned toward the door. He had a faint hint of mischief about him. Akieryon raised an eyebrow. "You've heard the rumor?"

"About how you were robbed on the way here and I saved your life?" When Akieryon nodded, Tempest grinned at him. "Yes, but I'm surprised *you've* heard already."

"Cori," Akieryon said, and Tempest gave a sagely nod.

"It's a masterstroke of Marek's. He's got at least four versions circulating already." When Akieryon stepped back and wrapped his arms around himself, Tempest took a swift step forward. "What's wrong?"

"I… thought he didn't like me."

"What, for dunking him in the fountain? I assure you, his sister's done far worse to him." When that failed to reassure Akieryon, Tempest added, "You're helping Caspar. That's the fastest way to get on Marek's good side."

"I didn't know he had one of those," Akieryon said. Chuckling, Tempest draped an arm over his shoulders and pulled him close.

"Don't worry about Marek—though you will have to get used to him, I suppose." Tempest's cool green gaze sobered. "Caspar would like you to start attending him in his presence chamber, just as I do."

Akieryon had no idea what that meant, and he told Tempest so.

"Just follow my lead," Tempest assured him. Akieryon looked him in the eye, squared his shoulders, and nodded. He trusted Tempest. He supposed he would have to come to trust Caspar as well.

The royal presence chamber, it turned out, was rather like the audience chamber in which Akieryon had first met Caspar, just a step less formal. The king sat at the far end of the chamber, a redhead to either side of him and a little swiveling writing desk at his right hand. About a dozen people lingered about the room, mostly in small clusters, talking to each other. Akieryon wondered how many of them had already heard Sir Marek's rumors.

Upon seeing them, Caspar rose from his seat and a hush fell over the chamber. He strode forward, his hands extended, beaming at them. "My friends," he said. "Welcome." He clasped Akieryon's hands warmly. "You must forgive me for not recognizing you at once."

Akieryon saw his cue, and he dipped his head appropriately. "The fault was my own, Your Majesty. I hid myself within Tempest's hospitality."

"After your ordeal, I shouldn't blame you. Come." His hand on Akieryon's shoulder, Caspar headed back across the room. Tempest followed them just a step behind. "You must get to know all of my friends."

Akieryon glanced around at all the faces watching them. "Are we all friends here?"

"Of course!" Caspar lied. He gestured broadly. "These are the people who help me with everyday governance." They were surrounded by people who stood to lose a great deal of influence, real or imagined. "And you've already met Dani and Sir Marek." Something wicked danced in the king's hazel eyes.

"Ah. Yes." Akieryon inclined his head. "Good to see both of you again."

Sir Marek's smile was benign, betraying nothing of his skill at disseminating lies. "Remind me again how you two met."

"We hadn't until just the other day," Caspar said, and Akieryon nodded his agreement.

"His Majesty and I have corresponded a great deal through a mutual friend, but it was all intellectual discourse." Was lying to humans wrong? Did morality even matter to an angel who could wield infernal magics?

Dani rolled her eyes. "Another of your boring Tymirin book people?"

"I believe they're called librarians," Tempest teased. Caspar settled back into his seat, and everyone else resumed their murmured conversations.

Day after day Akieryon spent his afternoons perched on a stool in a place of high favor at Caspar's side. In the evenings he curled into a comfortable chair, or tucked under blankets, reading book after book on human governance. He hadn't studied so hard since his Academy days. Once he understood representative government and elections in a broad sense, Caspar began to provide notes on his specific parliamentary system.

From what Akieryon could tell, Caspar's ideas were nothing short of a complete overhaul of the kingdom's political structure. He gave up all legislative power to his new parliament—almost. He had a vote in the parliament chamber, and also the power to decide any deadlocked votes. The more he read, the more Akieryon saw an underlying philosophy to Caspar's plans, a belief that one person should not—*could* not—bear the burden of governing alone. He reserved full command of foreign policy, as well as limited emergency powers (not to exceed ninety days unless approved by parliament). Caspar had left precious little room for future monarchs to abuse their power, such as it would be.

Setting aside the latest stack of papers, Akieryon pressed his fingertips to his eyelids. It was a lot to absorb. Clearly, Caspar had been planning this for years.

"Something wrong?"

Akieryon made a high-pitched noise behind his hands. Even with his eyes closed, he could still see Caspar's small, precise penmanship. "Eye strain," he said, a little shortly.

"Yes, reading Caspar's documents will do that." Tempest sounded amused as he set aside his book of sorcery. "Come to bed. It's far too late to stay up squinting at paperwork."

These were the moments Akieryon had come to cherish over the last few days. A week? Nearly two? Had he lived among humans so long already? When he put aside his reading for the night, when he and Tempest had put out all the lamps save for the one by the bed, then Akieryon felt the tension ease out of his shoulders. He climbed into Tempest's enormous bed and he nestled deep in Tempest's down blankets, where he indulged in a sense of peace he found nowhere else. Tempest draped an arm lazily across Akieryon's waist, and they talked quietly of unimportant matters until drowsiness overtook them.

Akieryon was aware, in an abstract sense, that he loved Tempest. It was inevitable, really. As inevitable as the pain of their eventual parting. Whether the end would come in three years or thirty years, Akieryon knew it would leave scars that would linger for the rest of his life, and so he avoided thinking about it. Tempest was human. So were Caspar and Dani and Cori—all people Akieryon counted as friends these days—and no amount of wishing could make them otherwise. This was the price of his freedom; he refused to make it Tempest's problem.

Most mornings arrived gently: a caress of sunlight, the breakfast tray in the antechamber, the delivery of more new clothes. Akieryon took his time eating and washing up and deciding what to wear. He hadn't had to choose his own outfits in centuries. Now he had more variety than he knew what to do with.

"You can't wear the same thing twice in one week."

Akieryon raised an eyebrow at Tempest's monochrome attire.

"They're used to me," Tempest said flatly, plucking the long vest from Akieryon's fingers and handing him another in a different shade of blue. "And you're the center of attention."

"Shouldn't that be Caspar?" Akieryon protested. "He's the king."

"Should has nothing to do with it, as you know perfectly well. This is your plan, after all." Tempest smiled at him. Teasing. Akieryon grinned back.

"Just checking."

"It's a good tactic." Tempest buckled his sword belt and selected several daggers, which vanished about his person.

"What tactic?" Akieryon asked warily.

"Distracting people with your innocent face and anxious demeanor." As he strode out of the wardrobe, Tempest added over his shoulder, "Probably most of them never even notice that you're a cheeky little shit."

"Hey!" Akieryon hurried after him, and they were laughing together by the time they stepped out into the corridor.

Their laughter died when they saw Sir Marek's silent page. The boy bowed, handed Tempest a folded piece of paper, and walked away.

"What's that child's name?" Akieryon wondered as Tempest unfolded the note.

"Lan," Tempest said absently. He frowned a little. "We're on. The representatives from Myrdis are arriving within the hour."

"Aren't they a day early?" Akieryon protested. He had to jog to catch up, for Tempest had already begun striding down the corridor. They hurried, and the distance to Caspar's presence chamber seemed somehow shorter than it should have been. Tempest shouldered between the guards and pushed the door open himself. This was normal enough not to warrant so much as raised eyebrows from Caspar's guards.

At the far end of the room, Caspar looked up from earnest conversation with Sir Marek. His face relaxed, and he beckoned for them to approach.

"Members of our parliament are arriving today," Caspar declared, loudly enough that a hush fell over the room. "I would like for our friend Akieryon to go and welcome them for us."

Feeling every eye in the room upon him, Akieryon bowed in the manner of a Seraph, with his shoulders rigid and his head bent low. His Lineage Mark was visible to any near enough to see it, but humans would think it merely a tattoo. "It would be my pleasure, Your Majesty," he lied. Beside him, Tempest shifted, awaiting orders.

"Sir Marek will accompany you," Caspar said.

Tempest tensed. Sir Marek bowed with a serenity that suggested he had expected this assignment. Akieryon shot Caspar an apprehensive glance. Caspar smiled.

"I'm putting my faith in the two of you."

The two of them, and also a small retinue of guards. Sir Marek set a brisk pace, marching them down to the ground floor, across a broad enclosure, and out a large double gate. This must have been the way Akieryon had entered the castle. He tried to take in the sights he had missed, but Sir Marek moved them along too quickly.

The city unfurled around them, broad avenues and busy markets soon giving way to narrower streets lined with tall, tight buildings. Their little company marched in a double column, allowing for traffic to pass them by in the other direction. Many people stopped and stared.

"Soldier," Sir Marek said, almost to himself. He hadn't spoken once since leaving Caspar's presence, and his voice startled Akieryon.

Realizing that he had fallen into step with the guards, Akieryon felt heat rising in his face. Redhead complexion, Dani had said, which made Akieryon a little less self-conscious about his tendency to blush at every opportunity. "The ducking I gave you wasn't proof enough?" He regretted his retort instantly. They were on a mission for Caspar. Now was no time for petty squabbles.

To his surprise, Sir Marek chuckled. "Tempest could have done that," he said, "and he's no soldier."

"No," Akieryon agreed quietly. "No, he is not."

Sir Marek made an amused noise. "Most of us aren't sure quite *what* he is these days."

"Human."

"You sure about that?"

Akieryon slanted a wry smile at him. "It's my job to know."

"Right. Demonslayer." Sir Marek paused, then added, "Is there good money in that?"

Akieryon wasn't sure how to answer. Good money? What did that even mean? Wasn't money just a means to an end? Payday meant going out with friends to Enoch's or Open Fifth. Payday fueled hobbies and gross indulgences alike. Money earned was neutral until spent. Akieryon shrugged. "Not for you, no."

Sir Marek snorted. He led them around a corner and into a noisier, smellier part of town. Butchers' wagons rolled by, and people of all ages hauled baskets full of fish up and down the street. Another turn revealed a row of jetties that stretched out into the river. It ran broad and slow here, ideal for docking flat-bottomed boats like the barge that made its way slowly toward them. Myrdis, Akieryon remembered from Caspar's maps, was a seaport. It made sense for their representatives to arrive by boat.

When the deckhands had made fast their moorings and the representatives had stepped in an apprehensive cluster onto the pier, Akieryon bowed and made a brief speech. He welcomed them on behalf of King Caspar, and congratulated them on taking part in this pivotal moment in their country's history. The representatives eyed him with varying degrees of skepticism. They ranged in size and shape and age, from grizzled old fishermen to a boy who looked little older than Lan.

Welcome thus extended, Sir Marek turned and led the group to their lodgings in the city. Along the way, he looked at Akieryon and raised an eyebrow. It remained raised until Akieryon said in an undertone, "I'm older than I look."

"If you weren't," Sir Marek muttered, "Tempest wouldn't bother with you."

"What's that supposed to mean?" Akieryon demanded, a little too loudly. A nervous hush fell over the representatives behind them.

"You tell me what it means," Sir Marek pressed, ignoring their astonished audience. "I'm not the one who refused when Caspar offered me a private suite."

Heat leapt up Akieryon's cheeks yet again. "It is as Caspar himself said," he insisted, lifting his chin stubbornly. "The safest place in the kingdom is at Tempest's side." He shouldn't let Sir Marek needle him, especially not about this.

"Sure, but—"

"Get down!" Akieryon reacted to the flicker of motion above them, his body moving before he registered what his eyes saw. Sir Marek ducked, and Akieryon used him as a vault, stepping from knee to elbow before springing from his shoulder, launching himself into the air. The sparking fuse of the bomb burned his hand as he caught it. He twisted in midair and threw it as hard as he could, with a little push of magic sending it straight up. It exploded high over the rooftops, harmless as any firework.

Akieryon landed clumsily, remembering only at the last possible moment not to show his wings. He hit the ground at a hard angle, wrenching ankle and knee before getting his hands under him to break his fall. Sir Marek was at his side in an instant, checking him for injuries.

"Tempest is going to beat my ass," he grumbled as Akieryon flinched from his touch.

"Nothing's broken."

"Doesn't matter." Sir Marek hooked an arm under each of Akieryon's knees and hoisted him onto his back. "Let's just get this over with."

"I can walk," Akieryon protested, though it would take a moment more for the pain to recede enough.

"Doesn't matter," Sir Marek repeated, growing more surly by the moment. The guards drew in close around the subdued representatives, and they all continued in silence the rest of the way to their lodgings. There, Sir Marek went to increase security, leaving Akieryon alone with the new arrivals for an awkward several minutes.

"We didn't come here to be killed," grumbled the representative from the joiners' guild, and the others agreed with him.

"Neither did I," Akieryon said. "I'm going to make certain this parliament convenes according to King Caspar's plans, with everyone fully intact." It had been his goal all along, but now someone had gone and made it personal for him.

"Good job catching that bomb," ventured the young one, who

represented the sailmakers. Akieryon smiled, and he inclined his head in thanks.

He would protect these people. Not for Caspar. Not even for Tempest. He would do it because he wanted to.

FAMILY

Upon their return to the castle, Tempest left to ward the representatives' lodgings against magical attack. Sir Marek surrendered Akieryon to the care of Caspar's personal physician, who wrapped his ankle and cautioned him to stay off his feet and keep his leg elevated as much as possible.

"How long?"

The doctor shook his head. "Ask me again in a week."

Medical recommendation or not, Akieryon still needed to make his report to Caspar. He made his way with care, favoring his injured leg only a little bit, all the way to Caspar's presence chamber. Caspar was not there. The single guard at the door suggested checking the inner atrium. A gentle enquiry of a passing footman led Akieryon back to the little garden where he had first met Sir Marek. He hesitated on the spiral stair. Voices drifted up from below.

"I should have sent Tempest." Caspar sounded sullen.

"I don't know that bloodletting in the streets would have been a better response," Sir Marek said.

"You could have been killed."

Something in Caspar's tone made Akieryon peer over the railing. He saw Caspar and Sir Marek standing near the fountain. Caspar fidgeted, chewing his lip and glancing nervously from Sir Marek's face to the fountain and back. Sir Marek reached for his hand.

"I'm fine," he insisted. "I'm here. You're not losing me that easily."

"I don't want to lose you at all." Caspar searched Sir Marek's face. Above them, Akieryon shrank silently back. This was a private moment, and he had no right to intrude.

"I'm here," Sir Marek repeated, his voice gentle but firm. "I'm still here." He lifted his hand to Caspar's cheek. Caspar leaned into the touch.

"You'd better stay," Caspar murmured. He melted forward.

"Always," Sir Marek said. And then they were kissing.

Akieryon recoiled into the shadows of the doorway. Sir Marek's bad attitude suddenly made so much sense. He loved Caspar. He was *in love* with Caspar. How much of an ass would Akieryon be to people if he fell in love with someone who insisted upon making a target of himself? Probably not as much as Marek, but still.

Akieryon stole another glance below, and immediately regretted it. Caspar had unbound Sir Marek's hair and buried both hands in it. Marek slid his hands under Caspar's shirt. Their bodies curved against one another with the ease of long practice. Probably years. Akieryon beat a hasty retreat, limping fast all the way back to Tempest's suite.

A short while later, Tempest returned to find him on the bed, his leg propped up on a heap of pillows. Tempest took in the sight with a scowl.

"You're injured."

"Minorly. It's my own fault," Akieryon added quickly. "After I threw the bomb, I landed wrong. I just… forgot?" He frowned, his words trailing away as Tempest sat beside him and began examining his ankle.

"Do you suppose it would cause more or less trouble if I healed this for you?"

Akieryon sighed. He had asked himself the same question only an hour earlier. "Probably more. Everyone saw Sir Marek carry me back to the castle. Let them see me limping for a few days." When Tempest eyed him with a sour expression, he added, "Anyway, my healing magics are probably better than yours."

"Oh, *are* they?" Amusement and challenge both rang in Tempest's words. Akieryon refused to back down.

"Unless you studied under an archangel," he said, "yes."

"I can't say that I have." Tempest gave Akieryon an appraising look. "Thanks."

"For what?"

"For taking care of things. The bomb." Tempest sat down beside Akieryon, and Akieryon could see worry in the set of his shoulders.

"So," he said, abruptly changing the subject. "Caspar and Sir Marek?"

Tempest laughed, and the sound raised Akieryon's spirits. "So you've caught them at last!" he said, as though doing so was some local rite of passage. "Aren't they gross?"

"Gross?" Akieryon repeated. Humans could be strange about one another's choice of lovers. He didn't want to think Tempest would be. He wanted to think of Tempest as the best of all of them.

"Yeah, all soft and..." Tempest waved a hand, searching for the right descriptor. "Schmoopy."

"*Schmoopy?*" Akieryon laughed. "Is this a human word I don't know?"

"You know," Tempest said. "When something is sugary and squishy and it makes you gag a little."

"Right, right," Akieryon said, still laughing. "And have they always been... schmoopy?"

"Oh, yes. Since Caspar was about seventeen, I think."

"Ten years?" Akieryon guessed. No one had actually told him Caspar's age, but Tempest nodded.

"Something like that. Except for that time when they split up for a few months because Marek was trying to push Caspar to find an appropriate princess to marry." Tempest kicked one foot off the side of the bed. "Be grateful you weren't here for that. The only thing worse than the two of them together is the two of them apart. You cannot *imagine* the pining."

Akieryon considered this. "So Caspar isn't going to get married?" He had a vague awareness that human kings ought to marry, and he assumed that if the law of the land allowed Caspar to be married to Sir Marek, he would have done so by now.

"No, he will," Tempest said. "He's going to marry Dani."

"*WHAT.*"

Tempest turned to raise an eyebrow at Akieryon, but failed as amusement creased the corners of his eyes. "Why, what's wrong with Dani?"

"They just, um." Akieryon struggled for the right words. "They don't act like they're going to be married."

"Of course not." Tempest flopped down, stretching full length beside Akieryon. A pillow rolled to a stop against the invisible barrier. "For one thing, they're not announcing it until after the parliament is settled. Let people try to kill Caspar for one thing at a time. Also, Dani's like me. She has no appetite for those tender emotions that cause people to make asses of themselves."

Akieryon considered what Tempest had said, and Tempest watched him with calm inevitability, waiting. "They're not in love."

"No," Tempest said.

"They're friends, though." When Tempest nodded, Akieryon pressed on, working out the details for himself. "And they've agreed to share a life together. And Dani doesn't mind Caspar being schmoopy with her brother?"

Tempest snorted. "As long as they don't do it in front of her."

"Right." Akieryon tipped his head back, considering. "Is this common? For Caspar to be marrying a friend and not his—his… um."

"It's better than most kings get," Tempest said, the sadness in his voice drawing Akieryon's eyes back to him. Then he shrugged and gave Akieryon a reassuring smile. "All three of them are content with it. Don't waste your energy worrying there."

"Right," Akieryon said again. He could have asked more questions. Instead, he lifted the edge of the blanket and he invited Tempest to join him. Without a word, Tempest burrowed beneath the bedding and curled against Akieryon's side. *He's tired,*

Akieryon realized. The arcane scents that typically clung to Tempest had shifted and intensified, while most of the green had faded from his eyes. "Just how densely did you ward that lodging house?" Akieryon wondered, not really expecting a response.

Tempest tipped his head against Akieryon's shoulder. "Seth himself would have to work to break it."

"Who's Seth?" Akieryon wondered, but only a soft snore answered him. He had asked before, and he would have to ask again later.

Tempest slept through suppertime, and Akieryon stayed with him. Late in the evening someone delivered a meal tray. Akieryon waited a little longer, until the water clock chimed the hour. Then he got up, retrieved the tray, and brought it back to the bed. Tempest didn't stir until Akieryon held a spoonful of custard to his lips. After that he ate with gusto, demolishing a heap of butter buns, a plate of bacon, and the rest of the custard in moments. Akieryon sat back and watched, pleased to see a bit of bright green returning to Tempest's eyes. At last Tempest noticed his stare, and sheepishly offered a half a bowl of poached pears with soft cheese. Akieryon grinned at him.

"You clearly need to recover your strength." Akieryon pushed the bowl back into Tempest's hand. Tempest looked like he might argue, but at that moment someone knocked at the outer door.

Akieryon hurried to answer, leaving Tempest alone with what remained of the food. There would probably be nothing left in another minute or so.

Akieryon pulled the door open. Caspar stood alone in the corridor, a slight smile tugging at the corners of his lips. "May I come in?"

"Oh. Um." Akieryon stepped back, automatically standing at attention as Caspar stepped into the antechamber. He pushed the door closed again. "Tempest is eating."

Caspar shrugged off the remark. "I'll see him in a minute. I came to talk to you."

Right. He never had given his report of the day's events. Akieryon suppressed a small grimace. "I just—"

Caspar caught him by the hand and clasped it warmly. "Thank you," he said. "A thousand times over." When Akieryon simply stared at him, he continued. "You saved Marek. You protected the representatives from Myrdis. As I hear it, you were the only one injured at all."

Embarrassment heated Akieryon's cheeks. "I made a foolish error. I landed wrong and turned my ankle." Then he frowned. "The bomb—it looked like a saltpeter grenade. Small blast radius, anyway, and a clay exterior. It would have caused more havoc than harm."

"But people would have been injured."

Akieryon nodded.

"Some may have died?"

Again, Akieryon nodded. He could feel shame creeping over his skin, but Caspar looked him in the eye and clasped his hand more tightly.

"Then accept my gratitude. My own true heart has not a scratch on him, and I owe that to you. The representatives from Myrdis are safe and I owe that to you as well. And you," Caspar added, looking toward the bedroom door with a twinkle of mischief in his eye.

"You're gross," said Tempest flatly. He leaned on the doorframe, half lazy and half weary. Akieryon hated seeing that this puzzle of a human had limitations after all.

"And you're predictable," Caspar shot back, his smile broadening. To Akieryon he said, "Myrdis is the largest city in Arum, which is Tempest's country."

"Was," Tempest corrected.

"Tempest has exhausted himself with magics for keeping the representatives from Arum safe," Caspar continued as though Tempest hadn't interrupted. "Which is why I have my cooks making up a fresh batch of pastries right now."

"Alright," Tempest said. "I guess I'll keep you."

"Even if I'm gross?"

"Don't push your luck."

A tray heaped high with pastries of all kinds arrived, and Caspar himself took it from the hands of the kitchen boy. "Thank you, Venin. Tell Pari these exceed expectations in every way." The child flushed and bowed and scrambled away, almost all at once. Smiling, Caspar set the tray on the low table and took a seat on the floor, just as Tempest often did. Akieryon eyed them curiously for only a heartbeat before he joined them.

"You're family now," Caspar announced genially around a big mouthful of something that oozed red jam when he bit into it. "I hope you understand that."

"Oh. But…" Akieryon glanced sidelong at Tempest, who had a pastry in each hand. "I'm not human."

Caspar waved the remark away. "Tempest told me. But you do have families where you come from?"

"Not me specifically." Realizing how easily Caspar had wrung information from him, Akieryon flushed hotly. "I'm a foundling, and no one ever wanted to keep me for very long."

"I think you'll find humans can be very, very clingy," Caspar said with one of his disarming smiles.

Tempest snorted. "Don't scare him off before Dani gets the chance to do it instead."

"I'm not that easy to frighten." *Unless you try to lock me away in the dark.* Akieryon picked up something flat and glossy and glistening with coarse sugar crystals. It was still warm. He took a bite. "Besides," he added, savoring the tart apple filling, "if being part of the family means late night pastry picnics on Tempest's floor, I'm all in."

Caspar beamed and nudged him with his shoulder. "Good man." To Tempest he said, "I like his priorities."

"You know what?" said Tempest, reaching for yet another pastry. "So do I."

Family. Akieryon had never wanted anything more in his life. In fact, he had spent more than a century yearning for precisely what Caspar offered him now. Fighting the stinging in his eyes, Akieryon screwed his face up into a skeptical expression. "Does this make Sir Marek an in-law?"

It turned out he could live with that.

CHARITABLE

ENTERPRISES

Caspar excused Akieryon from attending him in the presence chamber for the next two days. He appreciated the gesture, as well as the subtle reminder to everyone that the so-called expert had been injured in yesterday's attack, but by the middle of the afternoon Akieryon had grown too restless to remain in Tempest's suite. Someone had left a walking stick by the door. Smiling, Akieryon took it up and he leaned on it perhaps more than he needed.

He knew his way to the presence chamber by now, and he thought he could find the inner atrium if he tried, but he wanted neither of those places. He went looking instead for the training yard, which he had seen but briefly before. He promptly got lost. Three left turns and a flight of stairs should have brought him back to where he had begun, but he found himself instead at a door that bore a sign proclaiming QUIET PLEASE in large letters.

"I wouldn't go in there," said a voice behind him. "Not if you don't care for the stench of the poor."

Akieryon turned, his eyes narrowing as he matched a face to the voice. This was one of the nobles he saw sometimes vying for Caspar's attention. Sesoran, he thought, or something like that. He swallowed an urge to demand if this man had followed him. "I'm sure I've smelled worse," he said instead, his hand on the door. He hadn't meant to enter, but walking away now would give the wrong impression.

"Suit yourself." Sesoran shrugged in that careless way of the obnoxiously wealthy. "You've been warned."

Without comment, Akieryon pushed the door open. Beyond lay a rectangular room with tall windows, thick curtains, and benches lining the walls. A lone guard pushed the door closed behind Akieryon, who did not miss his glance of distaste at the retreating Sesoran. Smiling to himself, Akieryon made his way toward the door on the opposite end of the chamber. A young girl occupied one of the benches halfway between the two doors. She sat with her feet drawn up beneath her, and her eyes remained fixed on her hands, where her fingers twined over one another in an endless dance. When Akieryon walked past, she never looked up.

The next door opened into a corridor lined with smaller chambers. Some doors stood open, revealing two to four beds in each, separated by clean white curtains. A hospital, Akieryon realized. Nobody had said anything about the palace having a hospital wing. As he walked slowly by, people went about their business and paid him little mind. The corridor turned a corner, and beyond lay what appeared to be offices.

A familiar head of red hair was vanishing into one.

Akieryon hurried to catch up with Sir Marek, and he found that his ankle did still twinge a bit. By the time he arrived in the doorway, he leaned on his walking stick in earnest. Sir Marek was deep in conversation with a professional-looking woman. He had his hand resting atop a stack of boxes, which sat on a somewhat cluttered desk. The woman picked up a mug and took a pointed sip. Akieryon knocked on the doorframe.

"Ah, Akieryon!" Sir Marek seemed pleased to see him, if a bit flustered. He made hasty introductions, and the woman—Matron Xene—smiled at him.

"A friend of Sir Marek's is always welcome."

Were they friends? Akieryon looked a question at Sir Marek, who picked up a small parcel from the top of the stack of boxes.

"And where might I find this girl Zeli?"

"She's usually in the quiet room," Matron said. Akieryon immediately thought of the child he had seen there. What was Marek about?

Sir Marek took his leave of Matron Xene and headed back

down the corridor, but he slowed his steps to match Akieryon's.

"I didn't know there was a hospital here."

"Not just a hospital," Sir Marek said. "There are lodgings upstairs, for people with nowhere else to go. The nobles would prefer nobody talked about it—this was Caspar's first project that pissed them off—so I'm not surprised you hadn't heard of it."

Akieryon raised an eyebrow at him. "Aren't you one of the nobles?"

"I'm also one of the exiles," Sir Marek said bluntly. "I know how it feels to go without."

Akieryon nodded, digesting this information in silence for a few steps. "Why are you here?" he asked, matching bluntness for bluntness.

"I bring my household mending every month," Sir Marek said. Seeing Akieryon's confusion, he continued. "As a knight, I can't wear anything that shows visible signs of repair or wear. Neither can anyone close to me. So I bring the worn and mended clothing to people who can get use out of it."

"And you do it yourself because…?"

"Because I'm a nosy bastard," Sir Marek confessed with a sideways grin. "I talk to people and find out what they're saying about Caspar."

"I know why you're so protective of him," Akieryon said

softly, and Sir Marek nodded.

"It's something of an open secret at this point."

They had arrived back at the door to the quiet room, so Akieryon said nothing as they entered. The child remained where she had been. The guard by the other door gave Sir Marek a vague salute but otherwise ignored them. Together they walked toward the girl.

"I'm Sir Marek," he said when they were still a fair distance from her. "This is my friend Akieryon. May we sit with you?"

The girl darted a quick glance in their direction. Then she pulled her feet closer beneath her and gestured at the bench.

"Thank you." Sir Marek sat where directed, and Akieryon took a seat a little farther away. "Are you Zeli?" The girl nodded, and he continued. "I have something for you, but I need you to answer a few questions first. Can you do that?"

Zeli considered. Then she thrust the collar of her oversized shirt between her teeth and nodded.

"Good." Marek kept his voice soft, and he spoke as though he had never in his life encountered the concept of haste. "Do you like horses?"

Zeli chewed her shirt vigorously while she thought about her answer. Then she nodded.

"I do, too. I have six fine horses in a private wing of the stables here. In fact, I'm looking to hire a new groom. Would you like to learn to care for horses?"

Akieryon blinked, and glanced between them. He had no basis for judging human age, but surely this child was no more than half grown. "Sir Marek—" he began, but Marek held up a hand, silencing him. Zeli nodded again.

Sir Marek unwrapped his little bundle, revealing a fine wool tunic identical to the one Lan wore. He held it out to Zeli. "Is this okay?"

Zeli hesitated, eyeing the fabric with distrust. Then, cautiously, she touched her fingertips to it. Her eyes lit up, and she pulled the tunic into her lap and kneaded it like a cat.

"Good," Marek said softly. "You will wear that while you are in my employ, is that okay?" Zeli nodded again, with more enthusiasm this time. "I'll send my groom Aren to come show you the way. You'll like him. He doesn't talk much."

Akieryon waited until they had passed through the guarded door before he said, "You just hired a child." He spoke more harshly than he meant to, especially as he was still a stranger in this country.

"I did," Sir Marek replied amiably. "For now, I will pay her simply to learn about horses. She'll also have a roof over her head, a warm place to sleep, and most importantly, good clothes."

"Why are clothes so important?" Akieryon couldn't help but ask.

"Zeli's parents brought her here because they didn't know what else to do. She would scream and cry every time they tried to get her to wear anything but the most threadbare old shifts. When she came here, Matron Xene gave her linens from my household, and she quieted. It's the texture, you see," Marek said. "She can't stand coarse or stiff fabrics, and her parents couldn't afford to buy things she could wear. Why are you smiling like that?"

"I think," Akieryon said slowly, "this is the first time I'm really meeting the man Caspar loves."

"Shut up," Marek said gruffly. Akieryon grinned at him.

They walked in silence for a little while, then Akieryon said, "I think Sesoran was following me earlier."

"Sesoran." Sir Marek's eyes narrowed. "You're sure?"

Akieryon hesitated. "Tall fellow? Looks like a weasel swallowed a kumquat?" Did they have kumquats here? In any case, his translation spell would provide a comprehensible equivalent.

Marek snorted. "That's Sesoran," he said. "Or his brother. What did he want?"

"I don't know." Akieryon glanced over his shoulder. "He turned back at the door to the quiet room."

"He would," Marek muttered. "He forgets himself. But you," he continued, his frown fading. "I don't think you were looking for the hospital."

"No. I took a wrong turn on my way to the training yard."

Sir Marek gave him a sharp look. "Dani won't go easy on you just because you've hurt your ankle."

"It's fine," Akieryon exaggerated. "I don't intend to spar anyone. I want to work through a few weapons forms."

"Doesn't Tempest have weapons enough?"

"Weapons without enchantments on them," Akieryon specified, and Marek nodded.

"I see your problem," he said. "It's this way."

"Tempest says he's not a sorcerer," Akieryon ventured as Marek led him through a side door. "But—"

"But he enchants almost everything he touches. Yes, he's lazy that way."

Lazy? Akieryon blinked. "I think he's more like a cat," he said. "He just doesn't waste his time with anything that doesn't interest him."

Marek opened another door, and Akieryon flinched from the fierce sunlight. "You must interest him a great deal," he said gravely. "Tell my sister I said not to kick your ass too hard."

"I'm not going to spar!" Akieryon repeated to Sir Marek's

retreating footsteps. Squinting out into the sunlight, he saw Dani leaning on a staff and grinning at him in a way that reminded him too much of his old colleague Michiel. Several guards flanked her, arrayed in assorted training gear.

Well this was just lovely.

PRACTICE

Dani thrust the end of her staff beneath Akieryon's chin, halting it a breath from his throat. He didn't flinch. Her eyes narrowed.

"If you're not here to spar, what do you want?"

Akieryon glanced past her. "I need to borrow a weapon."

"Weapons are earned," Dani said in as sharp and commanding a tone as ever Lord Sidriel might have used.

Akieryon tapped his walking stick against the side of his ankle. "I can pay you back in a couple of days."

"Take a knee, soldier!" Dani commanded, and Akieryon dropped instinctively to one knee on the sand. "At the ready!" He settled his center and lifted his hands in a guard position. A smirk curved Dani's lips. "Begin," she said softly.

She paced around him slowly, unhurriedly assessing his defenses. Akieryon felt her gaze rake over him again and again, but he was relaxed and ready. He listened. He waited. He let his eyes unfocus slightly as Dani's shadow passed over him yet again.

Her staff lashed out in a swift, sharp jab. Akieryon deflected the blow with the back of his forearm.

Dani continued circling him. She tested him with intermittent attacks, always single blows, each neatly deflected. Akieryon welcomed the stinging on his hands and arms. It felt good to spar again, even in this limited way. Like stretching a muscle too long disused. Like coming home.

When Dani's real attack came, it was swift and sharp, a series of precise blows almost indistinguishable from the feints she threw to distract him. Akieryon matched her movements, blocking and evading, letting his body remember what his mind may have forgotten. She was good, surely a master of her craft. As with martial arts, so with magic: humans could learn anything in any world, and their only real limitation was time.

Akieryon had time on his side.

It took a while for an opening to present itself. He had ducked to the side, and Dani was just fractionally slower recovering from the swing than she had been a moment ago. Akieryon's arm snapped out and around the staff, securing it in the crook of his elbow as he grabbed for it with his other hand. Dani jerked the weapon away, but by then Akieryon could roll with the movement, tucking the staff close as he went. The moment it wrenched free of Dani's grasp, she stepped back and planted both hands on her hips.

"Well earned," she announced.

Come back up to kneeling again, staff at the ready, Akieryon looked around. A small crowd had gathered, and the sun had climbed a fair bit higher than he had expected. Everyone wore expressions of approval. Slowly, he lowered the staff.

Then he discovered he needed to lean on it a little to stand up. His ankle throbbed in protest, and he suppressed a grimace.

"I guess we know why Tempest's bangin' him," declared a sandy haired guard. Without comment, Dani walked over and cuffed him upside the head. Everyone laughed, and Akieryon found himself relaxing despite the flush warming his cheeks. Soldiers were soldiers, no matter where he went.

Dani indicated the weapons rack, and invited Akieryon to select whatever he wanted. Taking up a blunted sword, Akieryon saluted her with it. Dani saluted him back. The other guards gathered around them in a loose circle, which made Akieryon unreasonably nervous. Assuming a neutral stance, he closed his eyes and focused on his breathing. Whatever he did now, they were all going to watch him. Short of leaving, he could do nothing to stop them.

He concentrated instead on the space between light and shadow. Pulling at the balances of the cosmos, he sent a fine thread of light dancing along the edge of the sword. Distantly, he heard a hissing intake of breath. It didn't matter. He had work to do.

Akieryon worked his way slowly through a series of sword forms, each movement trailing fire and shadows. This was only the most fundamental of duel magics, but it felt good. It felt strong. It felt like he could cut the cosmos into pieces if he but willed it.

A part of him wanted to try.

Rather than shying from his darker impulses, as he habitually did, Akieryon reached for the feeling and held it close. He wanted to destroy something. He fed the thought with the ache of centuries of solitude. The light on his blade blazed brighter, and the shadows deepened and thickened. Akieryon reached with his free hand, and he gently lifted the dancing light away from the shadows.

The balance tipped wildly. If he released the magic now, it would explode. Instead, he drew it inward, filling himself up with celestial power. The light in his hand narrowed to a pinpoint, then vanished entirely. The shadows…

Destroy, he thought, focusing, channeling the power he had absorbed into that deep, terrible, hungry part of himself. *Anything. It doesn't matter what.*

The shadows crawled along the blade, slower now, seething with his intent. He teetered on a precipice of his own making. Fed by five centuries of solitude, the darkness thickened into oily smoke. The power uncoiled within him, feral and unfamiliar, but unmistakably a part of him. Akieryon knew he was slipping an instant before he lost control of it.

"Get down!" The infernal power burst out of the point of the blade and into the ground. Sand and droplets of molten glass flew in all directions. This was the power that had stripped the flesh from Master Seikhiel's leg. Akieryon had to control it. Until he learned, he was a danger to everyone around him.

As the sand settled, he looked around. Dani's guardsmen had all dropped to the ground and covered their heads. Akieryon nodded, appreciating their reflexes and their unquestioning obedience. It had surely spared them a few injuries. As they began to lift their heads, Akieryon knelt and began digging in the center of the blast zone.

"What," said Dani, stepping up behind him, "in all seven hells was that?"

"Nine," Akieryon corrected automatically.

"What?"

"It's seven Heavens," he said. "There are nine Hells." He worked his fingers underneath the fulgurite he had made, and he carefully lifted it free. It would still be too hot for anyone else to touch, but his own magic had made it. Now he needed to take it back to Tempest's suite and examine it.

"Why are there more Hells than Heavens?" Dani demanded.

She sounded offended.

Wearily, Akieryon pushed himself back to his feet again. His ankle screamed with pain. "There was an Incident," he said. "Two Heavens broke."

"How do you break Heaven?"

Akieryon ducked the question. "It was a long time before I was born."

For a moment, Akieryon considered the sword he had used. The dull, blunted metal now bore a gleaming streak of soot blue burned across it. He tilted it to the light, frowning, but he could sense no magic in it. He returned it to the weapons rack. Everyone else stood around, watching him with wary eyes.

"Until next time." He snapped Dani a smart salute. She returned it without hesitation.

"Any time, soldier," she said.

~⋅℮✦℮⋅~

The glass was black, and oily rainbows swirled across its surface. It had cooled by the time Akieryon returned to Tempest's suite, and yet it scorched the table when he set it down. He peered and prodded it, examining it from every angle. He stretched his mind, feeling the infernal energy of it. He had never encountered its like, despite having studied every known type of demon. This energy seethed with an unnamed hunger. It craved. It could devour worlds.

Or perhaps that was merely the flavor his centuries of solitude had given it.

The outer door opened. Irrational panic threaded through him, moving his limbs without thought. Akieryon snatched up a towel and tossed it over the fulgurite. It had started smoking by the time Tempest appeared in the doorway. He took in the scene with scarcely a twitch of one eyebrow. He made a casual, almost negligent gesture. The towel fell aside and extinguished itself.

His face aflame with shame, Akieryon stood in silence as Tempest prowled around the table. "Where did you get this artifact?" Tempest asked, his voice quiet and even. Akieryon shifted uneasily.

"I… I made it." Haltingly, Akieryon explained the feral magic that he had unleashed on the sand. Tempest listened with a slight frown of concentration shadowing his brow. When he had finished, Tempest reached out and picked up the fulgurite. "Don't—!" Akieryon began, but Tempest merely turned it over in his hands.

"Fascinating," he said.

Akieryon looked down at his hands. "I don't know what kind of magic I used," he confessed, his voice strained, little more than a whisper.

Making a noise that was at once noncommittal and thoughtful,

Tempest reached into a breach in the air and rummaged around for a moment. When his hand reappeared, he held a piece of flagstone a little larger than a saucer. He positioned the stone between two volumes of sorcery on the nearest shelf, and then he placed the fulgurite on the stone. "Better than the table," he pronounced with an air of authority.

"Sure," Akieryon agreed faintly. *Artifact*, Tempest had said. So they agreed that he had imbued the glass with some of the dark power that lurked within him.

"How's the ankle?"

So mundane a question jerked Akieryon out of his thoughts. "Oh," he said. "A little tender."

"Marek says the snobs are watching you."

Akieryon leaned a little on the table. Reminded of his ankle, he noticed its dull ache. "Isn't that the plan?"

A shadow crossed Tempest's face. "Don't trust any of them."

"Between them and me," Akieryon said, "which of us has access to unpredictable infernal magics?" He meant to make light of the situation, but Tempest's fleeting smile never reached his eyes. Akieryon limped across the little library to him. "It's fine," he said, serious now. "*I'm* fine. We'll find out who's behind the attacks, we'll protect Caspar, and the parliament will get started as well as these things ever do."

"Oh, no." Almost laughing, Tempest pulled Akieryon into a rough half-hug. "He's gotten to you. You are now infected with Caspar-ness."

"There are worse afflictions." Akieryon's stomach rumbled loudly. He glanced downward, then back to Tempest. "So what's for supper?"

"You are invited to dine with the king."

"Fffffffuuuuuuu—"

"Let's get you cleaned up," Tempest said with malicious cheer. He led the way to the wardrobe, leaving Akieryon little choice but to hobble after him. They would select an outfit, a bath would follow, and it would be a small eternity before he got to eat anything.

Well. He supposed this was the price of getting himself tangled up in human politics.

DINNER AND
A SHOW

Both Draycens met them in the corridor. Akieryon glanced from Sir Marek to Dani, and then to Tempest. Dani had opted to wear the uniform of the royal guard. Draped in velvet, with a bit of gold flashing at his shoulder, her brother far eclipsed her. It gave Akieryon a sinking feeling. He didn't know if he could handle a full dose of Marek twice in one day. Anyway, the Draycens' attire felt formal, and Tempest looked…well, he looked like Tempest.

"We're going to be late," Marek said. He turned and started walking down the corridor. Akieryon took a step after him, but Dani moved into their path and placed a firm hand on Tempest's chest.

"Every time," she complained. A little frown squeezed the corners of Tempest's eyes.

"I can walk with you as far as the door."

"And then what?" Dani challenged. "Will you go quietly back to your books?" She shook her head. "You declined knighthood when it was offered. You have to let Marek handle this."

"I don't like it," Tempest growled. The sound sent a thrill down the base of Akieryon's spine, but he was more interested in whatever the two of them were arguing about.

"This dinner is for knights only?" he ventured, and his heart sank as Dani nodded.

"He's smarter than you are," she said to Tempest. "Just turn around and go study your little spells, and leave us to take care of your pet project for a few hours." Tempest bared his teeth. Dani laughed and gave him a friendly shove. "Go on."

"I'll be fine," Akieryon assured him, and he hoped it was true. He had met some of the knights of Davenz over the last week or two, but he had little enough sense of them. Caspar had knighted only Sir Marek and a very few others who had rendered valuable service, as he put it. Saved his ass, Tempest said. The remainder of the knighthood consisted of individuals who had served previous regimes: Caspar's father, or his treacherous uncle.

They did not inspire much trust.

Armed with determination and little else, Akieryon squeezed Tempest's hand, then turned and limped away after Sir Marek. Dani caught up to them a moment later. Her sword jogged against her leg, evidence of her haste. Across the front of her right hip she had a conspicuously placed dagger—poignard, Akieryon automatically classified it—which he wondered about. Was it part of the uniform, or did Dani carry her weapons openly to deter bad behavior from the knighthood?

Akieryon wanted to glance over his shoulder, to look back and see if Tempest watched them walk away from him. He kept his gaze fixed forward. It wasn't enough, what he was doing here. It was never enough. It was too much. He wasn't meant to alter the course of Mortal lives. He was free. He was alone. What even was he doing here?

Dani nudged him with her elbow. "Don't look so grim," she said. "It's not an execution. It's just a bit of pageantry, showing you off to the snobs who think they're more important than they really are."

"Right," Akieryon said weakly. "Snobs." His confidence had hit an unexpectedly low ebb. Now every step down unfamiliar corridors filled him with resounding dread. He couldn't help anyone. He could never even help himself. What had he been thinking, offering to help Caspar? What did he actually expect to accomplish? He would fail. He had already failed. He was lost, they were all lost—

"Hey." Dani's hand gripped his arm hard enough to hurt. Or perhaps she knew where to find the most sensitive pressure points. "Breathe," she commanded. "Just breathe. You're a Demonslayer.

A few knights are nothing." She waited until Akieryon met her steady gaze, and then she squeezed. Her fingertips dug into the inside of his elbow for just a moment before she let go. "You've got this, soldier."

A few knights are nothing. "Right," Akieryon repeated. He stiffened his spine and squared his shoulders. "Let's get this over with."

Dani gave him a lopsided smirk. "You sound like Tempest."

Akieryon chose to take that comment as a compliment. He tried to center his thoughts as he followed the rest of the way to a dining hall he had not seen before. The guards at the door wore formal uniforms and held ornately etched halberds, which looked no less lethal for their beauty. One of them opened the door. Someone just within announced Sir Marek's arrival.

Akieryon hesitated in the doorway. "How many?" he whispered to Dani. She placed a hand in the small of his back and pushed him through.

"Twenty-two in total," she said in his ear. "But it looks like only about sixteen are here tonight."

Scanning the room, Akieryon shook his head. "There are at least thirty people here right now."

"Family members," Dani said dismissively. The two of them trailed Marek across the marble floor.

"Right. And what am I doing here?" Akieryon tried to avoid noticing Sesoran and his brother. He failed.

"Would you make a face if I said you're my date?" Dani laughed at the way he flinched away from her hand on his arm. "Relax! Caspar wants to show you off, of course."

"Of course," Akieryon echoed through clenched teeth.

Marek led the way across the dining hall, where he was heartily greeted by a broad man with graying hair and one sleeve tucked into his belt. "And here's your sister!" The man gave Dani a friendly thump on the shoulder, which she returned without comment. "And—oho, the king's new advisor?"

Akieryon itched under the good-natured scrutiny. "Friend," he corrected.

"He looks a little pale."

Akieryon felt heat creeping up his cheeks. "The ankle." He tapped his stick against the side of his leg. "I pushed myself too hard earlier."

"You should have seen him in the sparring ring," Dani said with a note of pride and a friendly shove. Akieryon swayed.

"It was a poor life choice," he said, only half teasing. "I'm Akieryon."

"Veirn." He extended his left hand, which Akieryon clasped automatically. Veirn grinned at him. "A warrior's grip. I like this one."

"Sir Veirn was commander of the Royal guard before me," Dani said in a tone that passed for fondness.

"Aye, until that last battle." Veirn lifted his shoulder to make his empty sleeve sway a little. "I like the slow life these days."

Dani snorted. "That's a lie."

"Can you prove that?"

"Wait," said Dani.

Grinning, Marek clapped Veirn on the shoulder. "So what's going to go wrong this time?" he said in a tone entirely too jovial for Marek.

"Oh, him." Veirn nodded at Akieryon. "Obviously."

Akieryon opened his mouth for a retort, but at that moment a door at the far end of the dining hall opened. Two guards stepped through, stood at perfect attention, and saluted. Right behind them came Caspar, only a little more finely dressed than Marek was. Conversations stumbled to a halt, and everyone who had been seated immediately stood.

Caspar stepped in front of the high table. His smile became genuine when he met Marek's gaze, and then he continued glancing around at everyone who had gathered. He made a short speech welcoming his knighthood, the crown's most valued friends. Then he beckoned to Akieryon to join him.

"I want you all to meet my good friend Akieryon," Caspar continued. "He's here to help us navigate this difficult transition." That part, at least, was mostly true. Akieryon wondered about the margin of his success. Probably small.

At Caspar's invitation, the knights formed an orderly queue, each coming forward to exchange polite words and, unfortunately, a formal introduction to the king's guest. Akieryon tried to keep all of their names in his head, but he probably lost a few. Marek made a point to clasp his hand like a friend. Were they friends? Or was this all for show?

After the introductions had been made, Caspar's knights remained standing in a half-circle around them. Caspar made a show of thinking. "Sir Sidemo," he said, "Sir Emnomen, and Sir Veirn, please honor my table this evening."

The rest of the knights dispersed to the other tables, giving Akieryon the impression that all of this was standard for these gatherings. Before stepping back, Sir Marek glanced up one more time at his king. For a fleeting moment, he let his heart show full upon his face, a love built on friendship and shared experience, yet so intense it might as well be worship. How had Akieryon missed it before? Then he blinked, and the expression of naked adoration was gone, replaced by a mask of bland politeness.

Caspar directed Akieryon to the chair at his right. Sir Sidemo he seated at his left, with Veirn at Sir Sidemo's left. *This is going to be dull,* Akieryon thought as everyone took their seats. From the chair beside him, Sir Emnomen gave Akieryon a calculating look.

"This parliament thing," he said. "It really works where you come from?"

"My home is ruled by—I think you'd call it a council?" Akieryon replied, choosing honesty. "But I've seen it work in other places. I travel a lot." *I've seen systems of government you can't even imagine.*

"Indeed? Where?"

"Places I've traveled? Anharrha," Akieryon said without hesitation, ignoring the probability that he asked where parliaments functioned. "Seyzharel. D'vear. Rhuln. Tolowent. Bin-Tary. Wesnet." He raised an eyebrow in challenge. "Shall I go on?"

Sir Emnomen scoffed. "Those aren't real places."

Smirking, Akieryon lifted his wine glass. "I'd be happy to tell the king of Seyzharel you said so. He might tear your arms off and walk away without ever even looking directly at you."

"Are you *threatening* me?"

Akieryon almost snorted wine up his nose. Then, affecting his best feigned innocence, he turned to look the knight full in the face. "Why?" he said. "Do I have reason to do so?"

Sir Emnomen sputtered, but a minor flurry of activity near the hall door captured Akieryon's attention. Liveried castle staff swirled around each other, some bearing platters of food, and some sampling small portions of the food carried by the others. Akieryon had never seen food tasters in Davenz before. He glanced at Caspar, but this was apparently normal. The serving staff began to circulate the soup course around the room. Someone placed a warm loaf of bread directly in front of Akieryon, and he forgot all about needling his neighbor.

He couldn't identify the soup—some sort of game stock with dumplings, maybe—but it tasted delicious. It was better with the bread. And Akieryon was so *hungry*. He tried to master his enthusiasm enough to be polite, with little success. The knights watched him, varying degrees of skepticism on their faces.

"Don't they feed you?" Sir Veirn teased, and Akieryon sent him a sheepish grin.

"I spent some time today in the sparring ring with the captain of the guard. It wasn't a wise decision."

Veirn's guffaw resounded through the hall, but Caspar turned to Akieryon with obvious concern. "You didn't hurt your ankle more?"

"No, no," Akieryon reassured him. "Your captain may be merciless, but she did allow me to take a knee."

From her place behind Caspar's chair, Dani choked back a

laugh. When Akieryon glanced at her, she caught his eye and mouthed *flatterer* at him. He raised his glass to her.

Sir Sidemo—who resembled a washed out and wrung out version of Sesoran—also raised a glass to Dani. "Ever charming, our Captain Danela."

"Captain Draycen," she corrected, and though her voice and bearing remained rock steady, Akieryon could see temper flare behind her eyes.

Sir Sidemo's gaze flicked across the hall, to where Marek appeared to be in the middle of telling some thrilling tale to a rapt audience. Sir Emnomen watched Caspar for any sign of irritation that his guard had spoken without anyone addressing her directly. Caspar sighed into his wine glass.

"Take more care," he said, and Akieryon wondered whether Caspar was speaking to him or to Dani. Probably both. "I don't like it when my friends get hurt."

Akieryon nodded. "Of course." He caught Dani's eye again. Her anger seemed to have receded. Good.

Sir Sidemo leaned forward to peer at Akieryon as waitstaff deftly replaced soup bowls with fruit and cheese. "Tell me," he said. "Where you come from, do you reprimand servants for speaking out of turn?"

Caspar's hand dropped alongside his chair, and he tried to

make a placating gesture without drawing attention. Akieryon fixed a bland smile on his face. "Where I come from," he said, "we give people the dignity of their actual job titles."

"And what is your job title?" Sir Emnomen prodded. Akieryon supposed he had earned the question.

"I'm—I was a soldier," he said. "It seems lately I've become something of a scholar."

"Is that how you ended up here?"

Akieryon shook his head. "Fate, rather." He slanted a smile at Caspar, who winked. "I met your king through pure chance. I only hope to repay him for his many kindnesses to me."

"Really?" A hint of malice curved Sir Sidemo's lips. "I'd heard you were busy repaying Tempest."

Akieryon's chest tightened, and blood rushed to his ears. The very last thing he'd ever want was to cause trouble for Tempest. And yet... "I owe Prince Tempest a life-debt. It is my duty to stay by his side until it balances." Some people only understand being outranked.

Beside him, Caspar choked, coughed into his napkin, then turned a reproachful eye on Akieryon. "Tempest has renounced the lands and titles his family held."

"Forgive me, my friend." Akieryon bowed his head to hide his smirk. "In my country, one's birthright is not so easily put aside."

"Tell us more about your country," Sir Emnomen prompted, perhaps to counter some of the rising tension. "What is it like there?

"You wouldn't like it there," Akieryon said, driven to bluntness by his irritation. "Your king might. The only class divisions are drawn more or less by age, with elders being the most highly valued. Everyone receives an equal education until they come of age. Some of our most important jobs are focused on helping others."

Sir Sidemo sniffed. "It sounds like a kingdom easily conquered."

Akieryon bared his teeth in a grin. "Others have made that mistake," he said. "Two of my teachers at the Academy are well known for having turned back the Lawless One's invasion."

"What kind of name—" A commotion near the door stopped Sir Sidemo's next barb. One of the tasters had collapsed.

Caspar was on his feet in an instant. Catching him by the wrist, Dani pulled him backward and stepped in front of him in a single economical movement. Akieryon didn't spare a moment for thought. He sprang up and bolted for the crowd at the door. Halfway there, his ankle rolled, and he stumbled. He pitched sideways. A shoulder bumped against his, steadying him, bearing him up again. Akieryon blinked, and Marek gave him a small nod.

Together they crossed to the door.

On the way, Akieryon snatched the flame from a candle. Closing his fist around it, he compressed it to a tiny pinpoint of intense light. The crowd parted to let them approach. Akieryon dropped to his knees beside the fallen taster—was he barely an adult?—and pulled the heat and smoke out of his concentrated candle flame. He thrust the magnesium-white light between his teeth and he inhaled, drawing it deep into his lungs. There it mingled with his life energy, turning a warm gold. Akieryon bent over the shuddering, wheezing young man, pinched his nostrils shut, and breathed golden light into him.

For a moment, nothing happened. Akieryon rolled the taster onto his side, then sat back and absently dragged the back of his hand across his mouth. A great tremor wracked the poor taster, and then the young man began to gag up phlegm and swirls of blue.

"Tykorran Blue," said Marek grimly.

"Cyanide," said Akieryon.

"I'll ask the dye-witches," Veirn said. Akieryon peered up at him.

"No," he said slowly. "I mean, you can, but the spell extracts the toxin in its nearest stable form. It may not have started as a pigment."

"So you're a sorcerer too." Sir Emnomen had come up behind

Veirn. Clearly he didn't like being left out.

Akieryon shook his head. "That was a basic Cleansing spell. Where I'm from, schoolchildren learn it." Indeed, he had moved almost entirely on reflex. He had time to regret it now. "Sir Marek?" he said quietly.

"Hm?"

"Could I borrow the use of your arm? I think I'm stuck."

Marek grinned at him. "I'm going to tell Tempest you were running on that ankle."

"Shut up," Akieryon grumbled.

It felt like they were becoming friends.

ONE BATTLE
AT A TIME

Caspar and Marek sat squashed together into a single overstuffed chair. Dani stood with her back to them, her arms folded across her chest, a scowl firmly on her face. Veirn stood at the window, gazing out across the darkened city. Tempest paced. He prowled the room like a caged animal, chewing ferociously at one thumbnail.

"Only a week more," Caspar said. He sounded thin and uncertain, ready to fade at any moment.

"I'm not leaving your side until this parliament business is done," Tempest growled. He stopped pacing to fix Caspar with a burning stare. "If you are in public, I am with you. No arguments."

Caspar sighed. "Is that really practical?"

"It's necessary," Marek said, his voice grim. "Until this parliament is settled, Tempest will resume his old post as your bodyguard. No arguments," he repeated.

"I relinquish my duty to him," said Dani, still not turning.

"Freely and without reservation."

"Next you'll be wrapping me in cotton batting," Caspar complained.

"Only if we thought it would help," Marek said.

"You'd undo it in five minutes," Dani pointed out. "Like trying to bandage a cat."

"Rude," grumbled Caspar.

A bit of mischief lit Tempest's green eyes. "For comparing you to a cat? Or for keeping you alive, with or without your consent?"

"It's just a patch," Caspar complained. "Until we can identify the actual threat, this is all stopgaps and half-measures."

"What about something a little bit more punitive?" Akieryon suggested.

Tempest flashed him a smile, brief but genuine. "You know, bringing you home with me might have been the second best decision of my life."

"What was the first?" wondered Veirn.

"Killing someone with his own magic."

"My fault for asking."

Caspar sent Akieryon a look that would have been sharp, had weariness not dulled it. "I won't be a tyrant," he said. "Not to any of my people."

"I would never suggest it." Akieryon spread his hands before him. "When a teacher can't identify the source of a disruption, they usually impose restrictions on the entire class, right?" When he received nothing but blank stares, he assumed that education here in no way resembled his own experiences. "Anyway, you don't need to restrict anyone's rights or freedoms. Just restrict their access to *you*. Make anyone who wants to approach you—I assume this would mainly impact the people who are accustomed to having access to the king, and they're also the ones who stand to lose the most when the parliament convenes—make them speak with Tempest first. Every time." Out of the corner of his eye, he saw Tempest nodding his approval.

"They'll be cross," Caspar predicted. "All of them having nearly unlimited access to my presence chamber is tradition."

"Tradition is based on trust. Trust, once broken, takes twice as long to build anew." To his relief, Akieryon saw Caspar steel himself, then give a small nod.

Veirn jerked a thumb at Akieryon. "So he's the real deal? I thought he was some kind of decoy you'd dug up to draw some of those idiots' ire."

"Real," said Caspar, "and also a decoy."

"He's Tempest's friend." Dani's voice carried a note of warning. "And he's been very useful so far."

"He's one of us now."

Veirn studied Caspar in silence for a moment. Then he lifted both hands in an exaggerated shrug. "You kids'll be the death of me. Well, I've got the alchemy guilds looking to see where saltpeter may have gone astray. Maybe that can get us somewhere."

"Maybe," said Caspar, but Tempest was shaking his head.

"*I* know how to make saltpeter."

Dani shot him a stern look. "You also know how to make a person wear his entrails as a hat. I don't think you count."

"And you." Caspar focused his weary gaze on Akieryon. "I appreciate your eagerness to protect my people, but you must stop causing yourself harm. Please."

Akieryon looked at his swollen ankle, which he had propped up on a cushion before him. "About that," he said. "I imagine enough people saw that my injury is genuine." He glanced around the room, accepting nods and scowls with equanimity. "It's no longer useful, then."

While Veirn scoffed and Tempest glared, Akieryon bent forward over his elevated leg. He rested his hands on his ankle, and he sank into a deeper awareness of his body. His mind slid between heartbeats and their lack, between blood and bone, between the minute electricity of life. Push and pull. Positive and negative. Gently he tilted the balance, pushing the pull—nudging, really—until inflammation ebbed. Tendons and ligaments tightened, leaving behind only bruises.

Akieryon blinked at the faces now staring at him. His human friends. How long had he been concentrating?

"You *are* a sorcerer," Veirn said.

"You must teach me." Tempest's voice, low and rough with hunger, made Akieryon grateful he had not yet tried to stand on his newly healed ankle. He might have collapsed back into his chair.

Caspar caught Tempest's eye and mimed wiping his chin and the corner of his mouth. Tempest responded with a rude gesture.

Ignoring the flush heating his entire body, Akieryon looked at Veirn. "That's basic battlefield Healing. Most soldiers know it."

"You must come from a very magical place, then."

Akieryon shrugged. "Moreso than here."

Caspar sank against Marek's side. Marek's arm tightened around him, offering reassurance. For a moment Akieryon thought he could feel the weight of their emotions, the pain and the fear and the weariness. The white hot flares of protectiveness. Uncertainty and anxiety for the future. It unrolled like a tapestry all around him. He could reach out and touch it. He could touch each individual emotion. The infernal magic sleeping within him stirred.

It was hungry.

Akieryon blinked, and the array of emotions vanished, taking the hunger with it. He didn't want to examine that too closely. Looking up, he saw Tempest standing over him, frowning.

"Are you okay?"

Akieryon nodded. "I'm tired."

Caspar must have been waiting for an excuse, for he promptly shooed them all out. All except Marek. Dani rolled her eyes, thumped Tempest on the shoulder, and bade them goodnight. Veirn complained loudly that he still had work.

Akieryon waited until they had returned to Tempest's suite before he spoke again. "About Sir Veirn," he began, and Tempest interrupted him with a short laugh.

"You don't trust him?"

Akieryon shook his head. "He's Caspar's spymaster, isn't he?"

"You caught on quick." Tempest sounded proud. "Now, show me that magic again."

Akieryon grinned. He had expected nothing less.

~❖~

Magic lessons kept them up half the night. The sun was already high when Akieryon awoke, and Tempest was long gone. Guarding Caspar. Akieryon found the usual breakfast tray, and when he was washed and dressed, he made his way to the presence chamber. The guards outside confirmed his identity, then waved him through ahead of a disgruntled-looking queue.

The next three days passed in much the same fashion, with evening magic lessons, days in the presence chamber, and delegates arriving occasionally. Marek masterminded another rumor, this one pointing the blame for Caspar's tightened security in several directions at once. Squabbles broke out between nobles, proving its efficacy.

On the fourth night, Tempest succeeded at separating pure light out of a candle flame. He looked from the pinpoint of light in his hand to Akieryon, his bright eyes wide, grinning like a child who had just discovered candy for the first time.

"I can feel it trying to pull itself back together," he said.

Akieryon nodded. "You're holding the keys to the universe." He took Tempest's hands, and he guided him through releasing the energy without letting it collide like a thunderclap.

Tempest looked down at their hands, then back to Akieryon's face. His eyes, fierce magic green, glittered with joy. Akieryon's heart flipped and clattered with answering delight. Instinctively, thoughtlessly, he leaned in for a kiss.

Tempest's hands on his shoulders stopped him. The rejection struck Akieryon full in the chest, like choking on ice. Flushing with shame, he ducked his head. "I'm—I'm sorry. I didn't mean —"

"You did mean it." Tempest didn't sound angry. He didn't

sound much of anything, really. Merely factual. "That's good to know."

Blinking, Akieryon lifted his head. "It is?" His heart stabbed several painful, sideways beats. "I thought you didn't like… I thought… um." Why could he not find the right words?

Tempest's grip on his shoulders tightened. "I'm not asking you to change how you feel. I'm asking you not to expect me to be normal about things." He gave a brief squeeze, then released Akieryon. As he stepped back, a hint of mischief tugged at his lips. "And I'm asking you to wait."

Wait? For what? Akieryon tried to ask. "You're not… upset?" he said instead. Cowardice.

Tempest frowned. "Why should I be upset?"

"Because I already know that you dislike… that sort of thing."

But Tempest was already shaking his head. "You gave no offense." The water clock chimed. "Come on. It's too late for this conversation."

Too late, by far. Akieryon allowed Tempest to lead him to bed. Nestled amongst the pillows, feeling Tempest's warmth against his back, he wondered that he could want more than this. Was this life not already more than he had ever dreamed of? Had he grown so greedy in his brief time among humans? What would he want next? Where would it stop?

Remembering the hunger that stirred the infernal magic in him, he shivered. Tempest pulled the blanket up and tucked it close around them.

Well. He didn't have to have answers immediately.

For now, this was enough.

~⊰❖⊱~

Dawn brought Akieryon a quiet determination to do better. To be a better friend to Tempest. He slipped out of bed early. After washing and dressing himself, he collected the breakfast tray and brought it to Tempest, who was just scrubbing sleep from his eyes.

"Did I miss something?"

Akieryon sat down on the bed and placed the tray between them. "No?"

"You're not usually up this early." Tempest reached for some warm bread. "Something on your mind?" he asked in all innocence, as though he had no idea what might trouble Akieryon.

I want you to know that everything is good between us. Akieryon squeezed some cheese between slices of pear. "I'm just worrying about… all the things." Still a coward, though.

"Fair enough," Tempest said around a large mouthful. "There's a lot to worry about."

Akieryon nodded. He wanted to curl up against Tempest's side and pretend the world didn't exist for a while. It wouldn't happen.

Tempest had to go to Caspar and keep him safe. Akieryon had to… keep up the ruse, he supposed. He sighed.

Tempest held a scone slathered in spiced jelly to Akieryon's lips until he took a bite. "Everyone is feeling pretty worn down." When he had safely transferred the scone to Akieryon's possession, he leaned forward, pressing their foreheads together. "One battle at a time, Demonslayer," he said softly.

Akieryon gave a dry chuckle. "You and I both know that's not how it works."

"We can try." Tempest got up to go get dressed, and Akieryon focused on the remains of their breakfast.

"Oh, yes," he muttered. "All we can ever do is try."

Tempest stuck his head back through the doorway. "What was that?"

"I'm going to try some more magic practice today," Akieryon told him. "Dani won't be in the training yard, will she?"

"Nah, she's too busy guarding Caspar." Tempest hesitated, his brow furrowing. "Be careful."

Akieryon thought about how the infernal magic made him feel, how hungry, how ready to unravel the universe. "I don't think I have the option not to be."

The magic came more easily this time. When Akieryon stood at the center of the sand sparring ring, oily black smoke seething down his blade, he closed his eyes, and he reached out for whatever the nearby guards were feeling. Awe. Fear. Excitement. Tiny threads of envy. Whatever he could grab, he fed to the magic crawling over the sword in his hand. He moved on instinct, and he tried not to let it frighten him. How could he touch their emotions? How could he pluck away bits to give to the hungry infernal magic?

Oh, there was an obvious answer, but he didn't much care for looking at it directly. Still, he'd had enough of cowardice for one day. He managed to release the magic without exploding anything this time—significant progress—and he returned the sword to its place on the rack.

"Quitting already?" called one of the guards. Akieryon shrugged.

"I'm out of time."

Out of time and out of ideas, but he could still help protect Caspar. Akieryon made his way back through the castle, chewing on what he knew. It still wasn't much. The bombing might be unrelated, but for now he had to assume it was all connected. The assassin and the poison, though. Would the person (persons?) holding the purse strings want to witness the murder attempts? Who had been present both times?

He had his head down, lost in thought, when he rounded a

corner and bumped into Cori. Akieryon caught her and steadied her, but fabric swatches and pencils flew in all directions. Stammering an apology, Akieryon hurried to help her collect her tools.

"How's your ankle?" The look the tailor gave him was just a little too shrewd. Akieryon took his time climbing to his feet.

"Feeling better today. I sincerely appreciate your concern." Likewise he appreciated Cori's nose for gossip. "Do you mind if I walk with you a little way?"

Cori blushed hotly, but she bounced on the balls of her feet. "Oh! I'd be honored!"

Akieryon fell into step beside her, heading away from the king's rooms, heading toward an unfamiliar part of the castle. For a while, he let Cori talk, let the crumbs of information fall where they may. The boy who had been poisoned was doing well. The cook was still furious, all these days later. Sir Marek had hired another urchin.

"You mean Zeli?"

Cori's steps slowed. "You know her?"

Akieryon shook his head. "I met her once, that's all."

Cori slid him a sideways glance that was far too knowing. "I hope she thrives, I really do. Sir Marek looks after his own."

"He had me fooled at first," Akieryon admitted, and Cori

laughed a bright, easy laugh that echoed off of the walls and ceiling, narrower here than the corridors Akieryon usually walked. Something sounded a little off. He tilted his head, listening.

"He never does—"

"Make a good first impression," Akieryon said, finishing the sentence with Cori. She laughed again. Akieryon drifted toward the wall, following the odd reverberation.

"He doesn't have to, of course, and may we all be so adored— What are you doing?"

Akieryon tested the edges of a panel, prodding it with his fingertips until he found the hidden catch. A portion of the wall swung open by a hand's breadth. "Did you know this was here?"

Cori tilted her head and pursed her lips. "No," she said, "but I bet Sir Veirn does."

Opening the door wider revealed a flight of plain stone stairs. Akieryon stepped through, and Cori caught at his sleeve.

"Where are you going?"

Akieryon looked at her, then gestured at the hidden stairs. "Down."

Cori gave him a skeptical look. Then she squeezed into the stairway after him and shut the hidden door. "Sounds reasonable."

Shaking his head, Akieryon gathered a tiny sphere of light above his open palm, and he began picking his way downward.

Cori kept close behind him, and shortly resumed her usual chatter. Akieryon listened in silence until she abruptly said, "What's Tempest like in bed, anyhow?" Akieryon stumbled and caught himself with a hand on the wall. The light flickered and nearly went out.

I also would like to know. Akieryon fought a rising blush, as though Cori would even see it. He drew a deep breath, and he gave an honest answer. "He cuddles."

"He *WHAT?* " Cori nearly shrieked in delight.

It struck Akieryon that most people had never seen Tempest's gentleness, or the warmth he shared with his friends. Most people had no idea how he could soften his voice. They never knew the extent of his affection, nor how demonstrative he could be when the mood took him. They only ever saw the king's taciturn bodyguard, the man with tattoos on his cheeks and blood on his hands.

Akieryon found he didn't mind the blood.

Voices drifted up from below, forestalling any need to reply. Akieryon gestured, and Cori's steps slowed. She might have held her breath as they both tiptoed to another hidden door.

"—absolutely no bread or ale," someone was saying, "or dairy of any kind."

"Yes, my lady," replied a second, wearier voice.

"No sauces," the first voice continued, and Cori nudged Akieryon.

"It's Lady Tonata DiSevi," she hissed. "Every time she arrives, she comes down here to explain her special diet to the cooks. Pari wants to hit her with something heavy."

"You must understand," Lady Tonata was saying, "I will become dreadfully ill if I consume any wheat or barley at all."

"I do understand, my lady."

"Excellent. Keep it in mind."

As footsteps moved away from the hidden door, Akieryon cautiously eased it open. Through the bustle of the kitchen, he saw a tall woman striding haughtily for the main door. Her dark hair, gathered under a beaded net, sported incongruous streaks of dark gold.

The kitchen boy Venin noticed them. Scrambling over, he hauled Cori into the kitchen and pushed the door closed. "What are you doing in there?" he hissed, trying to direct his ire more toward the tailor than the king's guest.

"It's my fault," Akieryon told him. "I discovered the hidden stair, and I let Cori explore it with me."

"You *let* me?" Cori looked like she wanted to kick him. "As though you could have stopped me!"

Fair point. Akieryon shrugged. "Sorry to intrude." From

halfway across the kitchen, a woman with impressively muscular arms bore down upon them.

"You," she said to Venin. "The soup." The boy snapped off a salute and scurried away. "You," she continued, to Cori. "What are you doing in my kitchen?"

Akieryon grabbed Cori by the wrist. "We took a wrong turn," he said in his most placating tone. "We're leaving."

"Sorry, Pari," Cori said. "We're not trying to add to your difficult day."

Pari waved them away, toward the main door. "Right, fine, get y'gone."

"You do miracles down here," Akieryon called over his shoulder. He couldn't see whether the compliment helped, or only enraged Pari further. Cori dragged him out the door.

"It's been fun," she said, "but I should get back to work."

Akieryon nodded. "See you around."

When Cori scurried away, back toward wherever it was that the tailors did their work, Akieryon paused, considering. Then he followed in the direction Lady Tonata had gone.

COUSIN

Akieryon trailed Lady Tonata along three hallways, until finally a closed door stood before him. He pushed it open, and discovered a scrap of garden walled on three sides. Not quite a courtyard. More of a nook almost forgotten between building additions. Here Lady Tonata sat on a stone bench, her hands in her lap, her gaze tracking the movements of tiny birds in a crooked old olive tree.

He pushed the door closed. When Lady Tonata glanced toward the movement, Akieryon mustered his best awkward smile. "I know what it's like," he said, "being different."

Lady Tonata looked him over with an appraising eye, and her shoulders moved as though with a soundless laugh. Then she indicated the bench beside her. "Aren't you Tempest's new… plaything?"

"Why does everyone say that?" Akieryon nonetheless accepted the seat Lady Tonata invited him to take beside her.

"Probably because you look so young and pretty."

"I'm older than Tempest," Akieryon pointed out with reasonable certainty.

Lady Tonata arched a skeptical brow at him. "He's thirty, you know."

Knowing nothing of human aging, Akieryon nodded anyway. "I was locked away in the dark for some time. Apparently it does wonders for the complexion."

Again Lady Tonata did that soundless laugh, but this time she actually smiled at him. "I see," she said. "He likes your sense of humor."

"I hope so." No, that wasn't fair. Akieryon knew he had made Tempest laugh, probably almost daily. Wit, dry and dark, seemed to please him, and that suited Akieryon just fine. "Are you here for the parliament?"

"Oh, the parliament!" Lady Tonata waved her hand in a gesture Akieryon could not interpret. "It's all my brothers ever talk about, but I thought I ought to witness this historic moment anyway." Her gaze sharpened. "What about you?"

"I hope to be useful," Akieryon dodged. "Parliament, I suppose, is a good place to start."

"Hm." Lady Tonata sat back again, all poise and little artifice. Akieryon counted himself no great judge of character, but he hoped she would prove to be less irksome than the rest of the nobility. "That remains to be seen." But her tone remained neutral skepticism, rather than the outright scorn Akieryon had come to expect. He nodded.

"We'll all find out together, won't we?" He ignored the approaching footsteps in favor of gauging Lady Tonata's reaction, but she looked up instead.

"What are we doing together?" Toxelom DiSevi—Akieryon managed to remember—threw himself down onto the bench at Lady Tonata's other side, then leaned forward to send an exaggerated glare in Akieryon's direction. "Should you be chatting up my sister, or will Tempest get angry?"

"Tempest doesn't get angry," Akieryon replied, a little confused.

"Toko," Lady Tonata chided, "you're intruding."

"When do I not?" Toxelom said, and he had a point. Their other brother Toredi complained loudly that Toxelom would speak over the king himself, given half a chance.

Abruptly, Akieryon could no longer contain his curiosity. "Is Tempest in the habit of bringing pretty men home with him?"

The DiSevi siblings blinked at him.

"No."

"Not at all."

"Well…there is the bard, isn't there?"

"Don't be daft, he's a bard. He hardly counts."

"Right. Comes and goes like a stray cat, doesn't he?"

"That's unflattering. Jynn is actually very sweet when you get to know him."

"Right. Creepy eyes notwithstanding."

Lady Tonata gave her brother a shove that nearly dislodged him from the bench. "Don't be a bigot," she said icily.

"Everybody thinks it!" Toxelom protested, which wasn't much of a defense. His sister glared, and he changed the subject. "Anyway," he said to Akieryon, "I thought you'd be in there." He gestured vaguely. "You know. Advising the king."

Akieryon shrugged. "He knows his mind. Parliament convenes in a few days. I guess I have a little time on my hands."

Inexplicably, Toxelom glared at him. Then Lady Tonata started to laugh.

"Oh, no!" She leaned forward, her arms crossed as though she could hold back her mirth, if only she tried harder. "Did they not let you in?"

Toxelom's glare became a full pout. "One DiSevi at a time!" He flailed his hands in a gesture of helpless frustration. "Can you believe that? His own cousins!"

"Family hasn't exactly been kind to him," Lady Tonata said, suddenly grave again. Toxelom made a noise like letting the air out of a balloon.

"Toniiiii," he whined. "Why do you always take his side?"

"Someone in this family has to," she retorted. "Now go away. You're scaring the hummingbirds."

When Toxelom had gone, grumbling all the while, Akieryon and Lady Tonata sat in silence for a time. The little birds flitted through the tree, and the shadows crept along the pavement. Akieryon cleared his throat.

"I was wondering—"

"Yes," Lady Tonata said, "my brother is fully an idiot."

Akieryon choked back a laugh. "Yes, I had noticed that," he admitted. "But you're the king's cousin?"

"On my mother's side mostly, yes."

Akieryon found the *mostly* somewhat troubling, but he refrained from mentioning it. "How is it that I'm just meeting you today?"

Lady Tonata sat back and stretched her feet out in front of her. "The boys got to drop everything and come make fools of themselves all over the capitol while I had to stay home to collect the rents."

"What's that?"

"The... rents?" Seeing Akieryon's genuine confusion, Lady Tonata tilted her head and squinted a little, obviously scrutinizing him. "The tenant farmers who live on our family's lands pay a percentage of their annual… yield… Where have I lost you?" she interrupted herself.

"Ownership of land?" Akieryon shook his head. "That's not really a thing where I'm from."

"No wonder Caspar likes you so much."

Akieryon grinned. "He does enjoy an outside perspective, doesn't he?"

They sat together long into the afternoon, deep in conversation. Lady Tonata explained inheritance of land, tenancy, and rent. Akieryon explained how in Heaven, the house in which he had lived was considered his, but no one owned the land, and no one had to pay to keep a roof over their head. Lady Tonata had him talking about himself and his home as easily as Caspar ever had, and only Akieryon's training kept him from using words such as *Heaven* and *Seraphim*. The resemblance between cousins had never been clearer.

"I'm glad you're here," she said abruptly, startling Akieryon. "My royal cousin needs more friends outside his little band of exiles."

"But I'm an exile too." When Lady Tonata squinted at him in that assessing way that Akieryon was beginning to recognize, he added, "I had to leave my home after I injured a superior officer in… in a training accident."

"That's not sensible. If it was an accident, why should you be punished for it?"

Because I would frighten people. No, that wasn't fair. "I think I almost killed him," Akieryon confessed. "My mentor. My teacher. He's… he's worth twelve of me."

"Given what I've heard of you, he must be something truly remarkable." Lady Tonata might have said more, but the door opened again. The tension in her shoulders eased a bit when she saw that it was only Sir Marek's silent page, Lan. "What, already?"

Lan bowed and gestured to the open door, all in one movement. With a sigh, Lady Tonata stood, then she beckoned to Akieryon. Together they walked back through the castle, following Lan to a room Akieryon had not yet seen. Sunlight streamed through tall windows, and sumptuous cushions littered every seat. Marek stood in a strategic sunbeam, smiling when he saw them.

"Lady Tonata!" He extended both hands toward her, which she ignored in favor of a hug.

"Well met, cousin," she said, visibly enjoying the way the word flustered him.

"Please—"

"What else should I call my dearest cousin's husband?"

"Stop that," Marek mumbled.

"What, embarrassing you? Doesn't Akieryon know already?" Lady Tonata turned. "You do know?"

About Caspar and Marek? "Obviously." Akieryon looked at Marek, who frowned intently at both of them. Was he upset? Should he have feigned ignorance?

"There, you see?" Lady Tonata was saying. "You're among friends, and we all know you are utterly devoted to him. That's good enough for me."

"I'm not his husband." The objection sounded threadbare, as though Marek had made it too many times already.

Lady Tonata patted him on the arm. "Keep telling yourself that."

"You are, in your own way, as obnoxious as your brothers."

"More intelligent, I would hope."

"That's not exactly difficult," Marek pointed out. "Come on." He led the way to another door and, seeing Akieryon's hesitation, he added, "Yes, you too."

"Don't worry." Lady Tonata nudged him. "You're not the main course."

This door led into the chamber where Akieryon had first dined with Caspar. He glanced at Marek, who nodded in a manner that suggested he might shove Akieryon forward if he lingered in the doorway much longer. Lady Tonata had already helped herself to a seat at the low table. She beckoned for the men to join her.

It felt like a curious echo of that long-ago night—it had actually been, what, a month?—when Akieryon had begun to feel at ease with Caspar and Dani. Sir Marek and Lady Tonata talked freely of family and lands and the management of both. They laughed together about people Akieryon hardly knew. Despite feeling like an outsider once more, he found himself relaxing. Surely Marek would not trust anyone who presented a threat to Caspar.

The front door opened, and Caspar stepped through. Tension melted from his shoulders as he entered, and then a sunny grin broke across his face. Sir Marek and Lady Tonata were on their feet in an instant, with Akieryon scrambling awkwardly after. Caspar threw his arms wide. "Toni!"

"Cousin." Lady Tonata bowed, appraised her king, and then launched herself forward for a hug twice as enthusiastic as the one she had given Marek. While they were occupied, Dani sidled through the door and closed it.

When Caspar at last released Lady Tonata, Dani poked her firmly in the back of the head. She turned, and her face transformed with pure joy. "DANI!"

"TONI!"

While the two women hugged and shouted over each other,

Caspar sat down and let his head drop onto Marek's shoulder. "Not much longer, my love," Marek murmured in a voice not meant for anyone else's ears. Caspar sighed and squeezed his hand. Akieryon looked away.

"You're looking particularly well." Lady Tonata held Dani at arm's length. "Punched someone lately?"

Dani shook her head. "New sparring partner," she said with a wink at Akieryon.

"Oh, no wonder." Lady Tonata dragged Dani over to the table and sat down again. "Where's Tempest?"

Dani grinned and nodded toward Akieryon. "Out looking for him, probably."

Lady Tonata raised one eyebrow. "It's like that, is it?"

"It is," said Marek, and Caspar dug an elbow into his side.

"You know how Tempest is. He assumes anyone he actually *likes* is somehow a helpless kitten."

"You are kind of a helpless kitten though," Dani said, and Caspar made a rude gesture.

"Stop flirting," said Lady Tonata. "You'll spoil my appetite."

Banter rolled easily around the table until the kitchen boy Venin appeared with platters of fruit and cheese. Then, while Lady Tonata picked delicately at a bowl of blackberries, Caspar planted both elbows on the table and leaned forward, abruptly all business.

"What do you want?"

Lady Tonata blinked at him. "I want something?"

"You have that look," Caspar accused. "The one that says you're about to ask me for something I can't give you."

Lady Tonata worked her jaw side to side for a moment, then slapped her palm down on the tabletop. "The DiSevi parliament seat," she said fiercely. "It should be *mine*. We both know my brothers are too stupid and too selfish to use it to good effect."

Shaking his head, Caspar sank back into a weary huddle. "The point of parliament is to limit my power. I can't just order your brother to give up the seat."

Lady Tonata glared at him. "I know," she said, sounding rather like she wanted to kick him. "For what it's worth," she added, sounding no less angry, "it's a good idea."

Caspar lifted his wine glass to her. "You'll find a way to convince Toredi that participating in government is actually boring and beneath him. It just might take a little while."

Lady Tonata grimaced. "You don't know how stubborn he can be."

"I'm pretty sure I do," Caspar said, mostly to himself. Roast pheasant arrived, and conversation moved on to other topics. No one mentioned the parliament again. The next time the door opened, Tempest walked in, surveyed the scene before him, and with visible reluctance sat down beside Caspar. Smirking, Marek murmured something, and Caspar dug an elbow into his side. Tempest reached for the remains of the pheasant.

"You've been busy," Lady Tonata said.

Tempest didn't look up from the food. If he looked up, he would have to see Caspar and Marek holding hands. "I usually am."

"Yes, but no one's scrubbing blood off the walls."

"Yet." Tempest grinned a sharp grin.

"Good to see you, too," Lady Tonata said. Akieryon realized that she meant it, and he relaxed a little. Anyone who casually teases Tempest about killing must be a friend, right? And yet, a faint thread of tension remained, drawn through Tempest's shoulders and down his spine. Akieryon waited until they were alone to ask about it.

"You don't trust her."

"Toni?" Tempest's face pulled into a faint grimace. "She's fine. She's just too close to the throne, and demonstrably cleverer than the nearer heirs. It's just…"

"Uncomfortable?" Akieryon supplied, and Tempest nodded. "She would be easier to poison than most people, though, wouldn't she? I don't think that's a desirable trait in a monarch."

With a short, surprised laugh, Tempest caught him in a rough hug. "How do you put things in perspective so easily?"

"Maybe because I'm old." Smiling to himself, Akieryon nestled into Tempest's embrace. This was enough. He could love this man with all the strength in his body and all the fire in his soul, and he never had to say so. He could be content, which itself was a new state for him.

He wanted to give it a try. He wanted more. He wanted to to turn his brain upside down and shake it until all the stupid, pointless wanting fell out of it.

Well. For now he would just enjoy what he had.

Two days later, the bard arrived.

ZERO HOUR

The previous day had been some sort of festival, most likely of a religious nature. Humans tend to crave divine favor. Angels, particularly younger ones, prefer benign neglect. Having felt the crushing weight of The Presence once, and considering that one time more than enough for his first millennium, Akieryon had opted to remain indoors.

Around midmorning of the next day, a small commotion erupted as one of the castle pages stood in the doorway of Caspar's presence chamber and announced the arrival of the bard. Caspar was on his feet in an instant, and hurrying out into the corridor, Tempest faithfully at his heels. Everyone else followed him in an excited wave of humanity. A little baffled and a lot curious, Akieryon accompanied them all to the entrance hall, where porters hauled away a battered old trunk. There, framed by the open doors, stood the bard.

This was the bard? The one Lady Tonata and her brother had mentioned?

He was a dragon.

Well, Akieryon corrected, of dragonkind. As the bard stepped forward, away from the glare of sunlight behind him, Akieryon saw more clearly the ineffectually tiny wings and serpentine, rattle-tipped tail that characterized his species. One of the unacknowledged dragonkin from the Shadowed Marches in the far south. They had lost both fire and flight, Akieryon remembered, but had evolved the strongest venom of any species of dragon.

"Jynn! Welcome back!"

With a faint jangle of strings, Jynn the bard ran forward into Caspar's eager embrace. Closer now, Akieryon saw that his skin had a cool, silvery sheen. His hair—no, his *plumage* he wore tied back in a neat plait, no doubt convenient for travel, and it exactly matched the metallic copper of his eyes. Some trick of refraction masked his pupils entirely, which probably explained Toxelom's remark about his eyes.

Jynn bounced from Caspar's arms into an enthusiastic hug of both Draycens at once. Then, whirling free once more, he dove upon Tempest, who laughed and spun him off his feet. Akieryon watched, fascinated. Joy rolled off of them in waves, bright and sweet like lemon cake.

Akieryon was *so hungry.*

Before he could stop himself, he had mentally reached out to touch their joy. Tempest stopped and looked at him. Jynn had wrapped both arms around Tempest's neck and twined his fingers through his hair, but he froze when he followed the direction of Tempest's gaze. All that delicious joy crashed down as though plunged into ice water.

"*Tempest.*" Jynn's voice was low and urgent.

"I know," Tempest said.

"Does he?"

"Not yet." Tempest gestured at Caspar. "We're a little busy here."

"Excuses," Jynn said. "I'm going to tell him." He took a step toward Akieryon.

"Don't." Tempest stopped him with a hand on his chest. "I want them to meet."

"I'm confused," Akieryon informed them.

"Of course you are." Jynn's fingertips drifted across the back of Tempest's hand in a soft caress, a lover's caress. Akieryon's stomach clenched in a way he could not reasonably pinpoint as jealousy. "He's obviously not explaining anything to you." To Tempest he said, "When?"

"When I'm not needed here."

Jynn scoffed softly. "So, next year?"

"A week or two," Tempest said, a flicker of annoyance

shadowing his brow.

Jynn smiled. "If you say so," he teased. He winked, and then he allowed himself to be swept along back to Caspar's presence chamber. Tempest quietly broke both arms of a man who took advantage of the excitement and tried to draw a knife. Then he handed him off to Sir Veirn, presumably for extensive questioning.

Most of that day passed in song and dance and outlandish stories. Jynn established himself as the unrelenting center of attention, giving Caspar a much needed rest. Late in the afternoon Dani decided that Akieryon needed to learn to dance. She dragged him around and kicked his feet to correct their positioning while Jynn absolutely shredded on a hurdy-gurdy.

When Dani had tormented him enough, she let him stumble to a halt beside Lady Tonata, who laughed and clapped along with the music. She looked bright and carefree, and it was a lie.

"I hope you're prepared to vacate Tempest's bed tonight," scoffed a voice behind them, and Lady Tonata whirled, her demeanor falling at once into righteous fury.

"Toko, *go away* and bother someone else."

Akieryon looked to Dani. "Are Jynn and Tempest really lovers?"

Dani wrinkled her nose. "They're friends," she said. "They fuck." She ignored Lady Tonata's smack to her arm. "But honestly the friendship is more important. If you want more details, you'll have to ask them."

Sure. Why not. Or he could die of mortification.

"Don't worry about it." Lady Tonata gave his arm a reassuring pat. "If there's anything Tempest is actually bad at, it's letting people go."

Sir Veirn appeared just long enough to murmur something into Caspar's ear. When he left again, he took Marek with him. Neither of them returned. Caspar smiled as though all was well. As afternoon wore on toward evening, Sesoran made a tasteless joke about the king's final hours of absolute power.

"Good riddance," Caspar said. "Either it corrupts its bearer, or else it destroys them. There is nothing else."

That remark killed the levity, and afterward people began to bid him goodnight. Caspar looked almost smug about it. Jynn played tunes that only just managed not to be lullabies.

When only a few stragglers remained, Jynn began to pack up his instruments. Akieryon watched, admiring the care he put into each movement. A normal person would worry, he imagined, or at least feel more than a faint suggestion of jealousy. He really didn't. Mostly, he felt a growing concern for his escalating ability to perceive and interact with others' emotions. It seemed to increase every time he attempted to use the infernal magic. What did it mean?

No. He knew what it meant.

He was a Demonslayer, and he could no longer hide from the truth. He had studied the races of demons who dwell in the upper Spheres of Hell and feed on the emotions of Mortals. He had even had to kill a few, the sort who went bad and caused disasters in order to generate more delicious fear and despair. If one had a taste for such things. His hand drifted to the back of his neck, to the Lineage Mark.

He was part demon. He was like those he had hunted. Nothing else made any sense.

"You okay?"

Akieryon blinked at Tempest. "Yeah." It was mostly true. "You've known him a long time?" He nodded toward Jynn, who had moved to Caspar's side and leaned in to plant a noisy kiss on his cheek. Caspar was laughing.

"Fifteen years. No, seventeen? I don't know, time is slippery. Come on," Tempest said with a faint smile. "Let's have a quiet dinner. It's the last peace we'll see for days."

Over glazed mutton and parsnips, Tempest deflected questions about the man he had captured. That, he noted, was not his problem right now. Afterward, he dragged Akieryon to his closet to select their clothing for the morning. This new interest in fashion baffled Akieryon until he had stacked his clothes, and Tempest proceeded to calculate exactly how many daggers he could hide therein. Oh, well, at least he was consistent.

"Are we expecting trouble?"

"We're preparing for the worst," Tempest said, his tone disarmingly light. He shucked his worn clothing and shook out the day's dirt with a faint pulse of magic. He put them away. "It's probably fine."

Probably fine, in Akieryon's experience, usually led to a bloodbath.

Tempest went to bed early that night, opting to rest instead of practicing celestial magic under Akieryon's careful tutelage. So he was definitely expecting trouble. Akieryon climbed under the blankets and curled against his side.

"You haven't asked."

Startled, Akieryon almost flinched back from him. "Asked what?"

"About Jynn." Tempest cracked one eye open and watched him. "And me."

Akieryon's heart rate jumped. He drew a deep breath. "If you wanted to be with him right now," he said calmly, "you would be."

A sharp breath hissed between Tempest's teeth. Pushing himself up on one elbow, Akieryon saw Tempest watching him more intently than he usually did. Something smoldering in his gaze made Akieryon feel hot and tingly, and maybe a little lightheaded.

"What?"

Tempest grinned at him. "Trust is sexy."

Akieryon blushed so swiftly and so fiercely he thought he might burst. "It's easy to trust you." A little grumpily, he collapsed back onto the mattress. "You're too direct." Except for whatever it was that he didn't want Jynn telling him. That, Akieryon assumed, was tied to Tempest asking him to wait.

He was willing to wait. He had time.

Perhaps Tempest held him a little closer that night. Perhaps he imagined it. Sleep came late, and brought strange dreams. People were frozen while trying to flee. The smell of smoke filled his nostrils. Someone sobbed his name. A thin, insecure voice wailed, and he needed to follow it. *Kie-nin, where're you?*

Hands on his shoulders pulled him out of his dreams. Gasping as though coming up from underwater, Akieryon stared dazedly at Tempest.

"Nightmare?" It almost wasn't a question. Akieryon grasped at threads of the dream, but it wisped away from him.

"I don't know." Akieryon scrubbed at his forehead. "It felt… wrong."

Tempest checked him over, but eventually he sat back, satisfied that no foreign magic had interfered with Akieryon's sleep. The sun had scarcely crept above the hills, but Tempest was already dressed, in rich velvets and embroidery and even tiny jet and pearl beadwork. Akieryon's mouth went dry.

"Is it time?"

"It's time for breakfast." Tempest pushed a pastry into his hand. "And then we go meet Caspar."

Akieryon wanted a cup of coffee, or possibly eight, to help shake the cobwebs out of his head, but he said nothing. The day would be stressful enough without him making demands. Dressed in charcoal satin and his fine blue coat, he followed Tempest to the royal apartments. Dani was already there, in her most formal uniform yet, with high collar and full sleeves and everything polished to a blinding shine. A contingent of similarly attired guardsmen flanked her. The sun crept higher.

The door opened, and Caspar emerged. As one, the guards knelt, and he pulled a face. Tempest took in his full length velvet coat, with gold braid and delicate filigree buttons, and he grinned.

"You're going to swelter in that."

"Says the man who wears black for every occasion."

Sir Marek followed at Caspar's heels. Tiny braids pulled his hair back from his face, each held in place with bits of crimped gold. He carried a purple cloak trimmed in otter fur carefully folded over one arm. Akieryon suspected that he had dressed Caspar himself, from the white suede shoes to the crown—not his usual plain circlet—set with sapphires. Caspar gestured for his guards to rise. Marek arranged the cloak over Caspar's left shoulder.

"He's very pretty," Tempest said, and Marek stepped back, flanking his king, hand resting beside his sword hilt. Caspar sighed.

"Let's get this pageantry over with."

The group of them processed down the grand staircase to the entrance hall, where apparently the whole of the nobility of Davenz had gathered. Caspar stopped five steps up from the bottom, and the guards arrayed themselves in ranks below him. Tempest and Sir Marek stood just one step below the king, and Akieryon positioned himself opposite Dani, at attention. A hush descended over the hall. In a distant corner, Jynn stuck a small stylus in his mouth and hunched over a sheaf of papers.

Caspar made a brief speech about progress and healing the wounds of the past through cultivating a better future. Ignoring the lukewarm applause of his peerage, he strode down the remaining steps with his head held high. The guards swung the doors wide for him. Reluctant nobility falling into his entourage behind the guards, Caspar stepped out into the morning sunlight.

Beyond the castle gates, the people had gathered. Caspar's entourage emerged, and a thunderous cheer shook dust from the walls. *The people are in favor of this parliament thing.* Who had said that? Lady Tonata? Sir Veirn? It seemed to be true. The citizens of Davenz chanted Caspar's name and threw flowers at his feet.

They loved him.

Caspar walked with his head high, his eyes constantly flicking over the crowds, his smile bright, broad, genuine. When hands stretched toward him, he reached back. His fingertips brushed against theirs, and people cheered louder than ever.

After weeks in the castle, watching the scheming nobility sneer behind Caspar's back, Akieryon gazed up and down the street, dumbfounded. These people *adored* their king. He could feel the truth of their joy, their excitement. Waves of giddy anticipation nearly knocked him over. He had to learn how to close off this newly discovered sense of his. He had to control it.

After they passed the lodging house where the representatives were staying, the cheering escalated. Tempest's wards pushed at the edges of Akieryon's awareness, even at this distance, and he smiled. They turned a corner, and ahead lay the Parliament Hall itself.

New, lime washed brick soared above the street. Columns flanked the entryway, supporting a sloped roof of clay tile. The windows stretched a full two stories high, gleaming in the morning sun. For a moment, Caspar stopped at the bottom of the steps, his head tipped back, contemplating the building in silence. Then he stepped forward.

At the top of the steps, Caspar turned around. A hush fell over the excited crowd, and he smiled. He made a longer, better speech, thanking everyone for joining him on this historic day, welcoming them to a new day, a new Davenz. "Progress does not come without struggle," he said, "and however fumbling they may be, I am honored to take these first steps forward with all of you."

Akieryon felt the roar of the crowd all the way to his bones. People jumped in place and climbed on each other, trying to get a better view. Some of the nobles looked like they might be sick. Caspar produced a silver key from somewhere about his person. Turning, he unlocked the doors. Two guards hurried forward to open them.

"This First Session of Parliament is now open!"

Akieryon stepped through the doors beside Dani. Everywhere he looked, sunlight glowed on polished wood. Before them, stairs diverged in two directions, curving around a central, open space. Desks were arranged in circles on the floor of the chamber, which sloped gently upward. Dani led Akieryon to the upper level, to the galleries that lined the walls, overlooking all. The room, Akieryon registered, was built as an amphitheater. Whoever spoke from the parliament floor, their voice would be heard.

Caspar walked to a desk that looked exactly like all the others, though this chair had a fancier cushion. He stood beside the chair, and he turned to face the representatives as they filed in. The guards directed them, and they found their seats had nameplates at the desks. Tempest murmured something that made Caspar laugh, and then he walked around the room, to a desk that directly faced the king's.

One by one, the representatives taking their places seemed to notice him there. A woman clad in rich yellows and blues—representing the confederated guilds of dye-witches, Akieryon later learned—squeezed Tempest's shoulder on her way past, and he winked at her. The representatives from the spinners, the weavers, and the leatherworkers likewise gave him subtle greetings. Akieryon blinked and leaned forward against the railing. Tempest was well liked?

When all the representatives had assumed their places, Caspar sat down. As one, the others sat as well. In the galleries, Akieryon was not the only one to remain standing, pressed close to the rail, straining his ears to catch every word. Caspar spoke a few words of welcome, then opened the session with an invitation for a few minutes of addressing any immediate or otherwise urgent concerns.

Mimoti DiPasha leaned forward and pointed aggressively at Tempest. "My lord king, what is *he* doing here?"

Caspar frowned and shook his head as though he had never heard anything more baffling in his life. "Why shouldn't the last survivor of the noble houses of Arum be included in these proceedings?"

"Yes." Xerishan Sinen, with a sneer on his thin weasel face, leaned toward Tempest. "How did you manage to survive that horrible coup?"

"Oh, no, I definitely died," Tempest replied mildly, almost cheerfully. "It just didn't stick."

"What do you mean, *it didn't stick?*" demanded Mimoti DiPasha. Across the room, unnoticed by most, Caspar was smiling.

"Someone fixed me."

Xerishan Sinen glared openly. "You have a friend who can bring back the dead?"

Tempest's eyebrows rose. "Friend? Oh no, no, I killed him. First opportunity. And no. He could manipulate time. It's not the same as a proper resurrection."

He could manipulate time.

I know something of what it is to be imprisoned.

Killing someone with his own magic.

Akieryon clutched at the railing as sudden realization staggered him. Time magic. That was how Tempest was so proficient. Akieryon's heart thundered in his chest. Humans potential was limited only by time. Tempest had found a way around that limitation.

Wildly, irrationally, Akieryon wondered if he would have to lose him at all.

Dani kicked the side of his foot, bringing him back to the present. Caspar was rapping on his desk, drawing all attention back to himself. He smiled. "If we're done questioning Tempest," he said, "does anyone else have any immediate concerns?"

If they did, they held their tongues about it. Caspar produced a sheaf of papers, and parliament began in earnest. While the nobility seemed absolutely confounded as to what to expect, the tradesmen had all brought notes of their own. Guild meetings, it seemed, trained good representatives. Before addressing more regulatory matters, Caspar established protocols for proposing, debating, and voting on legislation. Committees would be formed as needed, and would include diverse representation. Henceforth, any representative of limited literacy would be provided secretarial support.

Caspar yielded power to the people of Davenz.

Parliament was in session.

TRUTH

By some miracle, the day ended without a bloodbath. It did include a banquet, which has less blood and more food than the average bloodbath, but typically involves more threats of violence. This one took place in the same hall where the knights had dined. Akieryon tried not to think too hard about poison. An unexpected but welcome guest, Jynn occasionally joined the court musicians, but mostly spent the evening wedged between Tempest and Akieryon. He had his ragged sheaf of papers out on the table, and he scribbled furiously with his little metal stylus.

"This is why you're here," Tempest said. He sounded slightly amused.

"History is happening right now. It is my duty to record it accurately. And then to write wildly inaccurate songs about it." Jynn stuck the end of his pen in his mouth yet again.

"How does that work?" Akieryon asked, pointing at the stylus. Jynn reached into his pocket and produced another one, which he handed over without hesitation. The pen was a small metal tube, with a wax seal on one end and a nib on the other. Akieryon gave it an experimental shake, and Jynn grinned a sharp-fanged grin at him.

"Shadowmarcher design," he said. "It's filled with a mixture of minerals and powdered lichens that, when combined with our venom, produces ink."

"So you're writing with toxic ink?"

"Doesn't everyone?"

"I usually use lamp black," Tempest said.

Jynn wrinkled his nose. "Boring."

"But cheap and plentiful."

"Did you know," said Jynn, changing the subject, "this morning Tori DiSevi was complaining about Marek having a seat in parliament, and Marek said to him, 'Would you prefer my sister have it instead?' It must be nice having an argument that works one hundred percent of the time."

"It shuts people up," Tempest agreed.

"I can't imagine Dani having the patience for politics," Akieryon said, "but I do generally enjoy her company."

Turning to face him fully, Jynn grinned. "Yes, she did say the two of you spent some quality time together. When do I get to spar you?"

"Jynn, please," Tempest teased. "You've only just met him."

"When has that ever stopped me?"

Akieryon smiled at Jynn. "Choice of weapon?"

"Staff," the bard replied without hesitation. Interesting choice for a dragon. Akieryon nodded.

"Just let me know when," he said. Tempest was shaking his head at them.

"Enough flirting."

"It's never enough," Jynn objected. Akieryon merely sat and stared down at his half empty plate. Had he been flirting with Jynn? Did he *want* to flirt with Jynn?

Sir Veirn leaned down and said something directly into Tempest's ear. Tempest stood up immediately. "Keep an eye on Caspar," he said, before giving Jynn a pointed look. "Behave yourself."

Jynn gasped in mock affront. "My darling, I am never anything other than exceptional."

"Yeah, that's what I'm worried about." To Akieryon he said, "Don't take any shit from this guy." Then he walked away with Sir Veirn. Akieryon tried not to watch them leave. What good would it do?

Jynn grinned at him. "Well. Now I've got you to myself, haven't I?"

"I can't imagine there's much you would want to do or say that you wouldn't do in front of Tempest." Was that too blunt? That was probably too blunt.

Jynn gave him an appraising look. "First of all," he said, "there's kissing. Tempest isn't a big fan of—Oh, no, why are you blushing?"

Akieryon shook his head. "I wasn't exactly popular back—back home."

Jynn gawked at him. "No. You're telling me you—"

"Have little practical knowledge of kissing." Akieryon knew he must be blushing more furiously than ever. "Sad, but true."

"The Lenyr are going to eat you alive. You'll enjoy it, of course, but that's beside the point." Smiling as though he had not just casually wrung a humiliating confession from Akieryon, Jynn took a fresh sheet of paper and began scribbling music notation. "They're wrong, by the way."

"What? Who?"

"The people who made you feel unattractive."

Akieryon looked down at his plate. Suddenly, he no longer felt like eating. "If you say so," he mumbled. Fingertips on the back of his neck startled him. He flinched, and Jynn withdrew his hand.

"No?"

Shaking his head, Akieryon reached back to pull his collar away from his Lineage Mark. "Most people don't want to touch this."

Jynn half stood to get a good look. He sucked a breath through his teeth. "Well," he said softly. "That's a thing."

Akieryon hunched in a way his training should have prevented. "It's a Lineage Mark. I was born with it."

"I know."

"You… do?" Akieryon pulled his collar back into the correct position.

Jynn shrugged. "I didn't know what it was called, but—Ooh, dessert!"

The waitstaff had just brought in a fantasy of cake and custard, with candied fruit lining all the edges. Akieryon glanced over at Caspar, who was laughing with Lady Tonata, and he felt a twinge of guilt. He had not been keeping an eye on Caspar, as Tempest had requested. He had been paying attention to Jynn. He sat silently with his shame while the waitstaff brought plates of the glorious confection to everyone except Lady Tonata, who received a bowl of sugared fruit instead.

"Hey." Spoon in hand, Jynn nudged him. "What's wrong?"

"We're supposed to be protecting Caspar, aren't we?"

"He's fine. We were all teenagers together in Tymirin. Tempest likes to pretend like Caspar is made of spun glass, but really he's sturdier than he looks." Jynn said all of this around large bites of dessert. He ate as though he might never see food again.

"Someone *has* been trying to kill him," Akieryon pointed out.

"Yeah, I have a feeling we're going to see the end of that business very soon. Where do you think Tempest went?"

As though summoned by their conversation, Tempest strolled back in through the door at the back of the hall. He leaned in to say something into Caspar's ear, then returned to his seat. Promptly, someone brought him a plate of dessert. Jynn gave him a pointed look.

"Not yet. Veirn's working on it."

Jynn nodded. He finished his dessert and took a spoonful of Akieryon's. "So how long are you going to play parliament?"

"Caspar would *appreciate* my presence at the opening of every term, and also he'll let me know if there's something he particularly wants my vote on." Tempest shrugged. "I'm free to go by the end of the week, unless some gripping legislation comes up."

"Good." Jynn cut a glance at Akieryon. "Good."

Ignoring him for the moment, Akieryon leaned forward to grin at Tempest. "Caspar just wants you there to intimidate the rabble."

Tempest laughed a bright, surprised laugh that had people turning to stare at them. "Yeah, probably."

Jynn sat back, sipping his wine and watching them with a knowing smirk. He may indeed have had a little too much wine, for when he kissed Caspar goodnight as he had done the night before, he wobbled, and then laughed about it. He hummed to himself as he walked with Tempest and Akieryon back to Tempest's suite.

"There will be some splitting heads in parliament tomorrow," Tempest predicted.

"Good," said Jynn. "Maybe they'll be less inclined to bray like asses."

"I think that's a little much to expect," Akieryon said.

At the door, Jynn caught Akieryon by the hand. Tempest noticed, and made a small noise of annoyance. "Here we go," he muttered, his hand already on the door handle.

Jynn leaned close, looking at Akieryon in a way that made him feel hot and fidgety. "What?" The word came out too defensive, too wary.

"May I kiss you goodnight?"

Tempest made a noise in the back of his nose that might have been derision, or disgust, or merely amused distaste. He stepped through into his antechamber and closed the door.

Akieryon thought of how Jynn kissed Caspar on the cheek. "I… guess so?"

Jynn's knuckles brushed along Akieryon's jaw, and his thumb grazed his lower lip. "You're sure?"

Fighting and barely mastering an impulse to suck his lip into his mouth, Akieryon glanced at Tempest's closed door. No help would come from that direction.

Misinterpreting the look, Jynn eased a little nearer. "Tempest doesn't mind," he encouraged. "He's not exclusive with anyone. It's not in his nature."

Akieryon thought of his ill conceived attempt to kiss Tempest, and shame bloomed over his skin. "I…" *I wanted to kiss Tempest.* What he had wanted before was irrelevant. Jynn was here, and offering, and while Akieryon had never actually considered kissing a dragon man, he found he didn't hate the idea.

"I know." Jynn grinned, and his tail caressed the side of Akieryon's knee. "You have little practical experience. Shall we remedy that?"

Akieryon jolted forward, pressing his lips hard against Jynn's. Jynn gasped. One of his fangs scratched Akieryon's lip. It stung, but… in a nice way? Akieryon took two fistfuls of Jynn's shirt. Jynn's hands slid around Akieryon's waist, pulling him closer. He pressed one knee between Akieryon's legs, and he teased Akieryon's lips with his tongue.

It all felt surprisingly nice. Burning with curiosity, burning with something more urgent, Akieryon tried to mirror Jynn's movements. Jynn sighed a sigh that was half groan against his lips. Without deciding, almost without realizing it, Akieryon reached for the emotion behind the sigh. It felt warm and hungry, bright and heady like wine. Abruptly, Jynn pushed back from him. His hands on Akieryon's hips, he rested their foreheads together and drew several steadying breaths.

"Enough," he whispered, his voice a little rough. "Or else I'll drag you through that door and demand that Tempest change his mind about waiting."

The warm, intoxicating emotion melted away, leaving Akieryon feeling cold and hungry. He could wait. He could. "He won't."

"I can be very persuasive." Jynn's knuckles brushed against Akieryon's cheek in another caress. "And you're far too beautiful to keep in the dark for long."

A moment later, he had Akieryon firmly by the hand as he burst through into the antechamber. "Tempest! Help! Tempest, *why is he crying?*"

"Oh, no." In seconds, Tempest's arms had wrapped around Akieryon. He was safe here. Burying his face against Tempest's shoulder, he sobbed. "What did you say?"

While Jynn recounted what had happened, Tempest scooped

Akieryon up and carried him into the bedroom. Jynn repeated what he had said, and Akieryon made a small, pathetic sound against Tempest's neck. "Hush," Tempest murmured, gently stroking Akieryon's hair. Then he told Jynn where Akieryon had come from. Dimly, Akieryon registered that Tempest must trust Jynn, to just tell him everything like that.

When Tempest had finished, Jynn sat in silence for a moment at the edge of the bed. Then he nodded. "No wonder he loves you."

Akieryon tensed, expecting a rebuttal, or at least a noise of disgust. Tempest never loosened his hold, never halted the soothing motion of his fingers. "Mind your business," he said, but he sounded amused.

"You know I can't do that."

"Right. Bard." Tempest's arms tightened around Akieryon. "You won't put this in your songs."

"Who would believe me?" Jynn said, his tone too lighthearted to trust entirely. But then he wrapped his arms around Akieryon and Tempest both, and he leaned close, whispering into Akieryon's ear, "You're safe with us."

Slowly, Akieryon relaxed his grip on Tempest. Did he trust, really trust with his entire being, that he wouldn't have to be alone again? He could only think of one way to find out.

"It's so much worse than you think," he whispered.

Jynn's hand brushed against Akieryon's cheek, soothing some of the tears away. "You can tell us, if you want," he murmured. Then he repeated, "You're safe now."

Did Akieryon want to tell them? He drew a deep, shaky breath. "I'm told I was a foundling," he said, choosing words as precise as he could manage. "I grew up in foster homes—no more than a couple of years in each. People were eager to pass me on when they saw the mark on me. It was hard to make friends when all my peers picked up on the way none of the adults wanted me around. I went to the Academy." He shrugged. "It seemed the thing to do. I learned to be a Demonslayer, but even under Master Seikhiel's direct tutelage, I was an outsider."

"You say that name like we should know it," Jynn said.

"He's one of the most famous Demonslayers. And I… I nearly killed him." Pushing back a little from Tempest, Akieryon wrapped his arms around himself. "We were sparring, I got spooked by—I don't even remember what. I lashed out instinctively. I didn't mean to use infernal magic. I didn't even know I *could.* I flayed him to the bone. He could barely walk, but he took me and he locked me away."

"In darkness," Tempest said, his voice heavy with anger. "For five hundred years."

"But what if they were right to be afraid of me?" Akieryon

braced himself. He mustered his courage, and he blurted, "I think I'm part demon."

"Y—okay," said Tempest.

Jynn was nodding. "Half-breeds club," he said, lifting one fist. When Akieryon just stared at him, he added, "You tap your fist against mine. Like this." Taking Akieryon by the wrist, he demonstrated.

"Jynn is half elf," Tempest clarified. "Only the other Shadowmarchers particularly notice."

"Oh, well, draconiform traits are strongly dominant."

"We're not dragons," Jynn said, because they did not know. Akieryon let the subject lie.

"Maybe the people who were afraid of me were right."

"They weren't," Tempest said, his voice unusually forceful.

"But"—Akieryon glared when Tempest started to disagree again—"if I can't learn to control the infernal magic, I really will be a danger to everyone around me."

"You've been learning," Tempest pointed out reasonably. "You'll have it figured out soon enough." Akieryon wanted to argue, but why? Just so he could be right? To justify the way the other angels had treated him? None of that made any sense, and so he kept his mouth shut. It was surprisingly difficult.

Jynn stayed with them perhaps another half an hour before he kissed them both goodnight—on the cheek this time—and took his leave. Was he always like that? Akieryon opened his mouth to ask, at the same time that Tempest said, "Are they really dragons?"

Akieryon gave him a sly smile. Curiosity, he'd found, was the best way to engage Tempest's interest, and he found the trait quite endearing. "Sort of. There are many peoples who are descended from dragons but look, well, kind of like Jynn. *People,* but pointy in all the right dragon places. If I'm remembering correctly, Jynn's people are the only ones in the Mortal Realm, but I'll be the first to admit that I mostly studied demons."

"What are they like?"

Akieryon shrugged. "The ones in the upper Spheres of Hell are a lot like Jynn. Less venomous, but most of them can fly. The draconiform races of the Second and the Fourth Spheres are the only ones who retained the fiery breath. Though they can't do it until they reach their second stage of adulthood," he added hastily. "About four hundred years old."

Tempest processed this information in silence for a while. Then he said, "Do the ones with fire still have venom?"

"Of course they do." Akieryon grinned at him. "It's how they ignite the fire."

"Oh, well, of course," Tempest said, as though he should have thought of that himself. Akieryon nudged him, and they laughed together. Akieryon adored laughing together with Tempest. Nothing had ever felt so right.

That night, Akieryon slept soundly, nestled closer than ever against Tempest. In the morning, Tempest was gone. Jynn, however, appeared in time to ransack the remains of Akieryon's breakfast.

"Less pomp about parliament today," he said around a mouthful of sweet bun. "Which is great, because some shit's going down. You and I can walk down early and get good seats."

Akieryon eyed him skeptically. "Can you really just go wherever you want?"

"Fool's privilege," Jynn replied smugly. "As the king's favorite entertainer, I am permanently welcome almost everywhere he goes." Catching the look on Akieryon's face, he laughed a bright laugh. "Yes, that's really what it's called."

"Humans are so weird," Akieryon muttered. Jynn's smile sharpened a little.

"They are, aren't they?"

Jynn chattered the entire way to the Parliament building, telling wild tales of someone called Tak-Shaetven vanquishing man and beast alike with ease. He was partway through a fifth story when the great doors came into sight. Falling into step beside them, Marek scoffed.

"Does Shay know you talk about him that way?"

"It is my duty to spread his legend throughout the world," Jynn replied loftily. Then he slanted a grin at Marek. "You're chipper this morning. Did Caspar—"

Marek's hand flew up to cover Jynn's mouth. "Not here," he said, glancing at the crowds that lined the street.

Firmly, Jynn pushed Marek's hand away. "Careful of the fangs, darling," he said. "You don't want to startle the venom out of me."

The guards at the door saluted as they passed. Before they parted ways, Marek gave them a conspiratorial wink.

"I have a good feeling about today."

"I didn't think he ever had a good feeling about anything," Akieryon muttered as they climbed the stairs to the balconies. Jynn's laugh echoed through the hall.

WAIT, WHAT?

This parliament session started the same as the one yesterday, with Caspar asking if anyone had any pressing business to address. Jynn sat beside Akieryon, pen at the ready, gazing into the hall below with a sort of taut anticipation usually seen in guard dogs and racehorses. Akieryon was trying to follow the direction of his stare when Sir Marek cleared his throat.

"Sire," he said, "if I may?"

"This ought to be good," someone grumbled, and their voice carried through the entire hall. Jynn started writing.

Marek called Sir Veirn to the parliament floor. Sir Veirn came with documents. He had witnesses. He had proof, he said, of the source of the recent threats to the king's safety. Might he present his findings?

Akieryon noticed that guards had moved to block the doors. That couldn't be a good sign.

A murmur passed through the parliament hall. People who spent time in the castle knew of the attacks. Everyone else largely did not. Over the next ten or fifteen minutes, Sir Veirn presented a series of witness statements, transaction records, and, to general uproar, two signed confessions. Everyone leaned forward, waiting for a name.

"My lords, honored representatives," Sir Veirn said, not one to waste a dramatic moment, "we have in our midst a conspiracy spearheaded by one of your own."

Sesoran? Akieryon thought, a little uncharitably.

Sir Veirn drew a deep breath. He looked at Caspar, and he seemed dragged down by an immense weight. No, he wasn't being dramatic. He was truly, deeply sorry to burden his king with the knowledge he brought. He could delay no further. "My lord king," he said quietly, though his voice carried throughout the hall, "I wish it were not so, but I must stand before you now and accuse of treason: Lord Toredi DiSevi."

Toredi DiSevi sprang up to deny the accusation, and half of parliament seemed to start shouting over each other all at once. Caspar slumped in his chair, his head in his hands. Jynn paused in his frantic scribbling to let out a heartfelt sigh.

"Tori, why?" he murmured, his words almost lost in the growing din. "Caspar won't forgive you a second time."

"A second time?"

Toredi was shouting in Caspar's direction. Jynn shook his

head. "He sided with Caspar's uncle, back in the day. Caspar forgave anyone under the age of twenty-five at the time, which Tempest thought was a bad idea."

"I'm sure Tempest wanted to cut them all into little pieces," Akieryon said, and Jynn slanted a thoughtful look at him.

"No illusions, then?"

"I hope not."

Tempest had come to stand beside Toredi. His expression looked neutral, but his eyes glittered cold and hard as emeralds. Toredi started to yell something else, and then he was just. Gone. The hubbub in the hall escalated for a moment before subsiding into uneasy chatter.

"Tempest." Caspar sounded exhausted and exasperated.

"He's right here." Tempest held up an ink pot.

"Right." Caspar lifted his head just enough to press his fingertips to his temples. "Go with Sir Veirn to see him *properly* confined and available for questioning."

"He's available—"

"*Tempest.*"

Stuffing the ink pot in his pocket, Tempest turned and sauntered to the door. The guards moved aside to let him pass.

Caspar remained slumped for a moment more before he drew visible breath and squared his shoulders. He lifted his head, and he called parliament back to order. For the remainder of the day, they elected a committee for conducting a formal inquest, and they debated protocols for a treason trial. Exciting stuff. Jynn doodled in his notes.

"What's that?"

Jynn frowned first at the pair of spirals drawn in the margin of his notes, then at Akieryon. "Have you never seen the mark on your neck?"

Akieryon leaned closer, peering at the drawing on the page. Two opposing spirals drawn from one continuous line, with a wavy line crossing them. It gave him a vague and formless sense of foreboding. He shook his head, but Jynn caught his hand in a reassuring grip.

"It's yours," he said, his voice soft but earnest. "And it is what you make of it."

Akieryon stared hard at the mark on the page. He tried to imagine it belonging to him.

He felt a nameless ache deep inside.

~⚜❖⚜~

Everything moved quickly except for parliament. After some deliberation, Lady Tonata presented documentation showing suspicious withdrawals from her household accounts. Toxelom was held on suspicion of collusion, and probably taxed to the limit of his mental faculties under questioning.

"A little convenient," Jynn said around a mouthful of eel pie. "Toko wouldn't be a part of this, except by pure ignorance. He's stupid, not malicious."

"He said racist shit about you," Akieryon said, and then wondered if the word didn't translate properly. Jynn gave him a puzzled stare.

"Everyone does," Jynn said eventually, and Tempest nudged him.

"Not everyone."

Jynn smiled. "No, not quite. Anyway," he continued. "Toni is sharp enough to leverage suspicion to secure the parliament seat for herself."

"She'll make better use of it than either of her brothers would," Tempest said.

"Beside the point," Jynn insisted. "She's cunning. I like that about her."

"It's a reasonable tactical move," Akieryon said, and they both looked at him a little strangely. His cheeks warmed. "I'd do it. I mean, I don't have any siblings, so I suppose it's irrelevant."

Jynn arched an eyebrow at Tempest, and Tempest gave a barely perceptible shake of his head.

"She'd never cross Caspar though," Jynn said, a little too

loudly.

"No," agreed Tempest. "She got all the brains in the family."

That night, Jynn fell asleep in Tempest's bed, which was fine. It was certainly big enough for all three of them. Akieryon curled against Tempest, as usual, and he was at peace. When in his life had he ever been able to say that?

Tempest stayed long enough to be certain that the assassination attempts had ceased. He had no intention of lingering through the trial. One morning, Akieryon found the more practical half of his wardrobe packed into an impossibly small bundle. He looked from it to Tempest, who was still getting dressed.

"We're coming back, right?" He hadn't meant to sound so plaintive. Tempest turned, his expression softening.

"What did you think ambassadors do?" Seeing a flicker of panic cross Akieryon's face, Tempest stepped closer and caught him by the hand. "Caspar expects regular, in-person reports. Of course we're coming back."

Relief buoyed Akieryon through the remainder of the morning. He wanted to make decent farewells to everyone, but he wasn't sure what to do, so mostly he just followed Tempest around. A little before noon, they were ready to leave. A small crowd had gathered in the entrance hall to see them off. Akieryon shrank behind Tempest. Having none of it, Jynn pulled him forward and hugged him tightly.

"Take care of each other." Successfully extracting a promise from Akieryon, he turned to Tempest. "I'll be a week or two behind you."

Tempest opened his arms for the bard's enthusiastic embrace. "The Lenyr will be glad to have you."

Jynn grinned. "As frequently as possible, I hope."

Dani gave Tempest and Akieryon both friendly punches to the arm and told them not to get killed. Marek clasped Akieryon's forearm and called him friend. Akieryon was fighting back tears by the time he stood before Caspar.

"You'll always have a place here."

Akieryon managed a watery smile. "Always is a long time."

"I'll put it in writing." And then Caspar hugged him. Right there in front of everyone. "And be sure I'll call on you if ever I have need."

"You'd better."

Caspar turned to Tempest. "Three months," he said sternly. Tempest laughed.

"Of course," he said, hugging Caspar. "You'll see us before the rains."

Us. Akieryon's heart warmed at the thought. He followed Tempest out into the daylight, where a saddled horse waited.

Tempest mounted, and Marek boosted Akieryon up behind him.

"No bombs," he said with a wink, and Akieryon could only nod his agreement. As they rode away, he pressed his face between Tempest's shoulders, and he wept silently.

~⚜◆⚜~

Akieryon tried to remember the riding lesson from his first day with Tempest. That afternoon was rather a blur, and soon Tempest was teaching him again. The sun warmed him, and so did Tempest's hands, patiently guiding him through the correct movements. Akieryon struggled to concentrate.

Beyond the city walls, the houses and shops of the foregate quickly gave way to fields and orchards, well tended and sprinkled here and there with villages and small towns. The road more or less followed the river upstream, and Akieryon lost count of how many mills they passed.

In the fifth or sixth town, a woman dropped her spinning and rushed out to yell, "You've got a lot of nerve showing your face around here!" Akieryon blinked at her in surprise, and Tempest held up a placating hand, but when she came closer, her demeanor softened, she apologized, and she bade them good journey. Before Akieryon could ask about it, a man driving a team of oxen with a wagonload of hay had hailed them to tease Tempest for riding pillion with another pretty young man.

"Another?" Akieryon repeated, but Tempest was laughing.

"Maybe I'm just weak for redheads," he said.

Akieryon couldn't imagine Tempest having any weakness at all. He started to say so, but the carter was already telling them, "Watch yourselves. There's cutters about."

Tempest went still and rigid. "Where?" His voice was flat and cold, a murder about to happen.

The man driving the oxen spat off the side of the road. "Dunno. Heard it from Cabat in Broad Bend."

When they had parted ways, Akieryon asked Tempest, "What are cutters?"

"They hunt Lenyr for profit," Tempest said grimly. "They tend to take a piece back with them as proof."

Akieryon hesitated. "The Lenyr are *people*," he said, unable to keep the horror from his voice.

"You'll find that the worst things humans do, they do to each other."

Akieryon let the *they* slide. He had more on his mind at the moment. "Why are the Lenyr hunted?"

"They're different, and that scares people," Tempest said. "And landlords hate that they don't pay rent."

"This is why Caspar made you the ambassador."

"Gods, you're quick," Tempest said in the same appreciative

tone people often use to call someone sexy. Akieryon blushed. He didn't think he was quick; he just thought he knew Caspar by now.

They rode on in silence for a while. Time felt odd, almost slippery, so it came as no surprise when they soon arrived at the town of Broad Bend, which sat surrounded on three sides by a wide curve of the river. Tempest left Akieryon on a bench in the sunny front yard of the local inn and went to ask around about the cutters. The proprietor brought him a bowl of apple cheese soup and a heel of bread that tasted faintly like beer. It tasted amazing. Smiling, the innkeeper sat down opposite him.

"I know Tempest feeds you," she said, which seemed to be everyone's response upon watching Akieryon eat. Giving her a sheepish smile, he straightened his posture and forced himself to slow down.

"This is definitely the best thing I've eaten all week."

"And you dressed like that," the innkeeper teased. "Come on. What're you doing, following Tempest all the way out here?"

Akieryon almost said he had nowhere else to go, but he realized that that wasn't true any more. How strange. Blinking in surprise at himself, he told the truth. "I think I'm in love with him."

"Aye, well, y'could do worse." She was smiling though, so Akieryon assumed this was more friendly banter. "Y'wouldn't be the first to fall for a mysterious stabby man in black."

"Tempest isn't mysterious," Akieryon objected. "He's like a cat. He doesn't bother with things that don't interest him, and things that bother him tend to bleed."

The innkeeper laughed heartily. "Oh, I like you! Another soup?"

Akieryon looked down at his nearly empty bowl. "Yes, please!"

Tempest found them laughing over his third bowl of soup. "Hey, Mol." He gave Akieryon's shoulder a reassuring squeeze. "Any left for me?"

Tempest ate with enthusiasm that rivaled Akieryon's own, and the innkeeper Mol teased him about it too. Not for the first time, Akieryon wondered that the nobility of Davenz hated him, while everyone else seemed genuinely pleased to see him.

"How's the roof?" Tempest asked as they stood up.

"Perfect. As well you know." Mol gave him a one-armed hug, but also accepted generous payment for the meals. "Bring that cutie back around sometime!" she called after them, by way of farewell.

They headed north after Broad Bend. The land grew wilder, eventually giving way to forest on the left side of the road. Abruptly, they turned onto a narrow track that led deep into the trees. Birds chattered in the canopy, concerned more about their own business. Something moved in the underbrush. Everything smelled richly of encroaching autumn.

Perhaps half an hour passed before Akieryon could hear voices carried on the late afternoon air. The trackway opened into a small clearing. Three colorful wagons and five patchwork tents bordered the space, and people gathered around the cookfire, turning a wary eye toward the road. They tensed, until they saw who approached.

"Tempest!"

Half the group ran to them before they had even dismounted. Tempest was at once the undisputed center of attention, with everyone hugging him and kissing him and shouting over one another to tell him news. Akieryon stood a little back from the chaos, holding the horse's reins and trying to make sense of the cacophony.

"Where's Riol?" Tempest shouted, and everyone tried to answer him at once.

"A day farther on!"

"Captain's group went on ahead!"

"Running from you!"

"Wait, wait." Tempest held up both hands, and some of the chatter died down. "Your king left *you* in charge?" This last he directed at a young man who wore a beaded scarf to hold his dark hair back from his face. Everyone laughed. The young man in question seized Tempest by the ears and kissed him all over his face.

"You got a problem with that? Ambassador?"

Someone coming out of the forest brushed past Akieryon, heading for the hubbub. He moved like a predator, with single minded purpose and liquid grace. Akieryon tensed, despite ample evidence that Tempest was more than capable of defending himself. The stranger pushed through the crowd, which was slow to close behind him. Acting on pure—albeit keenly honed—instinct, Akieryon started forward, following the bobbing of the man's shaggy tail of auburn hair. Something was off about him. Untrustworthy.

He pushed the young man in the beaded scarf aside, and he planted himself directly in front of Tempest.

"You're back."

Tempest smiled. "I am. In fact—"

The auburn-haired man buried both hands in Tempest's hair, and he kissed him. Hard. Akieryon stumbled to a stop, feeling like he'd just been punched in the chest. This was nothing like Tempest's reunion with Jynn. No lemon-bright joy fizzed in the air. In fact, Akieryon could feel no emotions from them at all. Tentatively he reached out, pushing his mind toward the two of them, but still he felt nothing. As though the stranger was absorbing all of Tempest's emotions for himself.

But…

Only a demon could do that.

"Tempest!" Akieryon called out. People had noticed him now, and the colorful crowd was drawing back into an audience around the three of them. "Tempest, that's—"

The stranger had stepped back. He turned around, and he regarded Akieryon with a half-smirk that faded almost instantly to a look of astonishment. He stared, and so did Akieryon. The world stood still. The spaces between heartbeats echoed, ripples in the fabric of the cosmos.

The stranger's face might have been a mirror, so alike was it to Akieryon's own face.

ON THE MOVE

Akieryon's heart raced, and his palms had gone damp. The longer he stared, the more differences he could see, starting with the vivid black Mortal-Born Mark that swirled up his neck and over his jawline. He was leaner and sharper than Akieryon, and yet this man—this demon—was undeniably kin to him. Close kin. Almost a copy.

The demon's throat worked in several attempts before he managed a strangled whisper: "Kie-nin?"

"Akieryon," he said automatically. The demon wore a sleeveless shirt, and on one shoulder Akieryon could just see the sweeping edges of a double spiral Lineage Mark. That… made no sense. His gaze flicked to Tempest, a question he could not quite articulate.

Tempest shrugged. "I thought if the two of you met, it would save a great deal of explaining."

The demon clutched at his head with both hands. He looked pale and possibly near to hyperventilating. Tempest lightly touched his arm. "This can't be real," the demon gasped.

"Szearbhyn—"

"*Szearbhyn?*" Akieryon repeated, spitting the name that smacked him like a shovel to the face. "Szearbhyn *Soul-Stealer?* The notorious criminal, that Szearbhyn?" He stomped forward, and the demon Szearbhyn shrank a little, but met his glare with a stubborn kind of defiance.

"There is no other."

"I'm supposed to *kill you,*" Akieryon said. Confusion reeled in concert with anger. He looked away, looked at Tempest. "Master Niseriel specifically… he trained me to do it… he…" A horrible, vicious thought occurred to him. Taking Szearbhyn by the shoulders, Akieryon turned him to reveal the Lineage Mark in its entirety. It was exactly as Jynn had drawn in his notes. Akieryon stumbled back a step. "He wanted me to Fall," he gasped.

"Explain," Tempest said, sounding murderous.

Akieryon glanced between the two of them. He tried to swallow his growing anxiety, but it only seemed to get stuck in his throat. "An angel becomes Fallen only by killing another angel, or someone near enough to it. I've heard of angels Falling for having killed half-Nephilim, who are descended of angels and humans. And you're my… my…" Why couldn't he say it?

"Brother," Szearbhyn said with conviction. Akieryon hesitated, then nodded.

"You must be half angel," Akieryon reasoned. "So if I had completed my mission…" He cleared his throat, and he forced the truth out into the open, hating the bitter taste of every word of it. "Master Niseriel would have been rid of us both."

"Where is he?" Tempest demanded. Akieryon looked at him, startled out of his horror.

"You can't just storm Heaven and kill the commander of an entire regiment of Demonslayers."

"I won't know if I can't until I've tried it," Tempest replied sensibly.

"I mean don't," said Akieryon, his voice stern. He felt himself tipping past the point of rationality. He wasn't sure he cared.

"You're an angel," Szearbhyn said, his voice quiet, almost hurt. "Of course you're an angel. That's why they took you."

"I was *taken?*" Akieryon said, horror strangling his words. "I thought I was an orphan?" He glanced at Tempest, as though Tempest could help him at all.

"We were little," Szearbhyn said, "but I remember. I tore apart entire worlds searching for you."

"No." Akieryon was shaking now. "No, no, *no.* You became a criminal *because of me?!*" It was impossible. Everything was impossible. Maybe he was still in his tiny, dark cell, suffering the worst fever. Maybe…

"At first," Szearbhyn said with a careless shrug. "But I was good at it, and I like being a bastard."

"It caught up with you," Tempest pointed out.

This was too much. Akieryon braced his feet as though for a defensive stance. Szearbhyn would not attack him, probably, but the response had been trained into him over two centuries of careful tutelage. He struggled to breathe past an inexplicable weight in his chest. "You… Why do you have that?" He pointed at the Mortal-Born Mark on Szearbhyn's neck. It was impossible. Even if they were part human, he would have had to die to be Mortal-Born.

Szearbhyn touched the dark swirls, and a softness touched his features. "I was cursed into the body of a human child," he said. "A couple of decades ago. I grew up here." He spread his arms wide, indicating their rapt audience. "I remembered nothing of who I was. Nineteen years I was an ordinary Lenyr, and then the cutters came." His hand moved to his stomach, just under his ribs. "They killed me. Stabbed me. They released me." He grinned the same sharp way Tempest sometimes did. "I ate them, of course."

"Of course," Akieryon murmured, fascinated by the implications of the story. Szearbhyn must not have been simply confined within a human shell. He had to have been fully integrated into the mortal life force. The level of magical power such a curse would take—

"Come on." Szearbhyn held out a hand to him. "Let's sit by the fire, and you can tell me all about yourself."

Akieryon looked at the proffered hand. "There's really not much to tell." But he reached out. He took his brother's hand.

Akieryon explained again how he had spent his childhood unwanted in foster homes that never kept him for long. He told how he had become a Demonslayer. Then came Master Niseriel's cold, calculated cruelty. Then the accident, when he had used the infernal magic to flay Master Seikhiel to the bone.

"He's fine," Szearbhyn told him. "The so-called Sword of Heaven is back to business as usual, taking down all the high-profile demons."

"Except you," Akieryon said.

"Well I'm untouchable, right?" Szearbhyn thumped his chest and added smugly, "Half angel. Too great a risk."

His good humor faltered when he heard how Akieryon had spent five hundred years locked in darkness. "Then Zeph came and got me and pushed me through into the Mortal Realm. I crashed down in front of Tempest, and here I am now."

Tempest nudged him. "You left out the part where you charmed Caspar and Dani and even Marek."

Akieryon shrugged. "They'll forget about me soon enough." He hoped not, but all this attention had him feeling weirdly defensive.

Tempest bumped him with his shoulder. "They won't and you know it." Ducking his head, Akieryon smiled. "We're going back in three months."

A man sitting at Szearbhyn's other side leaned forward and quirked a hint of a smile at Tempest. "Is he going to make you be punctual this time?"

Akieryon was startled to see that this Lenyr man wore almost as much black as Tempest did. Following the direction of his gaze, Szearbhyn introduced him. "This is Xan," he said. "My betrothed."

Akieryon glanced between the two of them, then looked to Tempest, who nodded. He pointed at Tempest, and he pointed at Szearbhyn. "What."

"Lenyr aren't too bothered about monogamy," Xan said. "It's a personal choice here. I don't want anyone but Szearbhyn. Szearbhyn wants me and sometimes Tempest. We're all fine with that."

"And Tempest doesn't want anything to do with sweet, tender love," Szearbhyn said with a teasing grin in Tempest's direction. Maintaining eye contact, he lifted Xan's hand to his lips and began kissing knuckles, one after another.

"Do what you want," Tempest said. "You'll never be as gross as Varz and his husband."

As one, the three of them looked across the fire to where the young man in the beaded scarf was doting upon a heavily pregnant elf. Tempest shuddered theatrically.

Dinner consisted of a game meat stew and oaty flatbread. While everyone ate, a few people began producing assorted musical instruments from the wagons. Tempest noticed, and he shook his head.

"No party," he said sternly. "At least four people in Broad Bend saw cutters the day before yesterday." He looked to Varz. "We should rejoin your brother as soon as we can."

Varz pouted. "Just a little party? To welcome Szearbhyn's brother?"

"I can wait," Akieryon said. Safety first. Anyway, no one had ever wanted to throw a party just for him before, and he needed time to adjust to this new reality.

They compromised, which meant only two people played music while everyone relaxed and talked into the evening. The mood had become subdued at the mention of cutters, and no one seemed too keen to stay up late. Once everyone started retiring to the tents and wagons, Tempest took Akieryon by the hand. They walked together to a tent that had not been there earlier. Akieryon slanted a small smile at Tempest.

"This one's yours?"

"Ours," Tempest said softly. He held the flap aside, and Akieryon was almost certain that the interior of the tent was too large for the exterior. Small globes of light hovered near the canvas, and somehow didn't show through the outside. A heap of cushions and blankets occupied most of the space. Akieryon stepped inside and began shucking his travel stained clothing. As he set his coat aside, he realized that Tempest still stood beside the tent flap, just watching him.

"Are you going to stand there all night?" His smile died when he saw the look on Tempest's face.

"I'm going to keep watch."

"I can help." Akieryon reached for his coat again, but Tempest's hand on his wrist stopped him. Akieryon looked up into the fierce green of his eyes.

"You rest," Tempest said, his voice low and earnest. "You have a lot to process." His fingertips slid up Akieryon's arm, then down his spine in a way that drew him close and made his knees feel suddenly jellied. "I'll call for you if there is need," Tempest said directly into his ear. "I promise."

When Tempest had vanished into the night, Akieryon wasn't entirely certain how he had gotten tucked into bed. Tempest's pile of cushions was deliciously comfortable, though, and despite his racing thoughts, sleep soon overtook him.

~·❦·~

Dreams came confused and urgent. Tempest needed him. Szearbhyn called his name. Master Seikhiel told him to have patience. Caspar told him to stay safe. He took Tempest by the hips and he kissed him. It felt like Jynn's kiss. He tasted salt on his lips.

"Akieryon."

He startled awake to Tempest brushing tears from his cheeks. "Uhmmorning?" he managed, and Tempest gently tugged him into a seated position.

"You okay?"

I think I was lonely. Akieryon nodded. He wanted to cling to Tempest, but he managed to maintain his composure.

"Here." Tempest handed him a biscuit made from some kind of nut flour. "It's time to move."

Outside, the Lenyr were striking their camp with startling efficiency. Someone had hitched mule teams to the wagons. Several pack ponies stood loaded and ready. A chain of four people were passing wicker cages of poultry up into one of the wagons. Akieryon rubbed at his eyes and shrugged into his coat.

"Up you go." Tempest boosted Akieryon up onto his horse, then took the reins and walked up to the lead wagon. Varz stood there consulting an intricate piece of embroidery that, on closer inspection, turned out to be a map. "You do know which way they went, right?"

Varz gave him a sour look. "I'm not sure which crossing will get us there faster." His fingertip traced the blue line of the river.

"Take the nearer one," Tempest said. "I'll take care of the rest."

Soon they were under way. Tempest walked, leading his horse alongside the wagon. Sometimes he talked to Varz, who drove, but mostly he kept alert, watching the trees and the underbrush for signs of trouble. Szearbhyn rode on the highest point of the tallest wagon, working at a bit of rope with something that looked a lot like a marlin spike. He looked so ordinary. How could someone so notorious in so many worlds look just like any other Lenyr man?

They came to the river around midday. It ran broad and shallow, and they crossed it without getting water higher than anyone's knees. They kept going. After a brief meal stop, Szearbhyn abandoned his post on the wagon and swung up into the saddle behind Akieryon. His arm around Akieryon's waist set a strange electric sort of tingling spreading beneath Akieryon's skin. Szearbhyn shifted his grip when Akieryon squirmed.

"What do you want?"

Szearbhyn scoffed softly. "Not interested in spending time with your twin?"

Akieryon's breath caught a little. "Are we twins?"

"You really can't tell?" Szearbhyn gave him a brief squeeze.

Akieryon hesitated. "I don't trust you," he said, and Szearbhyn laughed.

"I don't trust me, either! We're going to get along just fine."

"Was that in doubt?" Was he worried about it? When had anyone ever worried about getting along with Akieryon?

"Well." Szearbhyn chuckled softly. "You *are* a Demonslayer."

"That was a lifetime ago," Akieryon murmured.

They rode in silence for a little while, and then Szearbhyn started talking again. Their mother had lived almost a century after Akieryon was taken, and she never gave up hope of his eventual return. Their kin were, as Akieryon had surmised, one of the many clans of demons who lived in the Ninth Sphere of Hell and fed on human emotion. Szearbhyn could not remember when he had first touched a soul.

Eventually, Akieryon began to relax. He talked in depth about his foster homes, and all the ways he had been unwanted. Szearbhyn hugged him tightly.

"You'll never be unwanted again," he promised.

"Never," Tempest agreed.

When the shadows began to lengthen into the afternoon, Varz

called for their little caravan to halt. The Lenyr made camp with the same ruthless efficiency that they had struck camp that morning. Tempest paced, gnawing at his thumbnail as he went.

"I was hoping we would catch up with Riol today," he said when Akieryon walked stiffly to his side. Two days in the saddle had made him ache in ways he had never anticipated.

"Tomorrow?"

"Probably." Tempest switched thumbnails and continued chewing.

"Want me to…" Akieryon gestured upward. "Do some scouting?"

Tempest looked to Szearbhyn. "Why do you never offer to do that?"

Szearbhyn reached out and caught Xan by the hand, pulling him close. "I'm more useful here," he said. "Protecting everyone."

Akieryon took a slow breath, then pushed his wings from energy to matter. "I'll do a quick spiral," he said. "I'll be back in less than an hour."

As Akieryon stretched his wings and sprang into the air, he heard Tempest continuing to tease Szearbhyn.

Sweet and keen, the freedom of flight coursed through him. It had been so long. So very long. Akieryon would have laughed for pure joy, if his mission had not been so grave. Twisting his wings against the air currents, he banked into a tight turn. Below, the Lenyr were looking upward, watching him.

Akieryon broadened his turn, sweeping over the edges of the camp, and then beyond. The treetops barely showed the first gold of autumn. As he soared outward and upward, he could see the fine ribbon of the river glittering in the distance. If he flew high enough, he would see the town of Broad Bend. He struggled to keep his eyes on the landscape below. His training kept him on task, and he steadily expanded his search.

There! At a point where woodland abutted an orchard, another, larger encampment stood. Smoke from three cookfires curled upward, and Akieryon counted five wagons. Immediately he turned back, winging directly for Tempest and the smaller camp.

"They're that way," he said before his feet touched the ground. "Not much farther on. Beside an orchard."

Varz brought out his map, and Akieryon found the place for him. "That's at the edge of Sinen land," Tempest said with a faint grimace, and Varz nodded. "We'll catch them before noon tomorrow."

That night, Akieryon went to bed alone again. He decided he didn't like it. How could he grow so soft so quickly? How could he depend on another person for his comfort?

How long could Tempest continue to go without sleep?

Akieryon lay awake worrying for longer than he should have.

216

PATH-MATE

The cutters came at dawn. Shouts dragged Akieryon out of yet more troubled dreams, and he had stumbled to his feet before he could shake the sleep out of his head. Barefoot and unarmed, he stumbled out into the misty morning. People screamed and ran for cover. Akieryon stood still and assessed the situation.

There was Tempest, already bloody to the elbows, a dagger in each hand. His full attention was focused on a man in light armor who stood holding an axe and hesitating. The man was definitely about to die.

"Come on!" Xan caught Akieryon by the hand and tried to pull him toward one of the wagons. "They'll hurt you!"

"They really won't," Akieryon said softly. As he watched, the man with the axe froze, his eyes going wide, and then crumbled to dust. For half a heartbeat, Akieryon thought this was some new magic of Tempest's. Then, through the settling dust, he saw his brother.

No longer wearing his human form, Szearbhyn had thick,

curling horns like a ram and a pair of small tusks springing from his jaw. His hair, unbound and untidier than ever, had doubled in length. Wings of black smoke shifted with his every movement. In one outstretched hand he held a pinpoint of misty light. A soul? Szearbhyn stuffed the light into his mouth and looked around for another victim.

He looked much more like what Akieryon would have expected of the notorious criminal Szearbhyn Soul-Stealer.

"I should… stop him?" Training warred with his inherent sense of justice.

"Why?" Xan demanded, and he made an excellent point. Akieryon grimaced.

"Because it's part of my job to stop demons from killing humans." Even if the humans were in the wrong? If they had initiated the killing?

Xan's startling cornflower eyes narrowed, almost in accusation. "Your job? You mean the assholes who wanted you to kill your own brother? Who wanted to get rid of you? That job? Sounds like they don't deserve you sparing them a single thought." He drew a sharp breath. "Plus, Szearbhyn's just protecting his family."

That much was irrefutable. Anyway, the moment had passed. Two mutilated corpses lay in the grass near Tempest's feet, and

Szearbhyn had eaten the souls of at least three more men. But the attack was over, and Lenyr were emerging from hiding.

Tempest went to wash up while the Lenyr struck camp. The pregnant elf, whose name was Lienne, moved among them, deftly tending to a handful of superficial injuries. Akieryon stood still, watching everything in a numb kind of a daze. This was… normal? He remembered how everyone had reacted to the assassin in the audience chamber. This was worse, and yet the Lenyr picked themselves up and carried on as though nothing out of the ordinary had happened.

"Hey."

Akieryon blinked and stared at Szearbhyn's demonic face. The Mortal-Born Mark was gone.

"You okay?"

Was he? Slowly, Akieryon nodded.

"You don't look okay."

"I let you kill humans," Akieryon said, and Szearbhyn scoffed.

"You didn't let me do anything. And you couldn't have stopped me," he added pointedly. Conflicted, Akieryon shook his head.

"If he hadn't done it," Xan pointed out, "Tempest would have."

"But Tempest is human," Akieryon objected. Szearbhyn and Xan exchanged a dubious glance.

"Ish," said Szearbhyn.

Varz gave the signal to move out, and Akieryon glanced around. "Where's Tempest?"

"He'll be along." Szearbhyn handed Tempest's horse's reins to Akieryon. "Mount up, Demonslayer."

"If it's all the same to you," Akieryon said, "I think I'd rather walk for a bit."

They had been underway for about ten minutes when Tempest caught up to them. He gave Akieryon's arm a brief squeeze, then trotted a few steps and hoisted himself up onto the wagon, settling beside Varz. They talked together in low tones for a while. Akieryon was starting to lean closer, instinctively trying to eavesdrop, when Szearbhyn sprang up into the saddle of the moving horse.

"What are you doing?" Akieryon struggled to soothe the startled animal. It jerked its head and danced a sidestep that nearly bowled him over.

"Taking it easy." Grinning, Szearbhyn tossed a round object up to Tempest, who caught it and took a bite. "Rest and digest."

"Yeah," Tempest said around a mouthful of whatever he was eating. "You won't be hungry until tomorrow at least."

Akieryon spent a while lost in his own head, considering the implications of what he had witnessed. Everyone knew that

Szearbhyn took souls. No one ever said what he did with them. If he reported this information to Lord Sidriel, would it be news? Or would he be revealing his location for no reason at all?

They came upon the other encampment a little before noon. It still sat in its place along the edge of the orchard, bustling with midday activity. Akieryon counted maybe twenty adults, and several small children ran underfoot with startling agility, never once causing a collision. Varz whistled. Everything came to a stop.

"They're back!"

The camp erupted into pure joy, so fervent and so abundant it nearly knocked Akieryon off his feet. In moments, everyone was hugging and kissing and jumping and shouting. Akieryon lost track of both Tempest and Szearbhyn in the chaos, but he saw Varz squeezed enthusiastically by a man who wore a red velvet ribbon around his full head of chestnut hair. The king, or captain, depending on who you asked.

Then, suddenly, he found himself drawn into the jubilation. Complete strangers were excited to meet him. People hugged him. People kissed him. People spun him around and danced for sheer delight. There was so much touching.

Eventually, Akieryon registered that people were calling him Szearbhyn's brother and Tempest's... Tempest's what? The word didn't quite translate. Life-companion-thing? UnSpouse? Akieryon grasped for it, but the meaning slipped away like a receding tide. A small child collided with his leg and wrapped both arms around his knee, overturning his concentration.

"Hello," he said, eliciting a giggle from the child. Immediately, Tempest appeared at Akieryon's side. He plucked the toddler up by the scruff.

"Mine," Tempest growled before passing the squirming child off to a barrel-set woman with impressively thick curls.

"You didn't react that way to anyone else," Akieryon pointed out. Tempest merely shrugged, so he added, "What is unspouse?"

"Unsp—?" Realization dawned, and Tempest laughed. "Is that how your magic translates it?"

"Yes. Sort of. It's a little… unclear."

"The Lenyr word for spouse literally means path-mate," Tempest explained. "Someone you choose to share your journey with. The addition of a negative indicates that a relationship is not exactly a marriage, but comparable in some regard."

"You sound more academic when you explain things," Akieryon informed him, and Tempest grinned.

"I read too much."

"No such thing." Akieryon hesitated, but he had to ask. "Am I your unspouse?"

Tempest's gaze wavered for the faintest flicker of an instant.

"If you like."

By supreme force of will, Akieryon managed not to throw himself into Tempest's arms. "Path-mate sounds perfect."

~⁙℀✦℆⁙~

The Lenyr decided to have a party that night. According to Tempest, the Lenyr never missed an opportunity to celebrate, so the two groups reuniting would have been reason enough. Akieryon joining them merely gave them greater cause. Someone started a haunch of venison roasting. Someone else supervised baking breadstuffs and making sweets. Varz rolled out a barrel that probably contained booze of some sort. People tuned various instruments, to the general delight of children and adults alike.

"Hey."

Akieryon frowned when he saw the serious expression on Szearbhyn's face. "What?"

"We need to talk. About Tempest."

"Oh, no," Akieryon groaned. "You're not warning me off of him too!"

"What?" Szearbhyn's face crinkled and puckered in offended confusion. "No! It's just, he bites."

Was that all? "Obviously," Akieryon said.

"Not cute little bites," Szearbhyn clarified.

"Do you think I'm delicate or something?"

Szearbhyn shifted uneasily. "Not, y'know, in a fight or whatever. But Tempest isn't *normal*. You have to be prepared for that."

"Nobody's normal," Akieryon pointed out.

"Right, but he's less normal than most."

Akieryon sighed. "Look," he said, "it's fine that he likes the rough stuff. I don't mind. I promise."

Again, Szearbhyn scrunched his face. "You said nobody wanted you around before, and now you sound like you know what you're talking about."

"Is that the problem?" Akieryon pulled his brother into a tight hug. "Thank you for looking out for me. I'll be fine. Really."

Apparently skeptical, Szearbhyn stuck close by Akieryon's side as the afternoon stretched toward sundown. Delicious smells filled the encampment and drifted into the trees beyond. The barrel-set woman, whose name was either Nac or Lilli, guarded the venison roast with a jealous wrath. People started dancing almost before the music had begun in earnest.

"They're very joyful people," Akieryon ventured, with a cautious glance at his brother.

"We live life to the fullest," Szearbhyn said with mingled sorrow and pride, "because a Lenyr life may end at any moment."

"Humans are so brief," Akieryon murmured.

"Lenyr tend to be briefer than most."

Akieryon followed Szearbhyn's gaze across the encampment to where Xan was dancing in a circle with three children who stood no taller than his waist. "Are you going to Make him?" he asked softly.

Szearbhyn Soul-Stealer, wanted criminal with a bounty offered for him in eight Spheres, gave his brother a scandalized look. "You do know how a Mortal-Born is Made?"

Akieryon nodded. "A Mortal who has absorbed sufficient demonic energy must die painfully."

"At the hand of his Maker," Szearbhyn said. "A demon. I would have to torture him. I would have to watch him screaming and crying and begging me to just let him go, until he had no more breath to beg." Soul-Stealer, demon who had toppled kingdoms, looked like he might vomit. "I can't do that to him."

Akieryon watched Xan in silence. How much demonic energy was enough? How much pain? Szearbhyn seemed pretty well informed on the details Akieryon's education had glossed over.

"I could do Tempest," Szearbhyn added in a philosophical tone. "It wouldn't even be that hard. He's been marinating in demonic energy for basically his entire life, and he would hardly even gasp before he was halfway dead."

Something desperate and feral clawed at the inside of

Akieryon's chest. "Don't. Just… don't."

Szearbhyn watched him, eyebrows arched in smug triumph. "See?"

"You're an asshole."

"So, I suspect, are you."

Akieryon let the comment lie. Slowly, he paced around the perimeter of the encampment, and his brother matched him stride for stride. "What's it like," he asked at length, "being human?"

"Everything feels more urgent," Szearbhyn said. "Time feels like it moves faster and slower all at once. Every little thing seems more important somehow." He grimaced. "It's frustrating. I don't know how they live like that."

"They don't know any other way." Akieryon reached for his brother's hand. Szearbhyn caught his fingers and gave them a squeeze. Again, that electric tingling rushed beneath his skin, the push and pull of magic trying to tell him something. What? What could the two of them accomplish together? What could they become?

Suddenly there was an arm around each of their shoulders, and only a familiar voice in Akieryon's ear stopped his elbow from meeting an unfortunate solar plexus. "Which of you adorable youngsters is going to dance with me?" Varz crowed, oblivious to the danger he had put himself in. Akieryon let out a slow breath and forced his muscles to relax.

"Varz," said Szearbhyn, "you're twenty-two."

"And you're twenty."

"I'm really not," Szearbhyn said. "I'm seven hundred and eighty-eight."

"Well now I know exactly how long I was imprisoned," Akieryon said. Immediately Varz spun him about, seized him by both hands, and dragged him toward the fires.

"You need to have fun," he announced, and Szearbhyn laughed at them.

Until supper time, Varz taught Akieryon dance after dance. He learned so many steps, he knew he would never remember them all in any sort of cohesive sense. It didn't matter. Varz twirled him madly between other dancers until, breathless and laughing, he finally collapsed into a seat near the fire. Nac-or-Lilli immediately pressed a wooden bowl into his hands.

Akieryon ate cautiously at first, to avoid burning himself, but soon forgot himself. Everything was hearty and perfect: venison and crusty bread and scalding root vegetables and little bits of buttery dough wrapped around tart berry filling. It tasted like warmth, like hearth and home. Deep inside, Akieryon ached for just one more night at Enoch's, belly full and ears ringing with the laughter of his comrades.

Lienne sank slowly onto the little canvas stool beside Akieryon. "You're settling in well."

Akieryon smiled at him, and then at Varz. "It's easy enough, with such a welcome."

Varz barked a short laugh. "You should have seen Tempest at first! He distrusted everything!"

"Yeah, he gets tetchy whenever anyone new is too near to Caspar," said a new voice. Another elf leaned over to plant a kiss on the top of Lienne's head. "He settled down pretty quickly though."

"My sibling Kirienne," Lienne said proudly. "*Yon*"—Akieryon's translation spell struggled and failed to hear the unfamiliar pronoun as *they*—"is responsible for the delicious roast venison tonight."

"Not just me!" Kirienne objected quickly, but Akieryon's academic interest had been engaged.

"Yon?" he repeated. "I thought elves had five genders?"

"It's seven now," Lienne informed him cheerfully. "Has been for a little over a century."

"Good to know."

"Kiri is the best hunter," Varz said proudly, "and Sis does magical things with fire and smoke and those arcane powders she's always mixing up."

Nac-or-Lilli must be the king/captain's wife, then. The family structure was beginning to make sense. A little bit. The sun dipped low into the evening, and people drew nearer to the fires. Not Szearbhyn, though. He danced with Xan near the edge of the encampment. Akieryon found himself smiling at them. Did he fit in here? Did he belong? He ached for it, but uncertainty remained.

"I hope you saved some of that energy," said a voice above his head. Dropping his empty bowl, Akieryon bolted to his feet and whirled to face Tempest.

Tempest had changed his clothes. He still wore his usual shades of black, but this time some midnight blue piping ran along some of the seams, and matching blue embroidery curled feather-like along the cuffs and collar. Akieryon blinked. He had never seen Tempest wear anything other than all black. He managed a vague gesture and a flippant remark. "Is this where you've been?"

"Perimeter check first," Tempest said benignly. "Party clothes second. Dance with me." It wasn't a question, or a request, or a command. Somehow, Tempest made the words into a simple statement. A fact. Akieryon felt heat flood his face.

"I'm not very good."

Tempest grinned. "Neither am I."

Akieryon couldn't imagine Tempest being truly terrible at anything. He caught him by the hands and pulled him away from the fire. "We'll be awful together, then."

Tempest watched him with the silent intensity of a cat studying someone new. His eyes glittered a particularly sharp green, and the voidspace smell hung close about him. Akieryon gave him a knowing smile.

"You warded the camp?"

"Just some basic alarms." He let Akieryon's arms settle around him, but made no move to dance. "I like to know when someone's approaching."

"I know." Akieryon swayed a little with the music, but it sounded oddly distant. "You also seem to like redheads," he teased, unthinking. Tempest frowned and silently repeated the word, so Akieryon clarified: "Szearbhyn. Jynn. Me?"

"Oh." Tempest blinked, then bluntly said, "No, I like wings."

Akieryon's breath caught. Heedless of anyone watching them, he tipped the balance of his wings, energy to matter. In the gathering twilight, they emitted a soft white glow. A low growl rose in Tempest's throat. He lunged forward and his teeth snapped down on Akieryon's shoulder, just below the slope of his neck. Akieryon gasped as a jolt of electric pleasure shot through his body.

"Mine," Tempest rumbled around a mouthful of Akieryon. Akieryon wobbled, and his knees stubbornly refused to be knees, so he held on tight and leaned his weight against Tempest. Tempest's arms tightened around his waist—tightened?—and lifted him up onto the balls of his feet. Every instinct in Akieryon's body screamed at him to kick his feet up, wrap his legs around Tempest, and hold on with all his strength. Instead, he folded his wings close against his shoulders, causing soft feathers to brush against Tempest's cheek. A raw, animal groan ripped from Tempest's throat. Akieryon gasped, half of his body freezing in unexpected fear, half of it coming alive in ways he had never known.

He was terrified. He was *exhilarated.* He wanted… No, that was all. He wanted. For perhaps the first time in almost eight hundred years, he wanted something he was allowed to have.

Later, Akieryon would have no clear memory of crossing the short distance to Tempest's tent. His back pushed the flap open, and it snapped closed again behind Tempest. He was much more aware of Tempest's mouth, moving with deliberation from his shoulder up his neck. Teeth closed on his earlobe. Gasping a curse, Akieryon fisted both hands in Tempest's hair, keeping him close, pulling him closer.

"No more… no more waiting?" he managed as buttons, clasps, and toggles parted at the lightest touch of Tempest's fingers. Tempest rumbled a low chuckle.

"No more waiting. You fit."

Akieryon would examine that remark later. For the moment, Tempest's teeth nipping at the corner of his jaw made thought a struggle. Everything was a struggle, everything except the need burning through his body and thundering in his ears. He turned his head a little. Enough. Tempest's lips grazed the corner of his mouth, and Akieryon reacted on pure instinct.

It was a big risk, possibly the greatest he had ever taken. At this crucial moment, with everything he wanted right in front of him, Akieryon kissed Tempest.

Instead of rejecting him, instead of retreating in revulsion, Tempest kissed him back. Tempest kissed him hard, tasting of raw desire. Akieryon dug deeper, reaching out to touch the need that Tempest felt. Lust was there, primal and dizzying, but underneath lay a solid, steadying warmth. Akieryon tried to examine the warmth from other angles, but it was all the same: honey-gold and smooth as a river pebble. It tasted like nothing Akieryon had ever experienced or imagined.

When Tempest finally broke away from the kiss, Akieryon wobbled and clung to him. It was too sudden. The light was too bright and the air on his skin chilled him through to the bone. Tempest's hands supported him, keeping him upright. Were they kneeling amid the heap of cushions? When had that happened?

"Slower?" Tempest asked, his voice somehow gentle despite the ragged edge of desire that rasped in Akieryon's ears and raised heat across his skin. Every nerve in his body was awake and humming with urgency.

"No. But..." Akieryon wanted to glance away. Instead, he tipped his forehead against Tempest's and looked directly into those magic-bright green eyes. "What if I—I might say something you don't want to hear." *I might say I love you.*

Tempest's fingers spread out over Akieryon's stomach and slid toward his hip. "I won't mind."

"Even if it's gross?"

A faint smile tugged at Tempest's lips. "I promise." He pushed Akieryon down amid the cushions and knelt over him. "Now," he said, "tell me what you want."

"Everything," Akieryon replied without hesitation. He reached both hands toward Tempest. "Show me everything."

THEY

In the small hours of the morning, the Lenyr camp had finally quieted. The stars wheeled overhead in their eternal, silent dance. Akieryon sat outside Tempest's tent, his head tilted back, feeling the rush of cool air over his fresh bruises and sore muscles. He stretched out his awareness all the way to the grinding and boiling of rock far below, and the freezing vault of the heavens far above. Everything in balance. Everything as it should be.

If the smell of the roast venison hadn't hung in the air, Akieryon would wonder if it was even the same night. Perhaps Tempest had stretched time for them. Perhaps the hours simply pass differently when spent enwrapped in another person. Enwrapped and enraptured. Akieryon shifted, testing the aches in his body. He could heal himself with a little effort. He didn't really want to, not yet.

Akieryon's hand drifted to the back of his neck, where Tempest had bit down hard. Did the bruise obscure the Lineage Mark? Did he want it to? He remembered Tempest's breath hot on his spine, moving from his neck to the space between his wings. He had buried his face in the soft down there, his arms tight around Akieryon's middle, his body taut and ready. Waiting. Waiting for Akieryon to say—

"I'm surprised you're not still in there."

A little stupidly, Akieryon blinked up at the silhouette looming over him. Szearbhyn. Sluggish like honey in winter, Akieryon's thoughts traced the shape of Tempest, now curled in his nest of cushions. "He's sleeping."

Szearbhyn sat uninvited beside his brother. "I still thought you'd be in there with him. Cuddling or something."

Akieryon tilted his head, considering. "I sleep beside him every night. Right now I just don't feel much like sleeping." Right now he wanted to feel the vastness of the universe.

Szearbhyn gave him a long, calculating look, but said nothing. For a while they sat together in silence, Akieryon lost in the turning of the Spheres, Szearbhyn keeping his thoughts to himself. Then a soft light spilled over the both of them. Together, they turned. Tempest stood holding the tent flap open, naked as a newborn.

"Hmm," he said, contemplating the twins.

"Hmm yourself," said Szearbhyn. He climbed to his feet, then offered Akieryon a hand up.

Ignoring him, Tempest looked at Akieryon with a thoughtful tilt to his eyebrows. "There are some things I can't show you without the help of another person," he said. "We could wait for Jynn, if you like, or…?"

Szearbhyn caught his meaning before Akieryon did. "I'm game if you are," he said, giving Akieryon's hand a small squeeze. Did he not notice the electric current humming just beneath their skin whenever they touched? The push and pull of their magic? Or did he simply not care?

Tempest was waiting for an answer, and for some reason Akieryon hesitated. This was weird, right? A normal person would say no. But then, what was the point of being a demonic angel if he didn't do things that were a little bit bad from time to time? Akieryon worried his lip between his teeth. He trusted Tempest. Wasn't that answer enough?

"It's fine," Tempest started to say, just as Akieryon blurted, "Okay." They blinked at one another.

Akieryon reached his other hand to catch hold of Tempest's fingers. "I did say everything," he said, "and I am a man of my word."

Something inscrutable smoldered deep in the shadows of Tempest's gaze. He tugged Akieryon back into the tent, into the warm, comfortable glow and the too-large interior. The flap slapped closed behind Szearbhyn, and Tempest smiled.

Dawn approached.

In the quiet and the stillness of the tent, he lay with all of his limbs wrapped around Tempest. His other self nestled close against Tempest as well, the missing piece, the key in the lock. They were drifting, afloat together in the boundless sea of reality. Everything blurred a little. Tempest's heartbeat slowed by half. Unguarded and relaxed, floating and falling, sinking deeper and deeper into dense interplay of energies…

With a gasp, They sat up.

They looked at Their hands, flexed Their clawed fingers for the first time. Their heartbeat jumped, sending a faint rumble through the tent. Blinking, They looked around. Tempest's magic showed everywhere, in patterns and random swirls, glowing and pulsing in every color and more. It was exquisite. They reached to pluck at a single thread of it.

Tempest awakened with a startled half-snort. Blinking, he scrubbed at his eyes, those eyes that ever burned with magic. "Szearbh—Akieryon…? What?"

They ran.

The tent spilled Them out into a misty pre-dawn. Beyond the circle of tents and wagons, beyond the luminous threads Tempest had bound through the perimeter, the worlds expanded and contracted, a living being that seethed and breathed and beckoned. They ran onward.

Trees rose out of the mist, their branches threaded with magic, with the balance of the universe. It skewed gently toward entropy. Limbs hung heavy with fruit. The immortal mycelium lay ready, stretched beneath the skin of the world, waiting only for a decent rain.

The sun eased its way across the horizon, still hidden in the mist. It didn't matter. Dawn tipped the balance, dark to light, and They felt it immediately. They breathed it in, drawing the morning deep into Their lungs. They were immense, brimming with the glory of the universe. They were—

Startled to hear someone approach. Dropping to a crouch, They backed against the nearest tree and bared their teeth. The footsteps paused. The mist parted, and there stood Tempest, magic rolling through him like rapids, over and around him like a thunderstorm.

We trust Tempest.

They straightened a little, rolling Their shoulders back and settling Their wings in a more neutral position.

But… do I trust Tempest?

Who was I?

"I brought you pants." Tempest held up a fistful of dark fabric.

They shifted, They considered, and then They reached one clawed hand toward Tempest. Tempest watched Them with undisguised fascination, studying every movement, tracing the threads of reality with his thoughts.

"I take it this is a surprise."

They looked up from tying the waist of the trousers. Meeting Tempest's too-green gaze, They nodded.

"May I?" Tempest lifted one hand, his eyes on Their wings. They knew what he did with wings.

"Mm," They said. Tempest didn't move. They tried again. They nodded.

Tempest's fingertips grazed the luminous white feathers at the tops of Their wings, then trailed softly down the wisps of black smoke curling below. He looked reverent, almost awed. Curiosity and wonder rolled off of him in waves, feeling like velvet and tasting of rich chocolate. They made a small noise in the back of Their throat, and Tempest withdrew his hand at once.

"Too much?"

"Everything."

Tempest nodded. "Are you singular? Or are you plural?"

They frowned, concentrating. They had the memories of Their separate Selves, but They had a new consciousness. More or less. It was as though They had always been there, sleeping just beneath the skin of the world, waiting for one wholly unguarded moment to bring Them forth. "A little of both," They said eventually. "Becoming I."

"Hm." Lightly, Tempest touched the sweeping curve of one of Their horns. "Are you permanent?"

"No." Instinctively, They knew They would become individuals again. "We—I don't know how long."

Relief hung thick in the air, a sticky custard of an emotion. A little saddened, They drew back against the cold, rough tree trunk. Tempest's eyes narrowed, but just barely.

"Are you afraid?"

"Yes. Are We—Am I unwanted?"

Tempest's calculating emerald stare softened to sunlight in spring leaves. "No. No, of course not. I just want to have my other friends also."

"I may… return?" They knew Their existence depended wholly on Their separate Selves. If the Selves so willed it, They would never return.

"I would like that very much."

A strange warmth filled Them, body and soul. Did They have a separate soul? Were the Selves only half-souls, that combined to form Them? Too many questions. Not enough time. Time slipped away like an eroding shoreline.

"Do you have a name?"

The question startled Them. No, of course not. And what was something without a name? Not a person, surely. Slowly, They shook Their head.

"Do you want—" Tempest's words ended abruptly, and he turned, his head swinging side to side with a predatory deliberation. They heard it too, the faint jingling of a harness. They bared Their teeth.

Out of the morning gloom came a solitary figure. It dismounted, then said in an unwelcome voice, "What the hell is going on here?" Tempest grimaced, but did not otherwise react.

"Sesoran Sinen," They snarled.

Sesoran flinched at the sight of Their claws and Their large, sharp teeth, but to his credit he did not back down. "You are on my family's land," he said. "Why?"

"Why do you follow Akieryon?" They countered. Sesoran's jaw set stubbornly.

"I need answers."

Tempest made an amused noise. "What kind of answers?"

"Why were you sneaking Lenyr into the castle under the guise of helping with parliament?"

This time, Tempest laughed outright. "Is that what you think was happening?"

"I'm no fool," Sesoran said, sounding hurt and defensive. "The Lenyr make camp here every year. I've seen him before."

"Szearbhyn," Tempest said. "You've seen Szearbhyn, not Akieryon. They look alike."

Sesoran raised a skeptical eyebrow. Perhaps he wasn't as useless as he first seemed. But the world was shifting, blurring. The threads of magic faded slowly from view. "I'll fetch them both," They said, and ran for the camp.

By the time They broke through the tree line, Their vision had doubled. They blinked and shook Their head and almost tripped over a goat. Heedless of the shouts of the few early risers busy about their morning work, They plunged through the flap into Tempest's tent. The world broke apart.

Akieryon and Szearbhyn tumbled in a sprawling heap amid the cushions and pillows. For a long moment, Akieryon lay still, his eyes closed, the thunder of his heart slowing. What had just happened?

"Why do you have the pants?" Szearbhyn complained, and Akieryon jolted out of his thoughts with a laugh.

"Luck, probably. Let's go deal with Sesoran, and worry about the rest later."

They dressed quickly, and hurried back out to the orchard. Tempest and Sesoran were watching one another with a wary sort of distaste when they arrived. Szearbhyn casually twisted his hair into a messy tail.

"What?" he demanded, and Akieryon wondered if some of his distaste for the man had somehow afflicted his brother through their connection, brief thought it had been.

Sesoran blinked at them. "There really are two of you."

"Three, apparently," Akieryon muttered. Their merged form had his own distinct personality. That and... well, he would worry about the magical implications later.

"Now that you're both here," Sesoran continued, "I can see the difference." He gestured at Akieryon. "You're better built, with a softer face."

"I think that's a compliment?"

"I'm the hot one," Szearbhyn said. No one argued with him, which wasn't great, because he would remember that later. Akieryon tried not to glare at Sesoran.

"I'm not him. He's not me. In fact, we've only known each other for a couple of days." He only just ground his jaw shut on an *Are we done here?*

Sesoran nodded slowly. His gaze traveled from person to person, as though he needed extra time to process this new information, before settling at last on Tempest. "Get out of my orchard," he said in a surprisingly conversational tone.

Tempest smiled a smile with sharp edges. "Good to see you too."

As they all walked back to the camp, Akieryon muttered, "He seems unhealthily invested in catching us out in a lie."

"Humans," said Szearbhyn with a shrug. "Everything feels more urgent."

"He's a jackass," mused Tempest, "but he may yet grow out of it."

Akieryon had doubts, but he kept his mouth shut. He had more pressing concerns. He thought about the threads of magic, plainly visible to their combined form. What else could he—they?—do?

Back at the camp, Kirienne handed each of them a steaming bowl of porridge. Szearbhyn emptied his pockets, producing several handfuls of olives and two underripe apples. Akieryon gave him a reproachful look.

"You were stealing!"

"I don't know how to explain to you that I do bad things."

"I am aware," Akieryon said. He hunched over his breakfast. What would Lord Sidriel say about all of this? What would *Lord Uriel* say about it? "We need to talk about the magic," he said, and regretted it instantly. Szearbhyn looked at him, eyebrows raised, cheeks bulging. He swallowed his mouthful of breakfast.

"What about it?"

Tempest made a thoughtful noise. "Angel magic functions on the balance of opposing forces. The two of you merged would be, what, the physical manifestation of that concept?"

"Something like that," Akieryon said unhappily. "I think that would be a pretty good reason for people to want to keep us apart." He stared down into his bowl his porridge, trying to imagine a limit to the power their combined form could access. Almost nothing came to mind.

"I'm not giving you back," Szearbhyn growled.

Tempest took Akieryon's bowl, set it aside, and pulled him into a tight hug. "It's a pretty good reason for you to practice."

Akieryon nodded against Tempest's shoulder. Practice. Of course.

"You don't deserve the way they treated you," Tempest murmured against his hair. "It doesn't matter what you can or can't do." He leaned back, holding and squeezing Akieryon's shoulders. "Personally, I think I'd be really nice to a person who could potentially unravel every one of my magics."

"Angels are idiots," Szearbhyn said. Without looking, Akieryon reached out and smacked his arm.

But perhaps he was right. Late that afternoon, the two of them sat facing one another, their eyes closed and their foreheads touching, trying and failing to merge. Even knowing him now, knowing the touch of his soul and the shape of his mind, Akieryon could not lower his defenses.

Perhaps he would never learn. Perhaps their other self would remain locked away forever.

Perhaps that was for the best.

"I may... return?"

No. No, he could not condemn their other self to an eternity of barely not existing. He had to keep trying. He had to learn how it worked. He had to fix this.

But he couldn't *think* his way out of it. He had to relax and trust and lower his damn guard. The only person he did those things with was Tempest. Perhaps Tempest could help.

Perhaps he leaned on Tempest too much.

Over the next few days, Akieryon settled into the rhythm of Lenyr life. Everyone worked throughout the day, tending their small assortment of livestock, procuring and preparing food, and practicing various artisan trades. Nac spun as fine a wool as anything he had seen at the castle, and also practiced joinery to maintain the wagons. Varz appeared to be a journeyman whitesmith. Tor, the eldest of the group at a mere forty, made the most exquisite glass beads. Szearbhyn appeared at first to do very little, but he and Xan would disappear for hours at a time and return with bags stuffed full of lichens and bark and other arcane ingredients. The dye-witches, Xan explained, paid a handsome price for their bounty.

Four days passed in relative peace, the only trouble roiling in Akieryon's mind. Why could he not merge with Szearbhyn? He could feel their other self just beneath his skin, awake and alert every time they touched. The more he tried, the more he failed, the more he perceived their merged self as a full and separate person. That raised still more questions.

Late at night, safe in Tempest's arms, Akieryon let himself consider that perhaps Master Seikhiel had been right to lock him away. Even on his own he was a threat. Combined with his brother, they had access to power few could rival. If he had remained under Master Niseriel's tutelage, what could have happened? What hell could he have unleashed on the upper Spheres of Heaven?

He was drifting, caught partway between sleep and awake when the tent flap eased open. Tempest didn't stir. Akieryon opened his eyes just as a hand skimmed over his shoulder, raising a familiar electric buzz. Szearbhyn settled beside him, curling against the side of him not warmed by Tempest. Akieryon relaxed again, and allowed himself to ease a little nearer to sleep. He counted breaths. His breaths. Tempest's breaths. Szearbhyn's…

"Let's do this," They said.

WHOOPS

"Again."

Tempest held up his hands, revealing a fine, half-spun thread of magic stretched between them. They snatched it from his grip, and They recognized the shape of it at once. One of Tempest's globes of light. They finished the spell, gazed for a moment at the tiny, glowing sphere, then unpicked it. The magic unraveled in a blink, and the light vanished.

"Fascinating," Tempest murmured, as though he hadn't seen Them do it twice before. But he liked the repetition. He liked consistency, and he liked proving that the first time hadn't been a fluke. It was reassuring, really. They knew almost as little about Themself as Tempest did, aside from the certainties.

They were certain that they could touch any type of magic. If They could see it, They could interact with it. They were certain that They could only exist for about half an hour at a time, at least until They practiced enough to maintain this form for longer. The power of Their existence was a physical strain, and like a muscle, it needed exercise. They were certain that Their presence caused ripples in the balance of the universe. And They were certain that

Tempest was Their friend.

"I can see how you do it now," They said. When Tempest merely arched expectant eyebrows, They added, "You're constantly collecting stray bits of wild magic and moving them through you. You've been doing it long enough that your magic kind of... has its own gravity. Perpetual motion of energies."

"You make it sound easy." Tempest gave Them a disarming smile. "Have you chosen a name?"

He asked every time the two of them talked. This was the third time. They scrunched Their face in concentration. Names were hard. "Maybe. Not yet. Almost."

Tempest nodded. He had chosen his name without giving it too much thought, but it suited him. "One more?" he suggested, lifting his hands again.

Slowly, They shook Their head. "I'm sorry. No. Sorry." The filament of magic running through Tempest's fingers was fading. They tried to hold on a little longer, to stretch Their capabilities.

The skin of the world rippled, just faintly, its complex web of energies flexing and reforming around something new. They looked to Tempest, who showed no sign of having noticed. "You're doing great," he said, his tone gentle, encouraging. "Next time we'll do more."

No, he had no idea. "Something's coming." They began to

stand, only to stumble as Their vision doubled. "I can't..." Can't leave yet. Must protect. Must... "Ah, balls."

Szearbhyn shoved himself free of Akieryon. "I'll take a look." He was off at a jog before Akieryon could argue.

"Something's coming," Tempest repeated, pinning Akieryon with the weight of his stare. "Can you be a little more specific?"

"Someone strong enough to be an Anchor." At Tempest's blank expression, Akieryon searched for an explanation. "Most Spheres are held up by the collective energies of their inhabitants. If enough of them died, say, in a cataclysm or something, the Sphere would collapse. But sometimes an individual becomes strong enough to hold a Sphere with little to no help. We call them Anchors." And Tempest certainly had the potential to become one, which Akieryon avoided mentioning.

"So if all the humans died, and all the elves and the Shadowmarchers—"

Akieryon was already shaking his head. "It would never get that far," he said. "Not here. The Mortal Realm is a protected zone."

"Protected like... like a nature preserve?"

Akieryon laughed. "Yeah, pretty much. If too many mortals started dying too quickly, they'd send angels to stabilize the Sphere."

Tempest arched a brow at him. "Has this happened before?"

Akieryon shrugged. Most likely.

But he really couldn't leave Szearbhyn to run off and deal with an Anchor from another Sphere all by himself. He sighed. "I'd better look into it."

"Is this a Demonslayer thing?" Tempest said.

"No." Akieryon grimaced. "It's an 'I don't trust Szearbhyn to handle it' thing."

Not waiting for Tempest's reply, Akieryon hurried after his brother. Away from the camp, away along the edge of the orchard, he began to sense wisps of foreign magic. Foreign… but almost familiar. It smelled like…

Like blood.

Akieryon broke into a run. Magic powered by blood came from the lower Spheres of Hell. If an Anchor from a lower Hell had come, if Szearbhyn picked a fight with them, it would surely draw the attention of the Demonslayers. Akieryon needed to stop this now, before it became a crisis.

The trail of magic grew stronger, leading him to a stand of myrtle. He broke through the copse and stumbled to a halt. Just ahead, Szearbhyn stood arguing with a dragon from Seyzharel. From his long crimson plumage to his almost luminous alabaster skin, the stranger was unmistakably royal. He wore flawlessly tailored silks, and a blue gem glistened at the center of his forehead. But he was whip-thin, despite the fact that his wingspan and the size of his backswept horns put his age at two hundred years at least. Why would any member of the royal family be so small?

"Pay me what you owe." The stranger's voice could have grown a frost on the trees. Akieryon knew nothing about him, other than that he was of Chaizhyn's get, a prince of the Fourth Sphere, but he did not doubt that Szearbhyn did indeed owe him, for debt or for offense.

"I've told you before, B," Szearbhyn said in a light, informal tone that was sure to set off an international incident, "fuck off."

Akieryon must have sighed out loud. They both turned.

The Seyzharel prince scrutinized him, his eyes a fathomless coal black. He glanced between Akieryon and Szearbhyn, arms folded, brows raised, wings set in a skeptical attitude. "What trickery is this?"

"No trickery at all," Szearbhyn said in that same get-someone-incinerated tone. "I have a brother."

The prince's lips curled in an unwelcoming, fang-baring sneer, and no wonder. That was no way to introduce someone to royalty. Akieryon's body slid easily into the sort of fluid, sinuous bow common to many dragon courts. If he could show his wings, he would raise them in salute, but he feared that white feathers would only escalate the current tension.

"Your Highness," he said in extremely formal Dragonish, "our new acquaintance honors me beyond measure."

"Oh, shit," muttered Szearbhyn.

The prince snapped his wings shut in a self-protecting gesture that should have been completely foreign to a dragon of his station. His midnight eyes were wide and wild. "Who are you?" he demanded, his voice tight with suspicion and laced through with something deeply unhinged. No, this dragon was not well. Straightening, Akieryon scrutinized him for signs of Hoarding Sickness. No fever. No lapses in grooming. He was underweight, but—

"My name is Akieryon," he replied automatically, his brain whirring. What was wrong with this dragon? "I meant no offense."

"Shit, shit, shit, shit," Szearbhyn continued chanting, like a particularly annoying incantation. "You don't *know*."

The prince's gaze flicked past Akieryon, but only for an instant. "And now you bring Mortals before me."

Tempest came to stand beside Akieryon, who was struggling not to ask Szearbhyn what he meant, and struggling not to point out that Mortals live here. In the Mortal Realm.

"Rude," Tempest said. So he had his own translation spell.

"Your Highness," Akieryon said, forcing his tone to remain neutral, "this human Tempest is my friend and companion. My path-mate."

The prince regarded him in silence for a long moment. Then he said, "Are you prepared to pay your brother's debt?"

"Baleirithys, come on," Szearbhyn said, drawing a glare from the prince.

"What does he owe you?" Akieryon asked.

"Blood," Prince Baleirithys said shortly.

Slowly, Akieryon shook his head. "It's against protocol," he said. "I'm not permitted to give blood to a demon without dire need."

The prince's gaze sharpened. "Not permitted?"

"Oh, no," said Szearbhyn.

A chill settled in Akieryon's stomach. "Doesn't... Is Seyzharel still on friendly terms with the Demonslayers?"

Baleirithys went unnaturally still. "Demonslayers," he repeated softly, acid in his voice. "Useless."

Well that was just hurtful.

"Rude," Tempest said again, drawing the prince's ire.

"Will you stand for his debt?"

"Not to you. Not as long as you stand here insulting my friends."

Baleirithys made a soft hissing sound, then turned again to Szearbhyn. "The blood," he insisted. "Pay it."

Something was seriously off here. Princes did not come personally to collect their debts. Princes did not turn up alone in rural Davenz. Princes did not look at Demonslayers with that wild, half-starved gleam in their eyes.

"Where are your guards?" Akieryon demanded. Baleirithys' attention snapped back to him, and he found he didn't like it at all. But Demonslayers did not quail before dragons, no matter if they teetered at the brink of irrationality.

"Guards?" Prince Baleirithys snarled, barely giving the word any voice at all. "Why would I remove guards from their post when I need no protection from this base brigand?"

"Right." Akieryon glanced sidelong at Tempest. "I'm not sure what happened to manners, and I'm sure Chaizhyn wouldn't approve—"

With an animal snarl and a flare of his wings, Baleirithys surged forward. Akieryon's hand flinched toward a sword he no longer carried, Szearbhyn swore loudly, and Tempest stepped between them, hands raised to push them apart. Baleirithys' teeth snapped. Tempest snatched his hand back.

"Did you fucking *bite* me?"

Baleirithys stumbled backward, both hands flying up to cover his mouth. What little color he'd had drained from his face.

"No." Akieryon was moving before the full horror of the situation reached his brain. "No, no, no, no." He grabbed Tempest's arm and gripped it hard, trying with all his strength to slow the flow of blood. He knew it was futile, he knew that neutralizing dragon venom was far beyond his skill, but he had to try. He reached for the balance of Tempest's blood, while trying stop the toxin from binding to Tempest's magic. It was a losing battle. Did he have time to bring Tempest to Lord Raphael? He would pay with his freedom. That was fine.

"Help me!" Akieryon shouted to his brother, who stood frozen in shock. With a sharp intake of breath, Tempest dropped to his knees, and Akieryon sank down with him. Still fighting to hold back the venom, to stop it ravaging Tempest's circulatory system while burning out his magic, Akieryon stretched his awareness between Spheres. He couldn't quite visualize the doorway. Tempest shuddered and slumped sideways against Akieryon. "I need a portal!"

"S'fine," Tempest wheezed through tightly clenched teeth. His free hand gripped Akieryon's shoulder, a little too hard. "Had worse," he lied.

"It's not fine." When had Akieryon started crying? "The toxin is in your magic."

"Yeah." A flicker of agony contorted Tempest's face, which had gone a strangely purple shade of gray. "Sucks." A trickle of blood, escaping his nose, blackened on contact with the air. No, Tempest was human. There was no time to bring him to Lord Raphael.

There was no time.

This was all the time they had.

Choking back sobs, Akieryon held Tempest as tremors ran through his body in ripples like earthquakes. He pressed their foreheads together. Tempest was clammy. "Don't leave me," Akieryon whispered uselessly, insensibly. "Please. Please, I love you."

"Hrnn. Trying." It was the first pained vocalization Tempest had let slip, other than gasps and hisses and ragged breathing. He was fighting the venom. He wanted to live. He wanted to stay.

He was failing.

Abruptly, Tempest heaved himself over onto one elbow, and he gagged up a startling quantity of blackening blood. He made a little, high-pitched noise in the back of his nose, shuddered, and vomited. Blood sweat dotted his skin. Worse, the green was fading from his eyes.

Akieryon curled his body around Tempest, fighting a losing battle with every scrap of magic he could muster. He was slipping.

He was fading. Akieryon had his wings out now, spread over the both of them, sheltering them. Tempest's pulse was thready and erratic beneath his hand. His breathing came in wet, bloody rattles. He groaned, and Akieryon sobbed.

"Mine," Tempest growled stubbornly, his hand gripping Akieryon's. It was a very dragonish sort of sentiment. He squeezed, with probably as much strength as he had left in him. "Mine." Then he gagged up more blood. How much blood did he have left in him? It streamed from his eyes and his nose, and it pooled in his fingers, making them swell and purple.

"Always," Akieryon whispered, holding him tightly. "For as long as you'll have me." He could no longer see through his tears, which felt like a mercy when Tempest's body seized and his lungs collapsed. When he stilled at last, Akieryon buried his face against Tempest's chest and wailed.

When his grief had melted halfway to rage, Akieryon lifted his head. Creator help him, he was going to kill that dragon. To his credit, Prince Baleirithys was not coward enough to flee from the death of the man he killed. He looked like he wanted to shrink before Akieryon's wrath, but he remained where he stood.

"Go," Akieryon rasped, his voice ragged with his tears. "Before I forsake my oaths."

Baleirithys hesitated for a moment too long. A portal opened, and a Ferryman stepped through. Some vague part of Akieryon's brain recognized her, but it wasn't important. Nothing was important. Nothing would be important ever again.

The Ferryman took in the tableau before her. Baleirithys and Szearbhyn stood side by side, differing shades of horror-struck. Akieryon huddled across Tempest's lifeless body, his face a mess of tears. A miasma of mingled magics slowly seeped out of Tempest. Sighing, the Ferryman rubbed her temples.

"Creator, but I hate this part."

She leaned over Tempest, ignoring Akieryon's bared teeth and feral growl. Lightly, she touched Tempest's brow. From the point of contact, a vivid black mark blossomed, uncurling like vines across Tempest's skin. Stepping back, the Ferryman stuck her fingers in her mouth.

Tempest's eyes flew open, blazing greener than ever, and he gasped a deep, rattling gasp. Shaking almost too hard to help, Akieryon rolled him onto his side, trying ineffectually to pound some air into newly reshaped lungs. Alive. Creator's breath, Tempest was alive. Akieryon blinked wet, gritty eyes up at the Ferryman.

"I've never seen the Making of a Mortal-Born," he whispered. It would be some hours before the full impact of it would sink in. Tempest was a demon. Tempest was a dragon. Somehow, it fit.

"Yeah, it never doesn't suck," the Ferryman complained around her fingers. She lifted her other hand, opening her portal again. "Be at peace, Soldier." She stepped through, and it closed behind her.

"Well, shit," said Szearbhyn.

"I…" Stunned, Prince Baleirithys reached out and flicked his fingers as though turning a page. The air cracked open, showing a bejeweled mirror behind him. "No." He stepped through.

"Hey, asshole!" Szearbhyn yelled after him, but he was gone. With an annoyed huff, Szearbhyn settled down to watch his brother fuss over Tempest. "I think we're square now," he muttered.

Tempest sat still for a long moment, taking everything in. He rolled his jaw and he tested his new, tiny fangs with the tip of his tongue. Then, shifting a little, he grimaced. Standing abruptly, he peeled away his clothes and set them ablaze with a brief gesture of disgust. He tilted his head, and a tiny rainstorm began to downpour directly above him. He scrubbed and scrubbed, unbraided his hair, rinsed his mouth out four or five times, and scrubbed some more. Tiny horns were emerging at his temples, and wings—a handspan so far—grew as they watched.

"Dying," Tempest declared, "is really gross."

Laughing and crying, Akieryon threw his arms around Tempest

and kissed him all over his beautiful, damp, alive face. Tempest tolerated it for a while, then pushed free of him. The rain had subsided. Apparently satisfied that he was clean at last, Tempest reached through a gap in the air and withdrew a fresh pair of trousers.

"I think my magic is stronger."

"It ought to be. Dragons are inherently magical," Akieryon informed him.

"Huh," Tempest said. He wiggled his wings, which were about the size of his head and showed no signs of slowing their growth. He made a face. "Everything itches."

"It should stop when the growth slows," Akieryon said. "I think."

Tempest studied his fingernails which, though still rounded, had thickened into claws. "You can teach me about my new self." He slanted a smile at Akieryon. "Demonslayer."

Akieryon grabbed Tempest's hand and gave it a squeeze.

"Right." Tempest glanced between the twins. "Who's hungry?" He laughed when they both grimaced. "Anything to get the taste of blood out of my mouth. If I never taste *that* again, it will be too soon."

"Oho," Szearbhyn laughed, "do I have some bad news for you!"

"Seyzharel dragons are blood drinkers," Akieryon said before his brother could gloat about it.

Tempest screwed up his face in comic dismay. "Seriously?"

AFTERMATH

Tempest sat beside the fire, eating everything anyone would hand him. Becoming a new species was hungry work. Akieryon sat at his side, longing to cling to him and doggedly not doing so. Tempest was alive. Of course he was alive. Akieryon wanted to weep with relief, but he had really cried enough for one day. Perhaps he should take a nap.

Szearbhyn nudged him. Looking up, Akieryon saw that Tempest had stuck olives onto his new fangs, to the immense delight of Nac and Riol's little daughter. Akieryon smiled, but his heart gave a weird little wrench. Tempest was the same as ever, if not somehow even more himself than he had ever been. Why did it almost feel a little as though Akieryon had lost him?

Sleep. He needed sleep. That would be just the thing to shake his thoughts into place.

He was about to stand up when he saw Tempest turn his hand over and look at the bite mark. It had already scarred, with spidery lines like lightning crawling out from the puncture marks. He made a show of chewing the olives, then said quietly, "I suppose I have to stop biting people." He only just didn't make it a question, but Akieryon was already shaking his head.

"You push your tongue up and forward against your teeth to express venom. The movement should be reflexive if you ever feel sufficiently threatened, which I doubt, because you're you." Tempest inclined his head slightly, and Akieryon continued. "You're fine to bite as long as you don't envenomate. Unless you intend to. Anyway, biting is quite common between lovers. But consuming blood directly from the flesh is considered extremely intimate, and therefore vulgar to do in public," he added hastily.

"That's reasonable."

Akieryon looked at Tempest. Rather against his own confused feelings, he had to laugh at Tempest's absolute sincerity. "Reasonable. Yeah. You're already a great dragon, you just need to learn the details."

The shock was probably wearing off. Akieryon really did want a nap. He stood up, and Tempest's jewel-bright gaze followed him.

"You're probably buzzing with energy." Akieryon managed a thin smile. "I need rest."

In the tent, Akieryon collapsed face down on the cushions. Oh, right. He had been pouring every scrap of magic he could muster into fighting the toxin. Probably some of his own life energy too.

Really, it was hard to remember.

Everything felt distant and hazy. His limbs were lead, and his thoughts drifted somewhere outside of his skull. Closing his eyes, he inhaled the warm, human scent of Tempest's bedding. He would smell like a dragon now, but his magic still carried that voidspace scent. That was fine.

Everything was fine.

He was so tired.

He opened his eyes when the bedding shifted against his side. Tempest's hand smoothed over his hair and down his back, drawing a soft sigh from Akieryon.

"Hey."

Akieryon rolled slightly to the side and managed a stiff smile. Had he actually been sleeping? "Hey."

Tempest nestled in and pressed their foreheads together. "How are you? Honestly."

"Me?" Akieryon fumbled for words. "You're the one who died."

"Yes."

Tempest waited for him to answer. Akieryon sighed.

"I feel like I could sleep for a week," he said. "I feel like I should have prevented it happening at all, and I feel like I've failed you. I feel like—I *know* that if Szearbhyn and I had remained merged for fifteen minutes longer, you would still be human."

"I haven't been human for a very long time," Tempest said, "except on a technicality."

Akieryon caught his hand and gripped it tightly. "I'm the only one here who can teach you about dragons, and my brain feels wrung out and useless."

"You're not here to be useful," Tempest reminded him gently. Akieryon closed his eyes so he wouldn't have to see the earnestness of his stare.

"I know."

"Do you?"

"No," Akieryon conceded, "but I'm trying."

Tempest made a thoughtful noise. He slid an arm around Akieryon and pulled him close. Akieryon choked back a laugh that was too close to a sob.

"I feel like a fool." When Tempest said nothing, he added, "I was absolutely out of my mind about losing you, and—and Szearbhyn *said*—"

Tempest pushed back far enough to frown a protective little frown at him. "What did Szearbhyn say?" The low growl held traces of a threat. Akieryon tried not to focus on it.

"That it wouldn't be hard to Make a demon of you."

"Well, no." Tempest relaxed visibly. "That doesn't mean you

were thinking about it when the venom hit. Are you sure you're not hungry?" He sat up and reached through a gap in the air. He frowned in concentration, grimaced, and finally withdrew two familiar-looking pastries, sugar crystals glistening on top. He bit into one. "Hot," he announced, but continued eating.

"Did you just steal from Caspar's cook?"

"Shush, no, that would be impossible." Tempest caught a blob of molten fruit filling before it could fall on a cushion.

"Pari is going to smack you so hard when she finds out," Akieryon said with an amused shake of his head.

Tempest ate a pastry and a half before he finally convinced Akieryon to have a few bites. "Still hungry," he complained. He lifted his hand to steal again, but Akieryon caught his wrist. Tempest gave him a quizzical look.

"You probably need blood."

"Isn't that against protocol?" Tempest's eyes widened slightly when he saw Akieryon pick up one of his daggers. "Wait—!" His words stopped in a sharp intake of breath when the dagger scratched across Akieryon's arm. The smell of the blood froze him, narrowing his focus.

"I'm not supposed to give my blood to demons," Akieryon said calmly, "because most blood drinkers gain magic from the blood they consume. I can make you more powerful." He offered his arm.

Tempest looked like he wanted to hesitate, or at least play at a feline sort of coolness, but instinct took control of his body. Seizing hold of Akieryon, he smashed his mouth against the cut and suckled hard enough to hurt. Akieryon gasped, and after a slight delay, Tempest softened his grip. Akieryon watched him, watched eagerness fading to contentment. He watched the flutter of black eyelashes against soft olive skin. Fangs scratched against his arm, not breaking the skin, not yet. Akieryon tried not to think too far into the future.

With one fingertip, he traced the vivid black swirls of the new Mark on Tempest's face. It made almost a complete circle at the center of his forehead, where the Ferryman had touched him. From there it twined down his cheek, somehow skirting the tattoos by his eye, before wisping out below his jaw. It was enormous, as Mortal-Born Marks went, easily twice the size of Szearbhyn's. Akieryon thought about the miasma of magic leaking out of Tempest, and immediately decided he never wanted to think about it again.

By the time Tempest released his arm, Akieryon was softly, absently stroking his hair. The dragons were right. Consuming blood from the flesh was definitely intimate. He had only just managed not to whisper *I love you* once or twice. Tempest sat back, a new shade of green sparkling in his eyes. He watched the last strands of his hair sliding through Akieryon's fingers.

"This is probably going to grow in red," he said, and Tempest recoiled.

"Why?"

"Because dragonish traits are strongly dominant." Akieryon avoided pointing out that Tempest's dragon traits came from the prince who had killed him. "It's going to change texture, too. Dragons look like they have hair, but it's actually plumage. Extremely fine feathers. You won't have to shave though," he added, almost an afterthought.

"Caspar will be jealous of that, at least."

"That's good, is it?" When Tempest grinned, Akieryon grinned back. He felt a little lighter. Strange. "Still hungry?"

Tempest tilted his head, considering. "No, I think that did it." He didn't test his magic right away, which probably counted as an admirable show of restraint.

"Seyzharel dragons—that's what you are now—are obligate blood drinkers," Akieryon reminded him. The cut was already mostly sealed, so he just pushed it a little farther along and rolled his sleeve down. "If you don't have blood often enough, you'll become anemic and sickly."

"I doubt that will be a problem." Tempest flashed fangs in a wicked grin. "You're delicious."

As he had intended, Akieryon blushed.

Akieryon curled against Tempest, and Tempest's arm encircled him. "I feel a little guilty," he confessed, and Tempest made a small noise of surprise.

"Why?"

"Because I'm glad you're a dragon now."

"These will take some getting used to." Tempest wiggled his new wings, now nearly the size of his torso. "But I think I like it. No pointless guilt."

Reaching up, Akieryon pushed his fingers into Tempest's hair —still damp—and felt for the tiny bumps that would grow into a ridge running the length of his head. Finding them, he smiled. "Dragon suits you."

~⚬⌒◆⌒⚬~

Tempest opted not to get used to his wings, not entirely. He used some magic that was not phase shifting to put them away out of sight. Akieryon didn't ask. Szearbhyn bothered him every few hours to see how big they'd grown.

"Cori will have fits if she sees these," Tempest said, not an excuse for coyness, merely fact. "Can you imagine her taking scissors to my wardrobe?"

"Not remotely." Akieryon frowned at Tempest's child-sized wings. "It looks like I'll be teaching you to fly in a few days."

"I want to do it!" Szearbhyn objected.

"Two things." Akieryon held up one finger. "One: your wings are smoke. Two: Tempest would probably be way too smug if we fought over him." He shoved two fingers in his brother's face.

"I'm right here," Tempest said.

"Fine," said Szearbhyn. "Who do you want to teach you?"

"Rathin," Tempest said without hesitation. "But he's not here, so definitely Akieryon."

"I'm really not feeling the love here," Szearbhyn complained.

"Your wings are smoke," Tempest and Akieryon said.

While Tempest and Szearbhyn continued the banter, Akieryon let his thoughts drift. Tempest's new little fangs caught the light with every smile, every laugh. He wondered what they would feel like when they broke his skin. He wondered if they would pierce all the way through his ears. Was that why dragons liked earrings? Tempest caught him staring, and he blushed.

"What?"

I want to know what it feels like to kiss you now. "Sex thoughts," Akieryon said, which wasn't a lie. For Tempest, kissing was about sex. It was a declaration of intent.

Tempest made a pleased little rumbling sound and looked at him like a cat wanting to pounce. Akieryon grinned and tilted his head in invitation.

This was fine. He didn't need to think about the pieces of himself that had shattered watching Tempest die. He didn't need to think about it, until hours later, when he found himself abruptly sobbing in Tempest's arms.

Lightly, Tempest touched the skin beside the fresh bite wound on Akieryon's shoulder. "Have I harmed you?"

His gentleness made Akieryon cry harder, but he managed to shake his head. He buried his face against Tempest's chest until he could force the words out. "Every time I close my eyes," he said, "I see you dying."

"You just need time," Tempest murmured against his hair. "You'll heal. You'll be fine. And I'll be right here with you. For as long as it takes."

A thought occurred to Akieryon. "You like taking care of me, don't you?"

"Yeah. Why wouldn't I?"

Akieryon gave Tempest a watery smile. "It's very dragonish of you."

Tempest digested this information. "Are dragons protective?"

"Very."

After a lengthy pause, Tempest said, "That prince. Will he be coming back?" *Will he hurt you or Szearbhyn?*

"I don't know," Akieryon said. "I used to know his family, but

I never met him before this morning."

Tempest gave a brief nod, disentangled himself, and planted a brief kiss on the top of Akieryon's head. Did he even realize he'd done it? Then, carelessly snatching up pants on the way out of the tent, he strode out into the night.

Akieryon passed a hand over the bite mark on his shoulder, and the wound sealed. He didn't waste energy doing more to heal it. He considered following Tempest, he even put on trousers of his own, but then he decided against it. Tempest would be back soon enough. In the meantime, Akieryon poured a little water in a towel and scrubbed his face clean. Everything was normal, he told himself, and the time had come to stop feeling upset.

He didn't want to call it by its name. Grief. Nothing deserved that much power over him. Especially not when Tempest was still here.

Tempest returned with Szearbhyn in tow, looking more disgruntled than usual. Tempest directed him to sit. He sat. "Now," Tempest said, sitting down opposite him, "you're the only one of us who knows this prince. Tell us about him."

"What, Baleirithys?" Szearbhyn screwed up his face in an expression of profound disgust. "You got me out of bed in the middle of the night to talk about *that* asshole?"

Tempest gestured for him to do exactly that.

Szearbhyn sighed. "As I hear it, he's mostly a good regent—"

"Wait," Akieryon interrupted, "regent? What happened to the king?"

"This is going to take all night," Szearbhyn complained. "Yes, regent. His father Thaghecii is allegedly in some kind of a magical coma. They call him The Sleeping King."

This was all wrong. "Thaghecii was never supposed to be king," Akieryon said. "His brother was Crown Prince."

"Right, well, something happened. The prince died, the old king vanished—"

"Chaizhyn was my friend," Akieryon said softly. Fresh grief wrenched at him, and he stamped it down.

Szearbhyn reached over and squeezed Akieryon's hand. "Thaghecii was not a good king. I don't know what he did, but Baleirithys is a little bit… not right."

"What do you mean, not right?" Tempest pressed. Szearbhyn shrugged.

"He rules what's left of Seyzharel competently I guess, but whenever he's in a particular mood—stressed, maybe—he comes to try to collect that imaginary blood debt from me. We bother each other. Maybe it's fun for him. Maybe it just helps him get his priorities back in order. Fuck if I know what goes on in his head."

"He's very thin," Akieryon murmured, as though that was

relevant. "Maybe he's not well because he's hungry."

"He's prince and regent," Szearbhyn pointed out. "He can eat whatever he wants."

"What I want to know," Tempest said with exaggerated patience, "is will he come back and start shit?"

"What, with you? Because he Made you?" Szearbhyn scratched his chin. "Hard to say. He might freak out and pretend you don't exist. Or maybe he will decide he has to correct his mistake and kill you more. I doubt he's ever been in this situation before."

"I'm not going to wait around to find out." Tempest looked to Akieryon. "You said that blood makes my magic stronger."

Akieryon nodded. "You have inherent blood-fueled magic now. Blood from more powerful individuals will give you a bigger boost."

"Right." Tempest plucked one of his globes of light from the air and rolled it between his hands. "And if I have blood from, say, a half dozen powerful individuals?"

"There's no limit to how much power you can gain by consuming it," Akieryon said flatly. "That's why Demonslayers aren't supposed to share our blood freely." He had broken that rule for Tempest, or had he? It was assumed that a dragon would share blood with his mates. Wasn't that what he was?

Tempest released the light back into the air and held one hand out to Szearbhyn. "May I have some blood?"

Szearbhyn grinned at him. "It's more fun if you bite me."

Akieryon thought of the fresh bite on his shoulder, and then tried not to think about it.

"Later," Tempest said, his gaze flicking to Akieryon, who struggled to interpret the glance. "I have an idea of how to deal with this Baleirithys. You can teach me to fly, and then we're going to Tymirin."

GOOD

Akieryon slept late the following morning. Awakening to a joyous cacophony outside, he fumbled for a shirt and stumbled out of the tent. All of the Lenyr were shouting and hugging and generally mobbing a figure he eventually recognized. Jynn. Right, hadn't he said he would be following about a week behind them?

Seeing Akieryon, Jynn pushed free of the crowd. "Here you are!" he crowed, and he lifted Akieryon off his feet in a bone-crushing hug. "Well? How are you finding it?" Setting Akieryon down again, Jynn glanced around, looking for Szearbhyn. "Tell me everything."

Everything, Akieryon reflected, was a lot. "Thank you," he said softly, his words almost lost in the general jubilation. "For wanting to tell me about Szearbhyn."

"So… brothers?" Jynn prodded.

"Twins. I had no idea, but he grew up with our mother, so he knew about me."

Jynn made a harrumphing sound. "A bit mean of Tempest to

keep something that big a surprise."

"He meant to spare me anxiety," Akieryon said, and he probably had. Akieryon was socially awkward enough to convince himself that his own twin would hate him.

"Don't make excuses for him. He's behaved badly and ought to be punished." Jynn's wicked grin suggested that Tempest would enjoy whatever punishment he devised.

Something in Akieryon wrenched painfully. "Have you seen him yet?"

"Ooh, yes, those *teeth.*" Jynn's unique copper eyes went half-lidded, and he hummed with pleasure. "And then when I asked him what happened, he just said 'I died,' which is just like him. *You'll give me all the details, won't you, darling?*"

"I will," Akieryon said, "but you won't like it."

"Later, then. It's good to see you," Jynn added, as though months had passed rather than barely more than a week. His thumb grazed Akieryon's lower lip. "May I?"

"You may."

Jynn's kiss was long and slow, full of delicious affection and desire. When he eased back at last, he drew one knuckle down Akieryon's cheek. "Ah, gods," he breathed. "Is Tempest done being possessive yet?"

"No." Akieryon blushed as he added, "He did say something

about sharing, though.”

Jynn groaned as though Akieryon had just stuffed both hands down his drawers and started feeling his way around. “You’d better not be teasing me,” he gasped.

“Only with intent to follow through.”

“You’re gorgeous.” Jynn kissed Akieryon on the cheek. “You *are* the hot one.” Taking him by the arm, he turned Akieryon to face toward where Tempest stood in earnest conversation with Riol. “You soften him, you know,” Jynn said quietly. “More than anyone other than Caspar.”

“Do I?” Akieryon thought about Tempest kissing the top of his head. He thought about swift hugs and interlaced fingers. “He trusts me to teach him to fly,” he murmured, mostly to himself.

“You’re good for him,” Jynn pronounced. “He needs to remember that he needs warmth and gentleness too.”

Akieryon watched as Tempest lifted the toddler trying to climb him and handed her to Riol. “As a male dragon,” he said, “he’ll develop a strong nurturing instinct. And he may become more protective.”

“*More* protective?” Jynn laughed. “Will he swaddle you in wool batting?”

“He’d better not.”

Jynn laughed harder. “You’re doomed, you know.”

Probably. Akieryon was fairly sure he'd known that from the start. Gentle hands rolling gauze across his eyes… had it only been a couple of months? He had lived several lifetimes in the turning of a season.

Spotting Szearbhyn at last, Jynn bolted across the encampment. He leapt upon Szearbhyn, throwing arms, legs, and tail all around him. Laughing, Szearbhyn staggered under the impact. Or the weight. How dense were Shadowmarchers?

"Tempest and Jynn were traveling together the first time we met them," said a quiet voice at Akieryon's side. Turning, he found the somewhat reticent hunter Kirienne. "Jynn was different then. Afraid to be his true self."

Akieryon could not imagine describing Jynn with words like shy. "That must have been a long time ago."

"Not really."

Akieryon watched Jynn and Szearbhyn as they clasped hands and bounced in place like schoolchildren. "I suppose," he murmured, "I know something of diminishing oneself in attempt to be more palatable to others."

Kirienne gave Akieryon's shoulder a friendly squeeze. "It's never worth it." With that, yon strode off away from camp and into the woods.

Later that evening, when everyone had gathered close to the

fires to enjoy rabbit stew and baked early apples, Akieryon asked Jynn a personal question. "I know you weren't raised among the elves," he said, carefully picking his way through the phrasing. "But have you ever given any thought to choosing a gender, as elves do?"

Jynn chewed slowly, his copper gaze fixed on the dancing flames. "Nah," he said at last. "My gender is bard."

Akieryon wasn't entirely certain what that meant, but he knew he would find out eventually. Throughout the evening, Jynn laughed and flirted with everyone, but he always stayed near Akieryon. He took out an instrument that resembled a tiny banjo, and he plucked a brisk accompaniment to a raucous round sung by all the Lenyr. He gave them a dancing tune on a little wood flute. He told stories and bawdy jokes, and everyone had a fantastic time.

When people finally retired to their own beds, he followed Akieryon into Tempest's tent.

"Now you're going to tell me," he said.

Akieryon sat among the cushions and hugged one to his chest. Haltingly, he related the events of the previous morning, watching Jynn's face all the while. He didn't describe the poison. Jynn went pale at the first mention of the bite. When Tempest entered the tent and came to sit with them, Jynn seized him and kissed him hard.

"*Don't* die by venom ever again," he said when he let Tempest breathe.

"Didn't plan on it. Didn't plan on it the first time, not that it makes any difference."

Jynn glared for a minute. Then he made himself a nest of pillows, reclined like an emperor, and said, "So are we going after him?"

"I'm going to deal with it," Tempest said. "You're going to stay here and look after the Lenyr."

"Boring!" Jynn complained, as though the Lenyr could ever be boring. "You know I'm good for a fight."

"I'm not taking you to a Hell Sphere," Akieryon said flatly. Jynn was too good and too precious for that, and anyway, visiting Seyzharel might awaken latent draconiform traits in him, and he didn't need that kind of stress.

"But you'll take Tempest?"

"Tempest will find his own way there without me, so it's less messy for everyone if I show him the way."

Jynn laughed a short, loud laugh, and he threw himself over to hug Akieryon around the middle. "Oho, he *knows* you!" he crowed to Tempest. "You're doomed."

"I don't mind," said Tempest.

"Well I'm staying right here," Jynn announced. "I was thinking I'd start by spending a couple of nights with Tor, but your harrowing tale—and I missed it by a day!—has changed my mind. You need me. Moral support bard.”

Akieryon wrapped both arms around Jynn and squeezed him tight. “Everyone should have a moral support bard.” He meant it, too. Even in their brief acquaintance, Jynn lifted his spirits and made him feel… loved?

Jynn shifted around and peered up at Tempest. “So are you going to go full dragon now? Like Rathin?”

“You’d never know it if I did.”

“Seyzharel dragons start out looking… a lot like you, actually,” Akieryon explained. “Bipedal, sharp teeth, wings. Their features become more draconiform over time. I’ve heard stories of thousand-year-old lower-Sphere dragons who have immense branching horns and scales and so forth.” He glanced at Tempest. “But also, you are what you eat.”

“Ah.” Tempest nodded gravely. “Like Szearbhyn.” Which was how Akieryon learned that his brother could gain physical traits from the souls he consumed. Were the horns his own, or had they come from someone else?

As soon as Akieryon had explained the blood drinking to Jynn, he was rolling his sleeve up and offering his arm to Tempest. “I don’t know how much magic I can give you,” he said, a little apologetic, “but at least I can make your venom stronger.”

Tempest eyed him hungrily. "I'll take all the strength I can get."

Akieryon didn't bother to point out that the blood Tempest had already consumed—his and Szearbhyn's—was enough to change his threat level in the Demonslayers' records. Let Tempest become the most powerful of his kind. Akieryon would never tell.

Jynn slept that night, and the next two as well, nestled in Tempest's hoard of cushions with them. His limbs added a comfortable weight to Akieryon's slumber. Softly, he kissed Akieryon awake in the mornings. It was nice.

"He's never had his own tent," Tempest said while Akieryon frowned over his wings, now grown large enough to attempt some basic gliding. "He bunks in with whoever will have him."

"In any sense of the word," Akieryon surmised. "I think his blood has made your wings grow faster. I told you he's a dragon."

"He'll never agree with you. He hears dragon and he thinks Rathin." Tempest stretched his wings experimentally. "Now what?"

Akieryon pushed his own wings from energy to matter. "Do as I do." For the next hour he guided Tempest through a series of exercises to stretch and strengthen his wings.

When he thought Tempest was ready, Akieryon closed his eyes and focused on a familiar destination: The Canyon of Tears in the

Ninth Sphere of Hell. He visualized it, stretched out for its solid, earthy energy, and pictured a doorway in his mind. When the images aligned, he reached through.

"Teach me that." Again, Tempest sounded hungry. Opening his eyes, Akieryon smiled at him.

"Flight first. Travel between Spheres later."

Akieryon watched Tempest take in their surroundings. The canyon looked much the same as it had on Akieryon's last visit, more than five centuries ago. The sandstone walls, banded in shades of rust, wept salt in fat white glittering bulbs. Wind and rain had weathered caves and towers of the rock. Far below, scrubby trees clustered along the canyon floor. He wondered if Master Seikhiel still brought cadets here for their first glimpse of Hell.

And wasn't it strange, that life should take this turn?

"You're smiling." Tempest sounded pleased. Akieryon took his hand.

"I was just thinking how I'm using my training as a Demonslayer to teach you how to be a demon."

Tempest stretched his wings against the strong canyon winds. Akieryon selected a long ledge on the opposite wall, and he demonstrated an easy glide. Tempest watched, then followed without hesitation. Akieryon's eyes narrowed in suspicion. Sure, the winds here were favorable for gliding, but that looked too easy.

He leaned forward, and he sniffed. Voidspace.

"You used magic for that."

Tempest shrugged. "A little course correction."

"Fine," Akieryon said. "But we're going to practice until you can do without the magic."

"I won't need to."

"Irrelevant. We're building muscle memory, which you do need if you're going to learn actual flight." Akieryon extended his wings, white feathers shimmering in the sunlight. "Again."

They practiced gliding for almost an hour and a half before Akieryon decided they had made acceptable progress for the day. He opened the way back, and he gave Tempest a wry smile.

"I'd say you'll be sore tomorrow," he said, "but that's not true, is it?"

Tempest grinned at him.

For a week they practiced gliding at the canyon. Finally Akieryon decided that Tempest was ready for real flight. He brought them through to the Ninth Sphere, and he froze. Someone else was there.

She sat on an outcropping of ruddy sandstone, her long brown legs hanging in the empty air. She wore her loam-dark hair in a couple dozen braids, which she had gathered into an overhand knot at the base of her neck. Her tawny wings she had tucked close against her back, where she carried two long, curved swords with garnets gleaming in the pommels. Akieryon's breath caught.

"I was wondering when you were gonna show up."

Akieryon managed, somehow, to find his voice. "Screams?"

She sprang to her feet and whirled with surprising agility, her deep brown eyes widening, cat-slit pupils narrowed in the midday sun. "Thinks-Too-Deep? You're *alive?*"

"Against the odds." Akieryon opened his arms for the hug he knew would nearly knock him off his feet. "It's good to see you," he murmured against Screams' hair.

Tempest cleared his throat. Grinning, Akieryon extricated himself most of the way out of his old friend's embrace.

"Screams-Like-Death," he said, "this is Tempest. My path-mate."

Screams sniffed. "A dragon, eh? This why I never saw you with a suitor of your own kind?"

"Not exactly." Akieryon smiled. "Tempest was human until a few days ago."

"And yet he reeks of magic."

"That's not new."

"Flatterer," said Tempest.

Screams sized them up. "You're not planning to come back to town with me, are you?"

Akieryon shook his head. "I can't right now. And I'd appreciate it if you didn't tell Summons-His-Blade that you saw us." It pained him not to visit old friends, but he could not risk discovery. Not until Tempest had squared matters with his demon sire.

"Done something naughty, have you?"

"Not yet," Akieryon lied. "What can you tell us about Prince Baleirithys of the Fourth Sphere?"

Screams gave him a wary look. "You're not taking on the Scion of Evil."

That was a bit dramatic. Akieryon pulled a face. "That's what they call him?"

"Eh." Screams shrugged. "Mostly in places where his father ruined everything. Which is most of the Fourth Sphere." She jabbed a finger in Akieryon's chest. "The kid's trying to fix things, so don't cock it up."

Akieryon stood his ground, but only just. "It's not up to me," he said, gesturing at the Lineage Mark sprawling across half of Tempest's face. "It's a family matter."

Screams looked at Tempest, and her lips peeled back in a grin that had too many teeth. "Well this is a first," she said, with the sort of relish that said *Run!* "Just wait until I tell Keeps-A-Piece that the *Blood Prince of Seyzharel* has a Mortal-Born! *And* he dresses like a stage assassin," she added smugly.

Akieryon grimaced. The sun had warmed the canyon, and the winds picked up, whistling in the depths. "Could you maybe keep it to yourself, just for a little while? No need to complicate a difficult situation further."

Screams rolled the thought around a bit, like tasting a fine wine. "I'll have to tell her you're not dead," she said at last.

"Fair enough. No Demonslayers, though."

"Oho, naughty naughty." Screams grinned broadly, her eyes glittering with delight. "A little side project here?"

Akieryon gestured at the canyon. "Right now, I'm teaching him to fly."

"Aye, and being too cautious about it." Screams looked to Tempest. "Am I right?"

Tempest, who had been observing her closely, raised his eyebrows and pretended otherwise. "A bit."

Giving him a broad, not-at-all-trouble grin, Screams-Like-Death stretched her wings wide against the afternoon wind. "Come on, kid," she said. "I'll show you some *real* flying."

"Kid?" Tempest repeated, caught between bemusement and a scoff. But Screams was already diving off of the cliff, and he happily followed her.

Akieryon sat down right where Screams had sat, and he

watched them: his old life and his new life, speeding through the twists and turns of the branching canyon, twirling like leaves on the air currents. He couldn't help but smile. He felt a warm blossom of contentment. Better than that, he felt certain that whatever the future may hold, it would bring many more sunny afternoons spent with people who made him smile.

Look, he told the past version of himself that still shivered in the darker corners of his mind. *We've made it. We're good now.*

He closed his eyes and he tipped his face toward the sun. He inhaled the clean, dusty scent of warm sandstone, tinged with a faint trace of some resinous plant.

Yes.

We're good now.

TYMIRIN

Screams-Like-Death managed to extract a promise that Tempest would come back to visit another time. He agreed to meeting more of the clan when they returned. Akieryon observed them with a wary sort of pleasure, thinking they must have had a lot of fun flying together.

"Next time," Tempest said, nudging Akieryon, "you're joining us."

"Yeah, maybe." But Akieryon smiled at the thought.

"No maybe. No excuses. You're flying with us." Screams hugged them both. "Come back soon. And *tell* me this time."

Akieryon smiled. "I will. I promise." Turning away, he started to feel for the familiar energy of the Mortal Realm. Tempest's hand on his arm stopped him.

"Teach me."

"You have to know where you're going to do it this way." Taking Tempest's hand, Akieryon interlaced their fingers. "Think of your destination. Picture it clearly. Sights. Sounds. Smells. *Feel* it, and reach for that feeling. Touch the energy. It should feel different to here."

"Got it," Tempest murmured, and Akieryon felt a faint vibration in Tempest's energy.

"Good. Now, take a little energy from there and a little energy from here, and tilt them until they align. Make it balance. Visualize a doorway, and step through."

Tempest stepped forward immediately. Akieryon wasn't ready. He stumbled, and Tempest caught him. "Like that?"

Akieryon looked around at the warmly lit interior of Tempest's tent. "Perfect." He made no move to step back out of Tempest's arms. "Now you don't even need me." He meant it as a joke, but the words stung as they came out. Akieryon let his head drop against Tempest's shoulder.

Tempest's arms tightened around Akieryon, and then his wings wrapped around him too. "Mine."

Akieryon nodded against Tempest's shoulder. *I love you too.* Words kept close in his heart. Words he would never say.

~⚬❧◆☙⚬~

The next morning, they set out for Tymirin. Jynn kissed them both silly before they left, adding a request that they "pass one along to that sexy Rathin."

"No," said Tempest, turning away. While he swung into the

saddle, Akieryon freed himself from yet another of Szearbhyn's suffocating hugs.

"Be safe."

Akieryon smiled. "You, too."

"Yeah, whatever." Szearbhyn boosted him up in front of Tempest. "If you're gone too long, I'll come looking for you."

"We don't want that." Akieryon twisted around to look over his shoulder at Tempest. "Let's get this done."

They made impossibly good time, hitting the Old Tymirin Road long before midday. It seemed they passed through a new town every quarter hour, and this time Tempest never stopped to chat with the locals. A glance at his face showed it set with stony determination. His eyes glittered like emeralds.

"Where are we?"

Tempest made a thoughtful noise. "We've just crossed into Tybexan."

"What are you doing?" Akieryon demanded.

"Traveling."

"I'm not an expert on Mortal Sphere geography," Akieryon said, "but I'm fairly confident we should not have left Davenz already. What magic are you using?"

"Just folding the road," Tempest said in a dismissive tone, as though everyone could bend space to his will. "I did want to be seen leaving Davenz, just in case. Now I want to try…" The balance of the world shifted, and the horse stepped from packed earth to pavingstones. The trees lining the road showed a riot of reds and golds.

"*Now* where are we?"

"Not too far out from Tymirin." Tempest sounded immensely pleased with himself. "If we keep up a decent pace," he added as though the horse had anything at all to do with their travel speed, "we'll arrive in time to have lunch with Sir Rynan."

Akieryon had stopped listening, his ears instead attuned to sounds drifting to them from ahead. Clattering, abrasive voices, and the unmistakable tension of something gone Wrong. He placed a warning hand on Tempest's arm.

Tempest gave him a brief squeeze, then slid from the saddle and led the horse the rest of the way up a small rise. On the road ahead, a man in a ring mail shirt and a blue tunic similar in style to the uniform Dani and her guards wore stood facing a half dozen men clutching an assortment of tools that could double as weapons —axes, billhooks, and the like.

"What ho, Daryn!" Tempest called out, and he trotted casually down the hill, leaving Akieryon and the horse to their own devices.

The armored man, Daryn, glanced their way, and his friendly, freckled face broke into a welcoming grin. "Tempest! You're back! These gentlemen of—Which militia did you say you're from?"

"Imperial Might!" called a voice from the back, and his fellows quickly shushed him.

"Right, those dickheads," Daryn said, his winning smile never faltering. "They seem taken with the idea that the best way to send a message to Her Majesty that they disapprove of her releasing occupied territories is to seize Copper's Mill."

"Mm." Tempest eyed the ragtag band, who squirmed before his scrutiny. "Common folk not getting their flour?"

"Not since yesterday."

"Shame." Tempest's tone remained philosophical, but Akieryon saw what everyone else had missed: his fingernails had, in the space of a minute or two, taken on a pointed, claw-like appearance. "Talks not going well?"

"We won't be intimidated!"

"Mm." Tempest tilted his head, bird-like. Dragon-like. "And what is it you're doing to the bakers? Intimidating them?"

Daryn coughed softly into one gloved hand. Akieryon held the horse well back, out of the splash zone.

"Our voice will be heard!"

"Sir Daryn." Tempest's voice had knives hidden in it now. "Is Her Majesty aware of this group's opinion?"

"Their representatives are pretty vocal about it every quarter."

"There, you see?" Tempest spread his hands out to his sides. The sunlight glinted on the edges of his claws. "She hears you. She knows. She simply disagrees with you. And in this big strong Empire you want, the lady with the dragon makes the rules, right?"

A general grumbling passed through the militia. One at the front of the group shifted his grip on his billhook.

"Right," said Tempest. His voice dropped deeper into his chest. "So, if we extrapolate that thought to its logical conclusion, then a dragon would be all that's needed to enforce someone's will, correct?"

Akieryon took a tighter grip on the bridle.

"This is a weird sort of 'might makes right' worldview?" Tempest prodded, clearly enjoying toying with his now-silent audience.

"S'not weird," someone mumbled.

"Right, then. What I say goes, and I say you dickheads need to go home." Tempest growled the last two words in the lowest depths of his vocal range, nearly vibrating Akieryon's back teeth. At the same time, his new wings shimmered into view, raised and ready for a fight.

The militia ran.

Letting his wings settle against his shoulders, Tempest turned and flashed his brightest, fangiest grin at his friend Sir Daryn. "Oh, yeah, and I'm a kind of dragon now."

Daryn looked him over, and he raised one eyebrow. "You might've led with that."

Tempest enjoyed driving the rest of the militia out of the mill. To Akieryon, he looked rather like a cat chasing creatures in a meadow. A few of them slunk away home sporting fresh claw marks, and Tempest rode into Tymirin contentedly sucking on his fingertips.

Akieryon peered around with interest. He had last seen Tymirin when he was still a cadet, some seven centuries ago. Now a sea of suburbs sprawled to either side of the river, a bustle of people and a riot of color. Beyond, the old city walls stretched austere and flawless, encircling the island just as they had hundreds of years ago. They rode across a lowered drawbridge, passing through an arch with the words *Yrrut sh'nesk Tymiri-En* cut deep into its apex. *Beyond lies the Sacred Dragon Isle.* Akieryon had always wondered about that. Which Sacred Dragon?

Within the walls, the city was built of stone and brick. Dragon iconography adorned absolutely everything. The buildings may have grown taller in the intervening years, but the layout of the streets remained the same: three broad avenues leading from the three gates to the Chandler's Market and the palace at its heart. In the old days, the keepers of flame and light had been the city's bankers as well. Did it still work the same way?

"Hasn't changed a bit," Tempest muttered. People swirled in and out of the Market, some busy and some merely sightseeing.

A man who stood a full head taller than most spotted them, and he shouldered his way through the traffic. He wore a bright scarlet tunic over the same style of ring mail that Sir Daryn wore. He was of middling years and middling complexion, and would have been utterly unremarkable if not for his height.

"You!" He pointed, and Tempest slid from the saddle with a rueful grin. "What trouble do you bring this time?"

"None but my good company. And him. He's trouble." Tempest gestured at Akieryon, who had dropped down to stand beside him.

"I can neither confirm nor deny that."

The unreasonably tall man scrutinized him. "Nah. He's a soldier."

"Why does everyone say that?" Akieryon complained.

"It's your posture." Tempest's tall friend winked. "Like a coiled spring, and perfectly in balance."

Posture. No one would ever say the same of Raaqiel.

Somewhere in the Market, a bell began to toll the hour.

Tempest grinned a sharp-toothed grin. "What's for lunch?"

The unreasonably tall man was none other than Sir Rynan, captain of the Tymirin Guard and Dani's old mentor. He saw the horse handed off to a groom he trusted, and then took them to a little shop wedged into the corner of the ground floor of one of the towering marble buildings lining the Market. Soon Tempest was contentedly demolishing an assortment of meat pies.

"The teeth are new," Sir Rynan commented, as though remarking how unseasonable the weather was.

"Newer than you think. Last-week new." Tempest took a long drink of sweet mint tea and volunteered no further information.

Akieryon picked at his own pie—some kind of poultry—and he watched them. Was Tempest being evasive for a reason? Wasn't Sir Rynan his friend?

"Where did you pick up your latest stray?"

"Crashed down from Heaven," was Tempest's cheerful reply.

Sir Rynan sat back, his arms folded across his chest. "We don't hear from you," he said pointedly. "Your king writes. So do Dani and Marek. You might be dead, but that they mention you from time to time. Why should I let you into the palace?"

Tempest shook his head. "I'm here to see Seth—"

"Of course you are."

"—and Rathin will want to see me."

Sir Rynan snorted. "Sure of yourself, aren't you?"

Tempest placed one hand on the table, palm up. Slowly, his claws appeared, not extending, not materializing, just joining this reality. "Yes," he said softly, his serious tone making Akieryon realize that he and Sir Rynan had been playing before. "I'm really very sure."

"What have you done to yourself?" Sir Rynan was also abruptly serious.

"I died. Again."

"Oh, is that all?"

Tempest shrugged. "I've spent the last week learning to fly. Just in case."

"Of course. Why not." Sir Rynan glanced at Akieryon, then looked to Tempest again. "Does your friend talk?"

"Not while I'm trying to figure out if you're actually angry," Akieryon said, and Sir Rynan chuckled, a sound like gravel at the bottom of a well.

"Fair enough. No, not really. Not really surprised, either. This one," he said, indicating Tempest with his own cup of tea, "turns up when he feels like it, stays as long as he likes, and kills whatever he thinks needs killing. Just like a cat."

"Fur-dragon," Akieryon said, smiling.

"What's that?"

"In Dragonish, the word for cat literally means fur-dragon."

Sir Rynan raised an eyebrow at Tempest. "Do you think Rathin knows that?"

"I don't know. Probably."

They would meet with this much-discussed Rathin eventually. Seth first, Tempest insisted. Sir Rynan paid for lunch and walked with them to Seth's private domain, which turned out to be the attic of the Royal Library. They entered through the front doors, passed the circulation desk, and threaded their way through maze-like stacks loaded with books of all kinds. Some books had faded, their covers almost illegible. Some still smelled of ink and glue. Pewter-colored cats lounged in the sunlight streaming in through tall windows. Everywhere Akieryon looked, hardwoods glowed with loving polish.

He felt right at home.

In the deepest corner of the library, nestled between two tall shelves of scroll cases, a staircase twisted tightly upward. Tempest led the way, his steps almost eager. Sir Rynan cut off any possibility of Akieryon retreating and losing himself among the books. The stairs passed through an upstairs storage space, and ended at a closed door. Tempest walked right through it, as though it were mere illusion.

"Normal people knock!" Sir Rynan called after him.

Akieryon lifted his hand to knock, and then he felt the peculiar magical resonance of the wood. "I see!" He pushed his hand forward, expecting to meet resistance at some point. Rather, the effect was something like standing on a deadfall. The wood caught him and pitched him through to the room beyond. He stumbled to a stop and stood blinking, trying to get his bearings.

The attic stretched the length of the library, with the space informally divided using shelves and workbenches. At the center was an open area, with a circle carved into the floorboards. A bucket of chalk and a box of candles stood nearby. Everything had a vaguely cluttered, in-active-use sort of appearance.

"Hm?" A honey-toned voice carried in the open space. "Now what have you brought me?"

Several strides farther ahead now and not slowing, Tempest gave a fond shake of his head. A flicker of movement drew Akieryon's eye. A tiny dragon launched itself from the top of a bookshelf, and Tempest held up one arm like a falconer.

"Cay, you old bookwyrm, how are you?"

The tiny dragon Cay arrested his flight mid-dive. Hissing, he swooped into a heap of boxes beneath the nearest workbench.

"Oh, dear, what have you done this time?" A lean man of perhaps Sir Rynan's age materialized out of the clutter and peered at Tempest through a pair of gold-rimmed spectacles.

Tempest shrugged. "I died again."

"Stop doing that. You've upset my brother." The man, Seth, started to pace around Tempest when he glanced toward Akieryon. "What—!" His hand flew up to shield his eyes, and he ripped the spectacles off. "What are you?" Tempest forgotten for the moment, he trotted over to circle Akieryon. "You're positively radiant!"

"Um…"

"Isn't he gorgeous?" Tempest sounded smug and possessive. Seth ignored him.

"Are you… corporeal?" He extended a cautious hand, which Akieryon clasped just to watch him flinch. "Amazing!"

"Akieryon," Tempest said, doing a poor job of concealing his amusement, "meet Sethian K'varaz, an actual sorcerer."

"He downplays his own skills," Seth said to Akieryon. To Tempest, he added, "Don't think you're not next, you upstart. Yes, Sir Rynan, come in!"

Sir Rynan peered around the door. "Nothing blowing up in here?"

"Not today, old friend."

Akieryon pointed. "What kind of magic is that on the door?"

"That? Nothing, really. Just a little trap for wandering supernatural entities. They like to eat my supplies, you know. What are you?"

"Manners," muttered Tempest, which seemed a delicious irony.

Akieryon glanced between Seth and Sir Rynan. "It's safe?" he asked Tempest, who nodded. Akieryon pushed his wings from energy to matter. Seth gasped, a sound of pure delight.

"Don't touch."

Seth jerked his hand back and shot a halfhearted glare toward Tempest. "I've only seen lesser angels," he said.

"Spirit-Forms," Akieryon corrected gently. "They're not lesser. They just dwell closer to your world." And have no access to physical bodies.

"Fascinating. You'll have to tell me all about it. You." Seth rounded on Tempest. "Show me."

Tempest grimaced faintly. Then, stepping into a slanting sunbeam, he showed his full dragon form. His wings had grown larger, Akieryon noted, and the little horns at his temples were about as big as the end of his thumb. Beneath the workbench, Cay hissed and made a rattling sound.

"Hush, you. You're far too small to eat." Stepping fearlessly forward, Seth pressed one thumb against Tempest's lip and pushed it upward, revealing the full length of one fang. "Hm. Blood-drinker teeth?" Not waiting for a response, he touched one finger to Tempest's forehead, right where the Ferryman had touched him. "Your magic is stronger."

Tempest lifted his wings a little. "Dragon things."

"So I see." Seth stepped back, folding his arms across his chest. "What kind?"

"Seyzharel. It's a Hell Sphere."

It's *in* a Hell Sphere. Akieryon fought with almost physical agony against correcting the minor inaccuracy. He ground his teeth and clenched his fists, and he watched Seth turn abruptly away and start rifling a bookshelf.

"Demon dragon? Dragon demon? Which is correct? Are you South's progeny? No, of course you wouldn't know that. Cay, where did I put that treatise on the dragons of Hell?"

Cay made a bitter, warbling little growl from beneath the workbench, and Seth sighed.

"No, you don't have to come out. Just tell me where you saw it last."

"Sorry," Akieryon interrupted, taking a tentative step forward, "but you know about the Cardinal Dragons?"

Seth froze and stood blinking at him. "Well... doesn't everyone?"

"They're myth," said Sir Rynan. "Aren't they?"

Seth grinned at him, before resuming his search. "My dear friend, what is a myth but a truth dressed up for a fun evening out? And no, the answer to whether or not they exist is not Yes or No, it's a great big We Don't Know, and isn't that exciting?"

Akieryon bit down on another reply. The humans didn't need to know. A little mystery was good for them.

Tempest caught his eye, and tilted his head, a question. When Akieryon made no reply, he said, "I'll tell you everything I know so far about being a dragon."

Seth paused, his hand on a dusty scroll. "For what price, my boy?"

Tempest scuffed one foot on the worn floorboards. "Not a price. A favor. I need to confront the demon who did this to me. He's an unknown variable, proven to be volatile, and I don't know how powerful he really is."

Seth leaned against the shelf and folded his arms across his chest. He waited, his eyebrows raised, expectant.

Tempest shifted his weight, and he gave Seth an awkward, hopeful little smile.

"May I have some blood?"

ISLE OF DRAGONS

Rathin could not join them that afternoon, which Tempest said was fine. Akieryon wondered what duties could keep an Imperial Dragon occupied. Tempest sat at one of the workbenches and described their encounter with Baleirithys for Seth. He described dying, which Akieryon tried not to hear, but heard anyway, and he described the transformation afterward.

"It's all a little muddled," he confessed, "and fading fast, but that's what I do recall."

"It's fascinating." Seth glanced up, then looked back to his scribbled notes. He had exchanged his gold-rimmed spectacles for a pair with one smoked lens. "Go on."

Cay had emerged from his shelter of boxes just far enough to snuffle at Tempest's boots. When Tempest glanced down, he yelped and bolted for cover again. Tempest sighed. "He used to like me," he said to Akieryon.

"He still likes you. He's just alarmed, and he'll get over it." Seth jabbed his pen at Tempest. "Talk."

Tempest shifted a little, and Akieryon thought he had never seen him less confident. He was anxious about what Seth would think? Really? "Magic is different now," he said quietly. "It feels different. Smells different. Tastes different." He met Akieryon's questioning stare. "*You* taste different."

Akieryon blushed, and Seth snorted behind one hand. "Different how?" he prompted, and Tempest shook his head.

"Like… the difference between having a stuffed nose and not? Everything is clearer. Richer. Brighter. And I can do spells without really thinking about it now. Just, I want a thing and I do it."

Akieryon felt a leaden certainty that he ought to discourage that sort of behavior, but casual use of magic was so deeply ingrained in Tempest's personality that he lacked the heart to do so.

"Tell me about the blood."

Tempest frowned at the empty cup in front of him. "I don't really taste it. The blood, I mean. I mostly taste the magic in the blood. Everyone's tastes different, but it all… tingles? Fizzes? That's not quite right. It has a taste that's also a feeling."

Seth scribbled notes furiously for a long moment. Then he produced a glass vial and held it out to Tempest. "A venom sample, if you please."

Tempest glanced at Akieryon. Akieryon butted against his shoulder and reminded him gently, "Up and forward." Tempest gave the vial a wary look.

A minute later, he was bent forward over the workbench, silently gagging. Without looking, he passed the vial of spit and venom to Seth. Akieryon wrapped an arm around Tempest, hugging him tight while glaring at a very chagrined sorcerer.

"That's… foul," Tempest managed. He wiped a faintly trembling hand across his mouth.

Seth rummaged in his pockets and produced a packet of waxed paper. "Licorice," he offered. "You hate it."

"I do." Tempest shoved a handful of licorice in his mouth. Almost instantly, the tension eased out of his shoulders. He leaned a little, pressing his whole side against Akieryon. "I'm glad Sir Rynan didn't stay to see that."

"You know he would pretend he hadn't seen." Seth held the vial up to the light, and closed first one eye, then the other. "I appreciate you. You know that, right?"

"You'd better." Tempest found Akieryon's hand under the table and gave it a squeeze. Seth's shrewd gaze followed the movement anyway.

It struck Akieryon that he could no longer touch Tempest's emotions, not since he'd ceased to be human. Seth though… Seth's pride and affection glowed warm and bright as new copper. It took all of Akieryon's willpower not to wrap himself in it. He wanted to roll in it. He sat with his chin in his hands, his eyes half closed, basking.

"Akieryon."

He blinked and straightened. Both Tempest and Seth were looking at him in that way that meant he hadn't noticed someone speaking to him. "Hm?"

Seth smiled a smile that was probably meant to look pleasant and persuasive. "What are you doing?"

"Oh. Um. Just…" Akieryon fumbled for words, as though he had been caught doing something wrong. "Sensing. Sensing emotions." His face had never felt so hot. Was he being unforgivably rude? Did Seth hate him now?

"Huh." Seth's eyebrows twitched a little higher. "Is that a common talent?"

"Not where I'm from," Akieryon said. Wincing inwardly, he looked to Tempest, but Tempest's eyes gleamed with amusement.

"He's going to want to study you."

"Oh, no," Akieryon said. "No, let's give him my brother instead."

Tempest's surprised laugh echoed the length of the attic. "That's the worst plan!"

"I know."

Seth glanced between them, and a slow smile warmed his

shrewd features. "Keep him," he said to Tempest. "Promise me. If you don't, I'll find a way to punish you."

"He's mine," Tempest said simply.

"Path-mate," Akieryon mumbled, blushing again.

"Good." To Akieryon, Seth said, "Keep making him laugh. It's good for him."

"I do my best."

"You make me sound positively dour," Tempest complained. Seth ignored the remark.

"Don't fuck it up," he said instead. "I'll know. And I'll find you and smack you."

"I could fuck it up a hundred years from now," Tempest said, just to be contrary. "You'd never know."

"I would know. And I would find a way to smack you."

Tempest considered. "Maybe." But he smiled.

The conversation rolled onward, Tempest explaining more of his experience as a dragon. The three of them passed a pleasant afternoon together, and then a page came to fetch Seth. He gave them an apologetic look, but Tempest shrugged.

"I still know the way to my room."

"Yeah, about that." Seth jabbed an accusing finger at him. "I have to open it once a month so it can be aired out."

This was apparently amusing. All the way out of the attic,

Tempest chuckled softly to himself. Akieryon followed him from the library through a warren of servants' passages, where nobody seemed to pay much attention to them. Even so, Akieryon kept glancing over his shoulder. He felt like they were being watched.

Tempest veered abruptly to the side, and he slid open a panel of wall. Beyond lay a tiny alcove nestled behind a tapestry. Taking Akieryon's hand, Tempest tugged him out of the passageway, out of the alcove, and into a corridor.

This was... more opulent than Caspar's castle. Gilt swirled along the edges of everything. Tapestries and portraits took up most of the wall space. At the end of the corridor, colored window panes threw rainbows on the floor. Akieryon looked at Tempest, who had stopped before a closed door. The smell of voidspace hung thick in the air.

"*How* much magic did you do to this poor door?"

Tempest grinned a little sheepishly. "I was a paranoid adolescent with very little clue how to behave like a human." He touched the door. It hummed with energy for a moment, then swung open.

"Yeah," Akieryon said, following him through the doorway, "but you chose to leave it that way."

The room beyond looked comfortable, but nothing like Tempest's suite in Davenz. The single bookshelf was half empty.

The bed looked large enough for both of them. A narrower, open door revealed a fairly small bathroom. Tempest gestured, and the tub began to fill. Akieryon peered around with interest.

"Have you been using magic to retrieve books?"

"Come over here," Tempest said, sounding amused. He touched Akieryon's sleeve, and then Akieryon's coat was in his hand. He gave it a shake and draped it over a chair. Akieryon looked at him, considering whether he should say something or not.

"That was more casual than usual."

Tempest shrugged. "Just getting the hang of this dragon thing." He might even have been telling the truth. His fingers came to rest on the buttons of Akieryon's shirt. "You seem to be getting along with my old friends." It was almost a question. Not quite. Was Tempest concerned?

"Cay was a surprise. I can't work out why my translation spell doesn't work on him."

"No one's does." Tempest gave an awkward little half shrug. "Only Seth can really understand him. You have to learn his body language, mostly."

"I like Seth," Akieryon announced, and Tempest visibly relaxed. Then he ruined it by adding, "I feel like I just met your dad."

Tempest scoffed and turned away. The tub stopped filling, and he began to strip out of his clothing. "I don't have a dad." His voice sounded strained. Akieryon lightly touched his back, but he stepped away into the bathroom.

"I'm not convinced you don't have two," Akieryon muttered.

"What was that?"

Shaking his head, Akieryon went to sit on the chair while Tempest climbed into the bath. He felt the awkwardness of the moment too acutely. Clearly Tempest had never noticed Seth's paternal feelings toward him. Should he elaborate, or should he let the matter lie?

"Hey," Tempest called from the bath. "Are you coming in here or what?"

Akieryon's head snapped up. Torn between *You're not angry?* and *Isn't that a bit cramped?* he settled on: "What?"

"Come here."

Hesitantly, Akieryon stood. "Why?"

The note of caution in his voice clearly amused Tempest. "I want to show you something."

"I assure you, I've seen you in the bath before."

Tempest laughed, and suddenly everything felt normal again. Akieryon stepped into the bathroom. Tempest beckoned, his eyes sparkling like emeralds.

"What—?"

Reaching out, Tempest took Akieryon's hand and placed it on the edge of the tub. Immediately, the bath seemed to triple in size. Tempest grinned up at him.

"You made a secret giant bathtub." Really, he shouldn't be surprised. "Why?"

"Jynn and I were teenagers in this town."

Well, yes, that did explain rather a lot.

Tempest tilted his head, an invitation. "Come on," he said.

Smiling, Akieryon reached for the buttons of his shirt.

~ ༄ ❖ ༄ ~

They stayed in for the evening, and morning found them curled together in the bed where Tempest had slept more than a decade ago. Akieryon lifted his head and peered blearily at the unfamiliar surroundings. Something was off, but his drowsy brain failed to identify what. His hand resting on Tempest's chest, he pushed himself up onto one elbow. Nothing was out of place, not that the room had much in it to displace. The bathroom door stood ajar, their clothes littered the chair and the floor, and—

"Don't startle him."

Akieryon frowned at Tempest, who still looked like he was asleep. Then a faint flicker of motion drew his attention to the single narrow window. There, on the outer sill, Cay pushed his nose against one corner of the glass. Akieryon's surprised laugh did indeed startle him. He fell backwards from the window, dropping out of sight for a moment before circling around and beating his wings against the glass.

"He's curious," Tempest said, still feigning sleep. "But he won't approach me directly."

"Because you're a bigger, badder dragon."

"Yep."

Akieryon relaxed again, resting his cheek on Tempest's stomach, and he watched. Cay alighted on the windowsill again, and began picking at the edge of one pane with his tiny claws. "Should I let him in?"

"Not now. He's not used to you yet, so he'll just flee." Tempest cracked one eye open. He moved one hand slowly, raking his fingers through Akieryon's hair before tracing his jawline and tilting his face upward. "Come here."

The soft rumble in Tempest's voice sent shivers chasing through Akieryon's body. He scooted into the crook of Tempest's arm. "Wherever you want me."

Tempest's fingertips skimmed down Akieryon's back, raising goosebumps all the way down. "I always want you. I thought you'd have noticed by now."

Akieryon's heart stuttered over itself. "Always?" The word

came out somewhere between a squeak and a gasp.

"Well, I'm not always paying attention to it, but yeah. You're delicious. You're fun. Jynn's right that you're the hotter twin." A twinkle of mischief gleamed in Tempest's barely-open eye. "And you make the most fantastic sounds when I bite you." With the speed of a striking snake, he rolled to pin Akieryon beneath him. Akieryon had barely managed a gasp when fangs sank into his shoulder, turning the gasp to a groan. His body arched upward, pressing against Tempest, aching for more.

"You're…" Akieryon's tongue flicked out, moistening his lips as though that could force the words out. "You're pretty good at hi-hiding it."

Tempest's hand moved over Akieryon's hip in a firm, hungry caress. "It's not relevant when we're not alone," he said matter-of-factly. Leaning in, he nipped at Akieryon's lower lip.

A knock at the door startled them both. Tempest's fang snagged Akieryon's lip, and the warm, metallic taste of blood bloomed between them. Tempest's tongue probed gently at the scratch, and his gaze slid to the side, but otherwise he held unnaturally still. Akieryon glanced at the door, then, remembering Cay, he looked to the window, met the little dragon's curious stare, and blushed hotly.

A card slid beneath the door.

Tempest flopped over onto his back and extended one hand. When Akieryon looked, the card dangled from his fingers. "Lunch invitation," he grumbled.

Akieryon nestled against his side and reached for the card, but Tempest seemed not to notice. He lay still, staring at the ceiling. "Tempest." With a fingertip, he tilted Tempest's face toward him. "What is it?"

"Lunch," Tempest repeated. He closed his eyes. "With Rathin."

Akieryon wished he could still touch Tempest's emotions. He wished he could know what Tempest was feeling right now, faced with the immediacy of showing the Imperial Dragon that he too was now of dragonkind. Tempest had grown up here. Rathin had clearly had some kind of formative influence. Akieryon shifted a little, pressed his ear to Tempest's chest, and listened to the steady beating of his heart.

"What are you doing?"

"Moral support?" Tempest probably wouldn't believe that. "Are you upset?"

"No. Well, a little." Tempest huffed an annoyed breath through his nose. "I can't be in the mood while thinking of Rathin."

Akieryon swallowed a laugh. "Anyway," he said, "Cay is still watching us."

"Yeah, I don't care about him though."

"You do care!" Akieryon prodded him gently in the ribs. "You were hurt that he was afraid of you!"

"I've known him a long time." Tempest shrugged. "I don't want to scare him. Not just by existing near him." He lifted his head to meet Cay's curious stare. "He's being a creep, though, if he really wants to watch us."

Akieryon sat up. "What's his deal, anyway? Seth calls him brother."

"He is Seth's brother. He used to be human."

Akieryon squinted at Cay. The little dragon was somewhat smaller than the average moggie. "I don't mean to be rude," he said, "but how?"

"How what?" Tempest spread his hands to the sides like a complete jackass. "It's apparently not that hard to make a human into a dragon."

"He's a lot smaller than a human," Akieryon pointed out. "Is he extraordinarily dense?"

"Only when he chooses to be."

"You know what I mean," Akieryon said, annoyed.

"I don't really know what Seth did with his excess mass," Tempest mused, his tone suggesting that he had never given the matter any thought.

"*Seth* turned him into a dragon?" Akieryon looked to the

window again. Cay tilted his head, observing intently.

"Mm." Tempest pushed up onto his elbows, making eye contact with the subject of their conversation. "Human Cay made some very stupid choices, and committed a little bit of treason along the way. He was scheduled for execution, but Seth convinced everyone that it was better justice for Cay to live out his days with all the autonomy of the average pet."

Akieryon considered, his gaze tracking every tilt of Cay's head, every twitch of his wings and flick of his tail. "It beats prison, I'm sure."

"Definitely. He wants me to open the window," Tempest added as Cay began to pick at the corner of one pane again.

"Not afraid of you any more?"

"He's still afraid." Tempest gestured, and the window eased open just a crack. "But he's more confident that I'm not going to eat him."

Akieryon looked at Cay, who tilted his head and peered back at him. Justice. What punishment would have been just for stripping the flesh from Master Seikhiel's leg? Perhaps Seth would know the answer, if he but asked.

Akieryon climbed out of bed. Cay startled, circled around, and alighted again on the windowsill. Tempest shifted just a little.

"The trunk by the bookshelf."

"What?" Akieryon peered around, noticing the trunk for the first time. It was small, and battered, and the lock appeared to have broken some time in a previous century. Akieryon knelt, and he opened it with caution. The hinges made no sound.

Within, he found his best clothes.

"Showoff," Akieryon said fondly. Reaching into the trunk, he selected a linen shirt with blackwork cuffs, and a comfortable pair of trousers. Tempest's soft chuckle followed him into the bathroom. It was fine. They were fine. They were going to have lunch with the Imperial Dragon. No big deal.

He wondered, just a little, whether this was the sort of situation that required diplomacy. Did he represent Demonslayers? Or, more broadly, angels? Or was he simply here as Tempest's friend? His path-mate? Akieryon's brain spun in place over these questions while he washed up and dressed.

When he emerged from the bathroom, he found that Tempest had not moved. Cay, however, clung to the very end of the bed, picking fastidiously at his claws while pretending not to observe Tempest. Akieryon grinned.

"I see you've won over one dragon."

"Not quite," Tempest said, "but we're getting there."

Akieryon nodded. He extended one hand for Cay to inspect, just as he might do for a cat or a dog. Cay sniffed cautiously, then recoiled with a clicking chatter of disapproval. "Do I smell funny?" Akieryon asked him. "Or do I just smell too much of Tempest?"

Cay gave him a reproachful glance, then burrowed into a fold of blanket.

"It's probably that second one." Tempest sat up, startling Cay, who shot out of the blanket and under the bed. When Tempest remained still for long enough, Cay poked his nose out and made a tiny, trilling noise. Tempest grinned. "No, I don't have any food in here. You'll have to go bother the kitchen staff."

Akieryon could easily imagine what kind of mischief Cay might cause in a busy kitchen. He studied the little dragon, who cringed into the shadows when Tempest stood and crossed to the battered old trunk. "It's fine," he said in a soothing tone for Cay, but the words were for himself. Everything would be fine. After all, they were among friends here.

Weren't they?

Akieryon thought of Tempest's reaction to the invitation, and he could not quite banish a whirl of anxiety.

DRAGON THINGS

An impeccably dressed steward led them to meet the Imperial Dragon. Rathin waited for them in a lavish solar, where the sunlight streaming through the tall windows haloed him in golden light. Plush rugs and velvet cushions littered the space, but Akieryon scarcely spared them a glance.

Rathin was lovely.

Objectively, Akieryon knew that Imperial Dragons were full shapeshifters. They could take on the likeness of any sapient creature they chose. Knowing it and seeing it were two separate matters. Standing there in the midday sun, Rathin looked perfectly human, and yet somehow *more* than human. It made no sense. Akieryon wanted to study him.

What would make a dragon in human guise choose to have a beard?

Upon seeing them, Rathin crossed immediately to Tempest and pushed his hair out of the way. His eyes narrowing, he inspected the new horns at Tempest's temples. Tempest and Rathin shared the same olive and raven coloring, but it seemed more on Rathin. His skin almost glowed with unnatural warmth. His hair and his beard ought to have had a rainbow iridescence.

"Hm." Rathin finally stepped back, still appraising Tempest. "How many days?"

Tempest shrugged. "Just over a week."

"Blood-drinker?"

Tempest nodded. "Seyzharel."

"South," Rathin said. He gestured to a table, which Akieryon had not noticed before. Four places were set, and platters of meats and fruits filled most of the space between. "Join me."

Akieryon glanced at Tempest, who was already taking a seat at the table. He followed in sort of a numb daze. No one acknowledged his existence. They were entirely on dragon time now.

Rathin plucked a quarter of an apple from a tray. "You want blood," he said, a flat statement. "Persuade me."

Tempest placed his hands flat on the table, palms up. The fresh scar caught the light, twin starbursts slashed with lightning. "The Seyzharel prince did this to me," he said. "He was irrational. Reactive and unthinking. He bit me."

Rathin drew a sharp breath through his teeth. He knew what that meant.

"I don't know if he's sick," Tempest continued, his voice quiet. Controlled. "I don't know if he's unstable. I just know that I need to protect my own. I can't leave this a question hanging over us forever. I must confront him."

Rathin chewed slowly, his gaze calculating. "You always were a bit of a dragon," he said at last. "And more than a little feral."

Tempest inclined his head in acknowledgement.

"What will you do when you confront him?"

Tempest's lips twitched, but only just. An almost-smile. "That depends on him."

Rathin watched him in silence, the thick kind of silence that hangs heavy with possibilities. Then, arriving at a decision, he pushed a cut crystal glass across the table toward Tempest. The red liquid within shimmered with a faint iridescence. Where had that come from?

The door opened. Tempest took the glass of blood and drank quickly, as though he thought Rathin might snatch it back from him. A guard held the door, and a woman stepped through. She was...

Small. She was small. She likely stood no taller than Tempest's shoulder. A circlet set with a constellation of sapphires held her dark hair back from her grave oval face. Her eyes were too large, too wide-set, and the same blue as her sapphires. When she saw

Rathin, a weight seemed to lift from her. She ran to him and leapt into his arms even as he arose from his chair to greet her.

"Your Majesty," Tempest said, also rising from his seat. Akieryon stood as well, watching the encounter unfold.

"Tempest," said the Empress of Tymirin. "What a rare pleasure this is. And who have you brought?" After Rathin had ignored him so thoroughly, the Empress' attention startled Akieryon. He fumbled for a response.

"This is Akieryon," Tempest said before he could blush too much. "He's mine."

The Empress smiled at him, and implored him to call her Tarys, and Akieryon had a firm sense that she had borne many sorrows in her brief life. She was, he remembered, about Caspar's age. She looked so much more haunted. Perhaps every monarch needed a Tempest of their own.

Lunch was pleasant enough, after Empress Tarys arrived. Tempest seemed on edge, though, and he and Rathin watched one another with a certain dragonish wariness. It came as something of a relief when the Empress wished them a safe journey home and took her leave of them.

When Akieryon asked about her health later, in the sanctuary of Tempest's bedroom, Tempest grimaced faintly. "Cay thought it would benefit her to try to break the soul bond between her and

Rathin." When Akieryon sucked a sharp breath through his teeth, Tempest nodded. Soul magic was dangerous for most people. Perhaps Szearbhyn could excel at it. "Seth doesn't know if Tarys will ever fully recover."

Akieryon looked at the dragon-shaped indentation on Tempest's pillow. Justice.

"Cay's intentions were good," Tempest continued as he stripped down to his underclothes. "But his actions—"

"Could have killed them both."

Tempest nodded a slow nod. "Now," he said, "if you will excuse me, I am feeling quite drunk. I shall lie down for a while."

Akieryon watched as Tempest eased himself into bed and curled onto his side. Why did Rathin's blood make him feel drunk, when neither his nor Szearbhyn's had? Was this a quirk of dragonkind? Rathin descended from a different lineage, that much was certain. Which, he did not know. The Dragon of the West, perhaps? If only he could ask Lord Gabriel.

Shaking away the thought, Akieryon meandered to the half-empty bookshelf and tried to select something to read. None of Tempest's books of magic caught his attention, and so he decided on exercise instead. He took his time stretching. Then he spent a little over an hour working through combat forms, letting his body flow from one stance to the next, feeling the power and control in his muscles. It felt good, but it couldn't quite banish the nagging feeling that he was trapped here. He wasn't a prisoner. He could leave any time he wanted.

He just couldn't return without Tempest. Probably.

Akieryon stretched again, then sat down on the floor and closed his eyes. He was far too tense for proper meditation, but he could still exercise his senses. He felt the floor beneath him, solid, well-worn wood that hummed faintly with Tempest's magic. He touched the sunlight and the shadow and the steady warmth of magic all around. Extending his awareness a little more, he brushed up against the emotions of the people in the corridor as they hurried about their day.

Someone was worried, a lemon-pith tang.

Someone laughed like peppermint fizz.

Someone was lost in a candy floss sea of new love. Too sugary. Akieryon looked away.

A familiar copper warmth appeared, moving toward them. Akieryon came back to himself a little too swiftly, and sat blinking in the afternoon light. He dragged himself to his feet and stumbled over to Tempest.

"Seth's here."

"Nmff," Tempest said into his pillow.

Akieryon shook him gently. "Wake up."

"No."

"Are you sure?"

Tempest pulled the pillow over his head. The matter settled, Akieryon went and opened the door. Seth was just raising his hand to knock. He blinked at Akieryon.

"How did you know?"

As greetings went, Akieryon had had worse. He briefly considered what a lie would be worth in this situation, but discarded the notion. "I sensed your emotions."

Seth's curiosity welled up, the sweet dusty green of curing hay. "How?" Then, mastering himself, he peered into the room. "So Rathin consented."

Tempest mumbled something rude beneath his pillow.

Akieryon thought to offer Seth the chair, but he crossed to the bed and sat. Without a word, he yanked the pillow from Tempest's head. Tempest swore and squeezed his eyes tightly closed. Seth opened his hand, and a single drop of blood glistened on his fingertip. This he held beneath Tempest's nose. Tempest's eyes snapped open. Just as Akieryon opened his mouth to protest Seth offering blood from the flesh, Seth snatched his hand away.

"Here you are," he said in a businesslike tone. "Now, tell me about it."

Tempest curled back against the headboard, gathering the

pillows around him like a nest. He glared a little, but didn't seem invested in it. Seth merely sat at the edge of the bed, patience personified. Tempest sighed, and he began to speak.

"Rathin's blood hit me like a brick," he said, his voice a little subdued. "Harder than yours," he added, nodding to Akieryon. "And I doubt he's more powerful than you are, so that doesn't make sense."

"You're probably a different enough type of dragon that it matters," Seth said.

"Opposing lineages," Akieryon said, and Seth extended one hand in a gesture of agreement.

"Right. I'll worry about what that means later. When the rest of my brain is functional."

Seth nodded. And waited. Tempest rolled his jaw and frowned in concentration.

"It was fine for a minute. Zingy, like your blood," he said to Akieryon. "And then it hit me kind of all at once. Like sweet hard liquor, sort of. My head is still spinning a little." Tempest flexed his hands. "I feel like I could rip a hole through the world. Just a little."

He probably could, but Akieryon wasn't going to say so.

Seth leaned forward and lifted one of Tempest's eyelids with his thumb. "How do you feel? Physically?"

"Light. And… larger? Does that even make sense?" Tempest pushed Seth's hand away. "Almost feverish," he added, "and a little headachy. I definitely need more sleep."

Nodding, Seth moved Tempest's hair aside. "Ah, just as I thought. Your horns are bigger."

"So I'm getting more dragonish." Tempest sank down and pulled the blanket over his head. "Great. I'm going back to sleep now."

Seth gave Tempest's shoulder a brief squeeze, then smiled at Akieryon. "Come on," he said. "Let's get some supper."

~⚬↺◆↻⚬~

Akieryon had thought that having a meal alone with Seth might be awkward, but he turned out to be pleasant company. Also Cay showed up after about ten minutes, so they weren't really alone for long. Seth knew that he was the nearest thing to a parent that Tempest had. He also knew that Tempest would never acknowledge it. They spoke of other matters, of the wider world and Caspar's parliament, of Dani and Marek, of the Lenyr and the home Tempest had found there. Seth loved him in a way Akieryon had always craved. It was warm and constant and Akieryon wanted to wrap it around himself like a blanket.

"May I write to you?" Akieryon blurted on sudden impulse. Heat flooded his face, but Seth's smile could have warmed the deepest winter.

"I'd like that very much."

Akieryon basked in Seth's warmth. The conversation drifted, but the glow of love remained. After the meal, Seth walked Akieryon back to Tempest's door. There he stopped, and he turned, his expression grave.

"I'm glad Tempest has someone who loves him like you do," he said, startling unguarded words from Akieryon.

"I was thinking the same of you!"

Seth smiled. "Good. Let's be friends, then."

"Friends," Akieryon agreed, offering his hand, but Seth swept him up in a hug instead. Then, as though it hadn't happened, Seth opened the door and turned away.

"Good night, Akieryon."

Tempest was snoring softly in his pillow nest. Akieryon undressed and climbed into bed beside him. Immediately, Tempest wrapped an arm around him and pulled him close. Something inside Akieryon unclenched, and he found himself blinking away tears. This profound sense of belonging was almost more than he could bear. It was everything he had ever wanted. It ached in all the cold and lonely corners of his soul. He shivered, and Tempest pulled the blanket tight around them.

Akieryon drifted. Late into the night, Tempest's hand moving down his side in a firm caress dragged him out of slumber. He opened his eyes to the darkened room. When Akieryon stirred, Tempest gave a rumble of satisfaction and began to nip at his neck. Oh, *yes please.* Akieryon buried both hands in Tempest's hair—there was now a distinct texture difference near the roots—and guided him. Tempest surprised him with a brief, searing kiss before nibbling along his jaw. Desire burned through Akieryon's veins, and he twisted his body against Tempest's, begging for more, more, more. Tempest growled. The sound of it rippled through Akieryon, heightening every sensation, narrowing his focus to the hands on his body, the teeth grazing his collarbone, and the hot rush of breath across his skin.

"Please," Akieryon gasped, and he felt Tempest smile against his chest.

Morning found Akieryon twisted up in a complicated tangle of bedding. Groggy and cautious of several assorted aches and twinges, he sat up and squinted across the room. Tempest was humming under his breath as he got dressed.

"You're in a good mood." Akieryon's voice sounded rough and dry. No surprise there. He looked around for the inevitable glass of water that Tempest would have left somewhere nearby. "Were you planning to tell Seth that—"

"That Rathin's blood made me super horny?" Tempest scoffed. "Hell no. That's none of his business." He caught Akieryon grinning into the water glass, and he scowled an exaggerated scowl. "Oh you bastard."

"Definitely."

Tempest threw a pair of trousers at Akieryon. "Up," he said. "We have things to do."

"Then perhaps you should have let me sleep." Akieryon stood up and started to dress. Tempest gave him a wry look.

"Don't pretend you wanted me to stop."

"I absolutely did not want you to stop," Akieryon agreed, accepting the shirt Tempest handed to him. "Just don't expect me to move too quickly for the next hour or so."

Laughing, Tempest dug through the battered chest for outer layers. He selected a short velvet jacket for himself, and then produced Akieryon's beautiful blue coat. "Breakfast first," he said. "Then farewells."

"So soon?" With a twinge of sadness, Akieryon thought of the pleasant time he had spent with Seth. "Would it be okay if we came back sometimes?"

Tempest paused and turned to face him fully. "You like it here?"

"I like Seth," Akieryon said. "And I like Cay, and I wouldn't mind getting to know the others better." He watched Tempest with a creeping wariness. There must be a reason he didn't visit?

Tempest exhaled a noisy breath through his nose. "Fine," he said dismissively. "Travel is easier now."

Was that truly the only reason? Tempest focused his attention on buttoning his jacket. When he tipped his head forward, a startling flash of color caught Akieryon's eye. Coat in hand, Akieryon crossed to him. "Wait, hold still." He reached up and pushed Tempest's hair back, exposing the roots. They were a fierce blood red. Akieryon told him.

"No." Tempest strode to the bathroom mirror, then stood there for a long while, scrutinizing his reflection. Akieryon finished dressing before checking on him. Tempest crinkled his nose at himself. "I don't hate it," he said, sounding surprised.

"Monochrome no more," Akieryon teased.

Lightly, Tempest touched his crimson plumage. "It's… flat. The individual strands. They're not round."

"Feathers," Akieryon reminded him. "Tiny feathers that look like hair."

"It'll take some getting used to." Abruptly dismissive, Tempest turned his back on the mirror.

"It's time to go to Seyzharel."

PRINCE OF
SEYZHAREL

They collected the horse from the Guardsmen's stable after enduring a bone-crushing hug from Sir Rynan. Akieryon doubted he had earned a hug, but he accepted it anyhow. He was still wondering at it while Tempest secured the tack and led the horse toward the door. When he opened it, the early sun shone brightly in the courtyard beyond. When they stepped through, the morning mist in the Sinen orchard closed around them. Akieryon looked over his shoulder and saw the doorway fading behind them.

"Showoff," he said fondly.

The Lenyr greeted them with cheering and hugging and kissing and generally as much excitement as though they had been gone for two months rather than two days. Szearbhyn thoroughly checked Akieryon for damage, which was excessive and unnecessary. Jynn dipped him backward and kissed him dizzy, which was significantly more necessary.

After seeing his horse comfortably reunited with the Lenyr

livestock, Tempest announced that he had another short trip to make. Tor and Riol persuaded him to stay for lunch, which Akieryon was almost certain he meant to do anyway. No sense going to Seyzharel on an empty stomach. Tempest sat in the shade of one of the wagons and told Jynn that their friends in Tymirin were well, and he repeated it until Jynn believed him.

Akieryon paced the encampment. The time had come. In mere hours, he would bring Tempest to Seyzharel. In mere hours, he would see what had become of his friends there.

"Hey."

Blinking away dark thoughts, Akieryon looked up into his brother's face. When had Szearbhyn fallen into step beside him? He should have noticed.

"You don't have to do this," Szearbhyn said quietly.

"Of course I do—"

"No. I can take him."

Akieryon raised an eyebrow at his brother. "You hate the prince of Seyzharel."

"So much," Szearbhyn agreed amiably. "But you had friends there, right? Before the—the everything?"

Akieryon stopped walking. "You're trying to protect me."

Stuffing his hands in his pockets, Szearbhyn looked anywhere but at his brother. "I know you're in love with him," he said, "but you don't need to flay yourself for his sake."

"Szearbhyn." Gently, Akieryon took his twin by the shoulders. Reluctantly and with no small measure of wariness, Szearbhyn met his waiting stare. "I'm a Demonslayer—"

"Former."

"—and this is my actual job. I promise I can handle it."

Szearbhyn managed a small scoff. "No one's job should involve wrangling Tempest."

"It's not really Tempest I'm worried about." If Tempest fought Prince Baleirithys, if the prince died, would Tempest have to become the Anchor for the entire Fourth Sphere? That was a lot to ask of someone who had only been a demon for a week.

"I think you worry too much," said Szearbhyn, who had started this conversation by worrying about his brother.

Jynn came to fetch them for lunch. Szearbhyn stayed close by Akieryon's side until the time came for them to leave. He walked with Tempest and Akieryon away from camp, into the trees. There he fixed a firm scowl on his face, which he directed toward Tempest.

"I know you'll come back," he said pointedly. "Don't you dare come without him."

Tempest responded with a slow smile that didn't quite reach his eyes. "Why would you ever doubt me?"

It was time to go.

Akieryon took Tempest's hand, and he focused on the Fourth Sphere. He visualized the broad plains of Seyzharel, the towering cliffs, the tingle of magic carried on the breeze. It resonated in a particular way that made it difficult to align with the Mortal Realm. He closed his eyes, and he concentrated. When the balance was right, he stepped forward.

Silence fell like a blanket. Nothing stirred. Nobody laughed or called out. With a wrench of dread, Akieryon opened his eyes.

The plains were empty. Where once agriculture had supported a thriving dragon society, gentle ripples of low moss-grass stretched in every direction. The wind shivered in the fungal shrubs, but nothing wheeled in the skies. Dropping Tempest's hand, Akieryon slowly turned in place. There, some small distance down a packed dirt road, jagged walls jutted where he expected a city. Ruins, empty and abandoned. Turning again, faster, Akieryon searched the horizon. Nothing. Nobody. His hand covered his mouth to stop a cry of despair.

"Where…?" he gasped past his fingers. "They're all gone? All of them?"

And then he had unfurled his wings. And then he was in the air, and he was the only thing circling in the sky. The great cities of Seyzharel lay dead and empty. From above, he could see how the roads had suffered mild neglect, and in the distance the great black caravan of the Raven Clan crawled slowly across the plains. But no dragons. No dragons at all.

The wind ripped a sob from his throat as he crashed into a heavy landing. Tempest's hands steadied him, and Tempest's arms encircled him, holding him tight.

"What happened here?" Akieryon whimpered. He was shivering in the harsh sunlight. Everything was too still. Everything was too quiet.

"You can ask the prince," Tempest said grimly.

The prince. Of course. That was why they had come. Akieryon cast one last despairing glance at the ruins, at the bones of Seyzharel. "I don't understand how it could get so bad. A Demonslayer's most important job is maintaining the stability of the Spheres." He turned his gaze to the cliffs. There, the silhouette of Castle Seyzharel stabbed upward like a cluster of sharp teeth. That, at least, had not changed. "Come on," he said, stepping a little distance free of Tempest. "Time to fly."

"Why?"

"Because approaching a dragon stronghold unannounced by magical means is considered unspeakably rude, and often leads to mess."

"Ah." Tempest nodded. "So we save mess for later."

Akieryon led the way, though their destination was obvious. They approached from the east, keeping the sun ahead of them—it faded into late afternoon here—to make themselves as visible as possible. The castle, at least, looked in decent repair. Banners fluttered from the parapets, graceful spires stretched into the sky, and narrow walkways allowed foot traffic between towers.

"Whoa, what is that?" Tempest veered a little away from the castle as they brushed up against its defensive magic. The spell was as old as the castle itself, and had only grown in power since Akieryon's last visit.

"Wards." He pointed to a semicircular platform between the gate and the lift that brought flightless visitors up from the base of the cliff. "We land there."

As they circled around to land, six guards in smart blue and white uniforms gathered around the edges of the platform. A surge of relief swept over Akieryon. So there were dragons here after all. He hadn't realized that he had worried that he might find the castle as empty as the plains.

They alighted on the stone, and the guards all took a single step forward. The one nearest to the gate wore silver bands on his horns that indicated authority. Captain of the guard, most likely. Akieryon turned to address him, and recognized the face watching him with wary curiosity.

"Ynecii?"

Everyone looked to the captain, who shifted uneasily and settled his wings in a wider stance. Defensive. "Er, no. My name is Thanasc. You knew my father?"

Akieryon nodded. "Five hundred years ago," he said quietly. The guards exchanged glances that he didn't bother trying to decipher. His attention remained fixed on Captain Thanasc, whose gaze had flicked downward.

"Only Thrin's Dad was here at that time." He made *Thrin's Dad* somehow sound like that was the man's name. "State your business."

Akieryon gestured to Tempest. "I've brought a Mortal-Born—"

"We're here to see the prince," Tempest interrupted.

"I was getting to that," Akieryon complained.

Captain Thanasc cast an appraising eye over Tempest. He took in the little horns, and especially the crimson roots peeking out beneath Tempest's black hair. Then, apparently satisfied with what he saw, he nodded. "Follow me."

Two other guards fell in behind them as they followed Captain Thanasc through the massive gates. The interior of the gatehouse led to an even larger set of gates, and those opened into a paved forecourt. More guards appeared on the walls above, watching them with interest. Thanasc strode up the broad steps to the front doors. He never once looked over his shoulder. Akieryon looked around, but the only dragons he saw were all guards. Where were the civilians?

Captain Thanasc lifted one hand. He barely touched the doors, but they swung silently inward. The entrance hall was as grand and well-lit as Akieryon remembered, but so empty. No laughter echoed in the halls. No children practiced gliding from the grand staircase. A flicker of movement caught his eye, and he looked just in time to see a dragon who wore his plumage to cover half of his face melt back into the shadows, folded fabric clutched tight to his chest.

"What happened here?" Akieryon whispered. Speaking louder would have felt disrespectful, like shouting in a mausoleum. Yes, Szearbhyn had told him, but still it staggered him to see Seyzharel so barren.

Captain Thanasc gave him an incredulous glance. Then, shaking his head, he led them up the first sweeping arc of the staircase.

Akieryon knew the chamber where the captain left them. He had played chess with King Chaizhyn there. The blue mosaic floor and the tall windows remained the same, but the deep cushioned chairs and chess table were gone, replaced by a glass table and several narrow chairs that looked profoundly uncomfortable. The velvet curtains were a bit much.

Akieryon paced to the nearest window, which looked out over the forecourt. Three guards stood in a cluster near the gate, their heads bent in the universal posture of gossip. Talking about the visitors, no doubt.

"I don't like this."

Akieryon turned toward Tempest, who had unconsciously voiced his own thoughts. "Szearbhyn did say that Chaizhyn's son had wrecked their society, but I didn't expect..." He shook his head. This emptiness was almost too much. It reminded him of his imprisonment.

Tempest had frozen, his gaze fixing on the door. Akieryon moved silently to his side. When the door opened, he glimpsed one of the guards that had followed them, but only for a moment. Then Prince Baleirithys swept into the room, eclipsing all. Here, in his home, his lair, he was nothing like the half-feral creature from the woods. Here, he had *presence*.

Three layers of silks in shades of blue swirled with his every movement, enhancing the whip-thin lines of his body, adding grace to his already refined manner. His walk was a glide, his posture flawless, his wings just open enough to take up more than an ordinary dragon's share of the space. His crimson plumage gleamed in the afternoon light, framing him perfectly, not a feather out of place.

His gaze hardened and sharpened to cold obsidian when he saw them.

"Demonslayers are not welcome here."

Akieryon bowed low. "Blood Prince Baleirithys, Regent of Seyzharel—"

"You may go," Prince Baleirithys interrupted. "Now."

Tempest stepped in front of Akieryon. "He's mine," he said in that low growl that resonated deep in his chest, "and he stays until we're done."

Baleirithys' wings flared slightly, a flicker of a display of dominance, more instinct than choice. His eyes narrowed, and he tapped one claw—buffed to a glassy sheen—against his chin. For a long moment he stood in silence, taking measure of Tempest. Then, with a motion more like a leaf settling out of the wind than any action Akieryon would term *sitting,* he placed himself upon one of the chairs.

"Sit." He gestured one graceful hand in a vague acknowledgment of the other chairs. "Both of you."

Akieryon warily took a seat. Tempest remained standing for a moment more, watching Prince Baleirithys, and also the bespectacled dragon who had been been hidden from view by his lord's wing. He stooped down, his faintly reddish gold plumage obscuring his expression as Prince Baleirithys murmured something into his ear. Then he nodded, bowed with one hand over his heart, and removed himself from the room.

Prince Baleirithys watched Tempest with a cool expectation. Tempest watched him back, almost bristling, ready to deflect any attack. A faint smile curved Baleirithys' lips.

"Speak your piece."

Tempest kept his hands above the table in a nonthreatening position, but he spoke in even tones that almost came out forced through his teeth. "You came to my world and you killed me. What you intended is irrelevant. You owe me a life. Now you will leave me and mine alone." His eyes narrowed the barest fraction. "That includes Szearbhyn."

Prince Baleirithys contemplated him in silence, his eyebrows arching slightly at the mention of Szearbhyn. His lips pursed, and he tilted his head to one side, birdlike. "I do believe you are quite willing to fight me," he said at last, and Tempest tensed with the effort of not starting up from his seat. Baleirithys let his wings settle closer to his slim shoulders. A tiny smile crept across his face. "Welcome to the family."

"I—what?" Tempest visibly deflated.

"Your blood ties are to me," Prince Baleirithys said. "It is my right to claim you as my son and heir."

Tempest frowned. "Are you sure you want me? A week ago I was human. Kind of."

"Your words prove you dragon enough. And that you come here to confront me, bringing magic enough to breach my wards."

"I did nothing to your wards," Tempest said, a little defensive.

"No." Baleirithys' smile widened. "But you could have."

Tempest looked a little put out that this prince had the measure of him so easily. "Fine," he said. "Let's assume you're right about me. Won't it cause trouble for you to have a former human in your bloodline?"

"You're misunderstanding," Prince Baleirithys said smoothly. "You're of my lineage, whether I want you or no. Acknowledging you openly now will prevent more problems than it will raise." A faint frown creased his alabaster brow. "Do humans discard their offspring so easily?"

"Some do. Some don't. Humans aren't really easy to describe in general terms, except by spite and stubbornness."

"Good."

Tempest's eyebrows twitched upward. "Good?"

Baleirithys extended one arm in a sweeping gesture just as the door opened again. "You see here the survivors of horrors past. We are the stubborn ones."

An adolescent dragon slipped through the open door and

soundlessly closed it. Akieryon would have guessed he was a year or two shy of eighty, based on his slight frame and delicate stubs of horns, but his wide, haunted blue eyes and his lack of wings suggested that this youngster had seen more than his share of trouble. He carried a roll of parchment as though he had never held anything so precious in his entire life.

"Oh?" Prince Baleirithys turned an indulgent look upon the youth. "Where is Yrich?"

"Yrich had to be somebody else, my prince." The young dragon bowed low while presenting the parchment, which his lord took without much care at all. He unrolled it upon the table. From where Akieryon sat, it looked like a register of the royal lineage, some ten generations long.

Prince Baleirithys held up one hand, and the youth placed a glass stylus in his waiting fingers. "Now," Baleirithys said, leaning forward over the parchment, "your name is… Thembysth?"

Akieryon blinked. He had not expected Prince Baleirithys to remember a name he had only heard screamed in anguish. "Tempest," Tempest corrected mildly, emphasizing the *p* sound, then demonstrating how to form it. Baleirithys nodded and set pen to parchment. While he wrote, the young dragon produced an elegant wood box a little larger than two fists together. Baleirithys handed back the stylus and took the box. Placing the box on the table, he opened it. Within, nestled in a bed of velvet, lay Seyzharel's Seal of State.

Prince Baleirithys turned the Seal upright, letting it rest on its broad face. The Seal itself was too large for the lineage document, but apparently that didn't matter. Baleirithys pricked his thumb on his own fang, and dabbed his blood onto a small, raised design at the back of the Seal. Then he took the Seal in both hands, turned it over, and pressed the coin-sized imprint beside Tempest's name. Akieryon squinted, and saw that Baleirithys' own name had no such mark beside it.

Baleirithys placed the Seal of State back in its box, closed the box, and handed it back to the wingless young dragon. Then he passed him the succession document. "Thank you, Tharaiyelagh." Tharaiyelagh bowed again, then withdrew. When he turned, Akieryon saw that he wore the back of his two-tone plumage—the darker color—cropped short. How peculiar. Dragons did not often favor haircuts.

"How old is he?" Akieryon blurted without meaning to. Prince Baleirithys turned a cold stare upon him.

"Does that matter?"

"Not particularly." Warmth flooded his face. "It just surprised me to see him working." In the past, the youth of Seyzharel had enjoyed a fair amount of leisure.

Frowning, Baleirithys tilted his head. "What else should he be doing?"

"I was a bodyguard at his age," Tempest said. "More or less."

The door opened again, and a dragon with a scarf over his plumage brought in a silver tray with three glasses and a little crystal dish. He placed a glass of blood before his prince, and another before Tempest. The glass that he set beside Akieryon contained a clear and faintly purple liquid. The crystal dish he offered to Prince Baleirithys, who plucked one round white object from it before waving it toward his uninvited guests. The unnamed dragon smiled a little as he set the crystal dish near Tempest's glass. Tucking the tray beneath one arm, he bowed, and then he retreated. The bowl contained little cakes or biscuits, or something similar.

"It's not poison," Baleirithys said, and it was almost funny, in a terribly dark sort of way. He proved his point by taking a delicate bite of the little cake in his hand.

Tempest took one, and then slid the dish to Akieryon. It contained spiced almond cakes, he discovered when he picked one up and took a cautious nibble. They were just the right balance of sweet and buttery, clearly the work of a skilled baker. Prince Baleirithys waited until he had taken a larger bite before saying, "So you knew my grandfather." Akieryon promptly choked on crumbs.

"Over five hundred years ago, yes," Akieryon managed after a long gulp of his wine. It was made from ember berries of the Fifth Sphere, sweet and smoky.

Prince Baleirithys looked away out the window, to Seyzharel's barren skies. "You've found this place much changed."

"You have no idea."

Baleirithys made a small, thoughtful noise and sipped from his glass of blood. "You won't mention him to me," he said, "nor speak of those times in my hearing."

In a flash of clarity, Akieryon really saw the dragon before them: a prince never formally acknowledged, too young for a regent and grieving a Seyzharel he had never known. Little wonder he had unhealthy ways of dealing with stress. "Never again, Your Highness," he promised.

Prince Baleirithys lifted his glass and inclined his head.

HOME AGAIN

After their surprisingly pleasant conversation with Prince Baleirithys, Tempest opened the way out of Seyzharel. A little overwhelmed, Akieryon took his hand and stepped through. He stopped and he stood, bewildered by the familiar plush rug underfoot, the massive bed, the open door showing shelves and shelves of books.

"Davenz?" It was a relief, coming home to Tempest's lavish suite after silent Seyzharel. Akieryon felt strongly tempted to crawl under the blankets and stay there for several days.

"I need to tell Caspar everything," Tempest said, "before someone else does." He went to the antechamber, and he checked the complex water clock. "He'll be busy with parliament for a couple of hours yet. How do you feel about a nap?"

"A nap sounds *delicious.*" Akieryon was already shrugging out of his coat when Tempest returned. They tossed their outerwear aside and collapsed into Tempest's marvelous bed, where they curled together like cats. Like dragons. In this familiar, safe place, sleep came easily.

The sunset had painted rich hues across the sky by the time they stirred. Akieryon washed his face and went into the wardrobe for a clean shirt, and he stopped, scrubbed his eyes, and yelled for Tempest.

"Oh, yeah, those are yours," Tempest said, grinning down at the tall, shiny, charcoal-blue boots that stood beside his shelves of shirts and trousers. "I didn't know when they'd be ready."

"Gorgeous," Akieryon said, and Tempest preened.

They took their time dressing. When they had finished, Tempest led the way through familiar corridors, eventually letting them into the room where they had dined with Caspar and Dani on a summer evening that had made them Akieryon's friends. A memory of smoke still lingered, and Caspar's uncle was in a bottle on the mantelpiece.

They had just made themselves comfortable when the outer door opened. Caspar froze for half a second, and then he beamed like the sun and opened his arms wide. Akieryon hugged him gladly. Together, they dragged Tempest into the embrace.

When Caspar had hugged them to his own satisfaction, he pushed free and gestured at Tempest's cheek and brow. "What have you done this time?"

"I died again."

"Stop *doing* that," Caspar scolded. He waved them to seats. "Go on, I know you're positively bursting to tell me everything."

Tempest told the tale, starting with Baleirithys' arrival. Caspar made for a rapt audience, leaning forward, gasping at all the right places. He leaned over and gave Akieryon's hand a squeeze when Tempest described dying in his arms. He interrupted four times to ask after everyone in Tymirin. Finally, when Tempest had finished telling him about Seyzharel, he sat back, a faint smirk playing about his lips. His hazel eyes danced.

"What?" Tempest demanded.

"You mean," Caspar said, with the exaggerated manner of someone accustomed to speaking to people who deliberately ignore obvious facts, "that now that you've died and become a demon…" He paused, almost unable to contain his glee. His smirk became a grin. "You're a prince again?"

Tempest exhaled loudly through his nose. "Oh fuck *off.*"

Like the true friend he was, Caspar laughed long and loud, until he subsided into wheezing giggles and scrubbed tears from his eyes, and Tempest ruefully laughed along with him. Akieryon grinned at them both.

He finally knew what it felt like to come home.

COMING SOON

Return to Seyzharel

in

Tools of the Trade

In which a feral young dragon learns about life, community, and politics

And look for more of Akieryon and Tempest in

The Shadow Prince

In which unrest in the Fourth Sphere of Hell draws far more attention than its inhabitants appreciate, and an ancient prophecy may or may not be involved.

ABOUT THE AUTHOR

Bethany Laurel is an aroace artist, writer, and copy editor who works as the ADHD compels her. In her spare time she's also working on a gluten free cookbook. She lives in Oregon's beautiful Willamette Valley with four cats, one witch, and several hundred WIPs.

Find Bethany chattering about writing things: @bethanylaurel.bsky.social

Find Bethany on Tumblr at your own risk.